First and Only

(Callaghan Brothers, Book 2)

Abbie Zanders

First and Only
(Callaghan Brothers, Book 2)

First edition. December 11th, 2014
Second Edition: October 28th, 2016
Copyright © 2014-2017 Abbie Zanders.

Written by Abbie Zanders.

All rights reserved.

ISBN: 1505849497
ISBN-13: 978-1505849493

This is a work of fiction. Similarities to real people, places, or events are entirely coincidental.

No part of this book may be used or reproduced in any form or by any electronic or mechanical means, including information storage and retrieval systems, without written permission from the author, except for the use of brief quotations embodied in critical articles and reviews.

The author acknowledges the trademarked status and trademark owners of various products referenced in this work of fiction, which have been used without permission. Any trademarks, service marks, product names or named features are assumed to be the property of their respective owners, and are used only for reference. There is no implied endorsement from the author of this work.

Acknowledgements

Special thanks to:

… to my wonderful beta readers

… to Aubrey Rose Cover Designs, for crafting an *amazing* book cover

… and to all of *you* for selecting this book – you didn't have to, but you did. Thanks ☺

Before You Begin

WARNING: Due to strong language and graphic scenes of a sexual nature, this book is intended for mature (21+) readers only.

If these things offend you, then this book is not for you.

If, however, you like your alphas a little rough around the edges and some serious heat in your romance, then by all means, read on…

chapter one

Being on a bus wasn't so bad. It got a bad rap, really. So yeah, okay, maybe it didn't smell all that great. Diesel fumes and body odor and that uniquely identifiable aroma associated with port-o-potties. Nothing a well-placed spritz of citrus and honey body mist couldn't cure. Lexi discreetly placed the tiny bottle against the inside of her wrist and squeezed. Now all she had to do was simply lift her hand near her nose and *voila*, problem solved.

Aside from that, the seats were relatively comfortable. As long as you didn't think about the personal hygiene of whoever occupied the seat before you, that was. Lexi squirmed, pulling away so less of her back pressed against the seat, fighting the sudden urge to scratch. And wash. She wasn't an overly fussy girl by nature, but her grooming habits were impeccable.

Of course, she could have just taken the limo, but Lexi had never been comfortable with the luxuries her position as master chef of the Celtic Goddess restaurant afforded her. Sometimes she just needed to return to her humble roots and get lost in the crowd. Besides, the two day trip would give her some much-needed time to think and sort out her conflicted feelings about returning to Pine Ridge, Pennsylvania, after so many years.

Lexi observed those around her discreetly, with surreptitious glances here and there from beneath ridiculously long, thick lashes, a gift of her mother's Greek genes. As much as she avoided direct social involvement, she did find people-watching to be an intriguing way to pass the time. It was fascinating, watching all of the subtle nuances of body language and facial expressions. In her mind, Lexi would craft a scenario for each of the "players", as she called them, often wondering how close she came to reality.

There wasn't much to observe today, though. The bus was less than half full, and she'd already dismissed most of her fellow passengers, feeling confident she'd thoroughly exhausted the most interesting possibilities. There was the plain woman huddling by herself in the back, most likely running away from an abusive relationship given the bruises she tried to hide. The heavy foundation, sunglasses, long sleeves and pants were all dead giveaways. Lexi offered the woman a small smile at one point – one that instantly conveyed understanding and empathy without pity, but otherwise left her alone, knowing that the last thing the woman wanted was anyone butting into her business.

The Mohawk-sporting pincushion a few seats up and over didn't offer much of a challenge, either. He was young – Lexi guessed no more than seventeen or so, judging by the scared look on his face when he let his guard down. A good kid at heart who got in with a bad crowd, probably. Given the duffel he kept beside him, he was on his way into the military. Lexi's theories were confirmed when the bus stopped near Dover and the kid didn't get back on.

Somewhere along the way, Lexi must have nodded off. When she woke up again, the bus was pulling away from yet another terminal. Damn. She would have liked the chance to stretch her legs and get the blood flowing again.

On the plus side, there were a few more passengers. Thankfully, there were still enough open seats that her solitude remained unthreatened.

She sighed, glancing over the newcomers through her dark sunglasses, adjusting the hood of her thin, lightweight shirt so that it put more of her face into shadow. The few conversations she could hear were subdued, blending in with the hum of the tires eating up the miles and the soft hiss of the overhead air vents.

The most recent additions held little interest. An elderly woman with bag full of yarn and knitting supplies. A tired-looking woman grasping the hand of a young boy. A young couple with their eyes glued to their iPhones. Lexi wondered idly if they were texting each other.

Her eyes were drawn to a woman a few seats ahead of her who kept shooting glances across the aisle. A forty-something trying too hard to look like a twenty-something. Too much make-up. Hair too blonde. Clothing made for Disney pop stars, not women of maturity. Her body was in pretty good shape, though, Lexi had to admit. She hoped hers would look as good when she reached that age. Assuming she did, of course. That might be a stretch, given her genetics and the knack she had for attracting trouble.

Lexi's gaze moved to what had captured the older woman's attention, and ... *hello*. She immediately sat up a little straighter, shifting slightly to get a better look at the man. Dark hair peeked out from beneath a baseball cap pulled low over his forehead. The slight profile hinted at strong, chiseled features, too. Shoulders too wide for the standard bus seat extended into her line of vision. A long, jean-clad leg stretched out into the aisle. As it always did, that particular combination of features made her heart beat a little faster.

The cougar reached across the aisle, her red-taloned hand landing on the forearm of the dark-haired hottie. The low murmur of voices mixed in with the white noise as the woman attempted to engage the man in conversation. Lexi couldn't blame the woman for trying. From back here the guy looked totally delicious. At least the woman had good taste.

With several hours to go and nothing else to hold her attention, Lexi watched the scene with mild interest. A few times, she was treated to additional glimpses which only supported her initial impression. His shoulders were very broad. The line of his slightly-darkened jaw and the curve of his neck was sinfully masculine. Occasional shifts or flicks of his hands when he talked were done with a grace and fluidity that suggested a confident man who was comfortable in his own skin.

Lord, but he was easy on the eyes. Well, the back of his head and slight profile were, anyway. She passed the time imagining what he looked like from the front, creating her own perfect fantasy in her mind's eye. *Creating* wasn't exactly an accurate word, because the face she conjured belonged to a real person, someone from her past who she'd never quite been able to forget. And from where she sat, this guy was a dead ringer.

She mentally kicked herself for not noticing him boarding, for not seeing his face. How she'd missed it, she had no idea. Given the way parts of him were spilling over the meager seat space, the guy was obviously tall and well-built. And, if the little bit of his face she had seen was any indication, he was gorgeous as well. Surely she must have broken some rule of feminine über senses by not feeling a shift in the cosmic energy within the Greyhound interior when he joined the motley crew of travelers heading north.

Lexi kept her gaze locked on him for longer than she should have, but found it hard to wrench her eyes away. Why bother, she rationalized, when the guy hadn't looked back her way once? And with nobody else behind her, it wasn't like she was going to get caught, right? Except that even as she was rationalizing, Mr. Gorgeous shifted slightly, then suddenly turned around and looked directly into her eyes.

Embarrassed, Lexi dropped her gaze immediately, feeling her face flush about a dozen shades of pink. She pulled her hoodie further around her face and shrank back into her seat. For the next hour, she stubbornly refused to lift her head, pretending to be engrossed in the paperback she'd picked up at the station. It wasn't one of the hot and steamy romances she preferred, but it looked interesting enough to pass the time.

Too bad it took her so long to realize she was holding it upside down.

* * *

Ian felt the prickling on the back of his neck and knew immediately that he was in someone's sights. By the tingle of awareness in other, more private regions, he also knew that it was a woman who was watching him. An unusual gift, perhaps, but one that had served him well in the past. He cleared his mind, relaxed and stilled his body, and let it wash over him as he extended his SEAL-trained senses.

Yes, definitely a woman. Behind him and to the left. He almost frowned, feeling a slight wave of disappointment. Not the little thing in the hoodie and shades, the one who had been catnapping when he had boarded? She was just a kid, wasn't she?

No, he decided after a few minutes. Definitely not a kid. A woman. A woman with enough intensity in her gaze to not only have his neck prickling, but to heat up his core temp several degrees at least. *Damn.*

He had to look, but it had to be done smoothly. Ian shifted slightly, glancing back down the aisle. Ah, yes, it was the hoodie. The small figure started as he caught her, her full lips parting slightly in what he imagined was a soft gasp at being busted.

He started to smile, but she was already looking away. It was hard to tell with the way the hood was shadowing her face, but he could have sworn he'd caught a flush of bright pink flaring across her cheeks. Even more surprising? He found it oddly arousing.

The woman beside him droned on and on. About what, he had no idea; he'd stopped listening a while ago. She was attractive enough, but a bit mature for his personal tastes. He just couldn't summon the interest.

Now the one in the hoodie, she was a different

story. Eyes hidden beneath the brim of his cap, Ian glanced back discreetly several times in the hopes of getting a better look, but her head remained steadfastly downcast, intent on --- he smiled with genuine amusement --- an upside-down paperback.

Ian occupied himself over the next hour by imagining what she looked like. Was her hair light or dark? Those eyes that had landed on him with such a penetrating gaze --- were they warm and soft, like chocolate or caramel? Or perhaps they were clear and faceted, like emeralds or sapphires? And her lips. Were they the dark, dusky rose they appeared to be, or was that just an effect of the shadows?

He was roused from his musings when he felt a hand lightly caressing his thigh. The woman next to him was saying something about excusing herself to use the facilities. The wink she included implied a not-so-subtle invitation to join her. It was an interesting proposition, but not one he was inclined to accept. Her absence did give him another idea, though. One far more appealing.

chapter two

"May I?"

Lexi started at the deep male voice near her ear. The gorgeous man from a few seats ahead was indicating the window seat next to her with a graceful wave of his large hand. She scanned the half-empty bus. Surely there were lots of other seats available. Why had he targeted this one? Watching from afar was one thing, but sitting next to him? Talking to him? That was something else entirely.

She was just about to suggest another location when their eyes met. The words she was about to utter froze upon her lips. Stunned shock raced through her as every bodily system went into sudden and total lockdown.

This man didn't just look like Ian Callaghan. He *was* Ian Callaghan, the man she had secretly loved and lusted over for the better part of her adult life. Even after ten years, she would recognize those perfect, crystal blue eyes and devastating, mischievous smile anywhere.

He offered her an apologetic smile. "Please,"

he said, his voice rumbling through her chest and settling somewhere between her thighs. "Have pity on me."

Somehow her heart resumed beating, and her mind began functioning again, though it was admittedly running at minimum capacity while the rest of her tried to process the man before her. Speech and coherent thought weren't fully back online yet, so minimal movements were all she could manage.

Lexi's eyes flicked toward the seat he had previously occupied. The blonde cougar was gone. In answer to her unspoken question, he glanced toward the bathroom. Ah, thought Lexi with equal parts horror and amusement. He saw his chance at escape and was going for it.

Without a word Lexi lifted her pack and prepared to scoot over, but Ian apparently had other ideas.

"I'll take the window, if you don't mind," he said quietly. She cast a doubtful look at his long, muscular legs. The well-worn denim clung to them, leaving little to the imagination and doing absolutely nothing but encouraging the ridiculous fantasies spawning uncontrollably in her mind. Fantasies that were all too familiar.

He grinned what had to be the sexiest half smile she had ever seen. Honestly, she thought, regaining more of her ability to think, that thing should be illegal for the all the effect it was having on her, and, she'd bet, every other post-pubescent female he had ever used it on.

"Don't worry," he whispered in a tone far too seductive for the back half of a bus. "I have a talent for fitting into tight spaces quite well." He added a wink for emphasis, and Lexi felt a rush of warm, wet heat between her legs. Yep, definitely illegal.

Without waiting for her to answer (which was good because she would have sounded like a babbling idiot had she tried to speak), he placed both his bag and hers in the overhead compartment --- dear Lord, every muscle in his chest and arms rippled right before her very eyes --- and slid in beside her. She tried not to think of his package passing before her eyes, mouth, and tongue --- and failed miserably. This man was her every sexual fantasy come to life, up close and personal.

Lexi tried to swallow, but ended up closing her eyes in humiliation when her throat refused to cooperate and she gulped audibly. She could have sworn she heard a small chuckle, but it was hard to hear much of anything over the blood violently pulsing in and around her ears.

His long legs brushed against hers as he somehow folded himself into the seat beside her and made it look graceful. Who knew the light touch of worn, faded denim could be so erotic?

He had only just gotten himself settled when the blonde emerged from the tiny bathroom space and proceeded up the aisle, freshly perfumed and sending Lexi into an immediate sneezing fit. The woman turned back to shoot her an irritated glance and noticed Ian now sitting next to her. Her glance quickly turned to a scowl.

Lexi chanced a peek over at Ian, who was now slouched down slightly in his new seat, arms crossed over his sizable chest, and ball cap pulled down over his eyes. Turning back to the woman, she offered a little smile and shrugged apologetically, but all she received was a whole lot of nasty through narrowed eyes, tightened lips, and a look that gave Lexi goosebumps.

"Is she gone?" he murmured so that only Lexi could hear.

"Yes," she whispered back out of the side of her mouth. "But I think she wants to kill me."

"I'll protect you," he chuckled in a low, soft rumble that reminded Lexi of a tiger's purr and set scores of butterflies alight in her core. He shifted so his broad shoulders touched hers, inclining his head toward her. He inhaled deeply, a smile curving those sinfully wicked lips. "Ahhh. Much better. Thanks."

A few minutes later, the steady rise and fall of his arms across his chest suggested that he'd fallen asleep. Lexi finally started breathing normally again. For as long as she could remember, Ian Callaghan had had that effect on her. Apparently ten years and twelve hundred miles had done little to dampen it.

She took the rare opportunity to study him discreetly. If she did it right, she figured, she could use what she saw as fuel for several weeks' worth of late-night fantasies at least. Because that's all they would ever be: fantasies.

He was harder looking than she remembered. Darker. Leaner. More muscled. More of a man, less of the boy he had once been, though there was still a roguish playfulness about him that she was sure had convinced a lot of girls to play naughty over the years. Lexi had always been one of the good girls, but the funny thing was, something about being so close to him made her want to be naughty, too.

She was able to discern the bottom of a tattoo extending just beyond his short sleeve. Of course. The Callaghan crest. She remembered Kieran going on and on about it, how he couldn't wait until he was eighteen so he could get one, too. Each of the Callaghan brothers sported the ink, customized with a design that symbolized their particular skill. Kieran wanted a dragon, something to indicate his passion with martial arts. She wondered what Ian's was. He'd always been super good with electronics, if she remembered correctly.

He smelled better than she remembered, too, and that was a bad thing, because even back then there was something about him that seemed to throw girls into instant heat. Whether it was the soap he used, or the deodorant, or just his God-given natural scent, he smelled good. So good she wanted to bury her head in his neck and lick him right then and there to see if he tasted just as fine. She sighed, a sound of secret suffering with which she was intimately familiar.

Ian neither recognized nor remembered her; that much was obvious. She wasn't sure if she should be flattered or insulted. Flattered, because she had really blossomed since the last time they had seen each other. Insulted, because, well, she would know him anywhere.

But then, she already knew Ian had never been interested in her. Even if she hadn't been a couple of years younger than him, she had never really been his type. On the plain side of being considered pretty, she was quiet and shy. The type of girl no one noticed unless she did something to put herself on the radar. Despite her instant and undeniable attraction to Ian Callaghan, she hadn't been willing to do what so many other girls were for a stolen night with the bad boy of the bunch. No, Lexi had always wanted to save herself for the right man.

She almost snorted. As if there was such a thing.

Oh, well, she thought with another quiet sigh. The past was the past, and none of it really mattered. Soon enough they would go their separate ways and she would never see him again. It was for the best.

* * *

Ian wasn't really asleep, but he found feigning slumber a great way to learn a lot about people who thought he was. They tended to let their guards down. Just like the tasty little thing next to him. The one whose light, delicate scent filled his lungs and invaded his body. The one who was surreptitiously studying him now under the protection of her hood and from behind those shades.

Within seconds of his innocuous deceit, she started breathing normally again. This told him several things. First, she tended to be rather shy and reserved. This held intense promise. Females that were shy and reserved on the outside often hid a deep passion within, and he was a great fan of passion.

Second, she was not the kind of woman who slept around, also a definite plus. Her reaction to him was not one of a woman experienced in dealing with highly sexual men such as himself, but more like the gentle girl next door. He had always leaned more toward the darker, the forbidden, so it was a bit of a surprise to find himself so intrigued by this woman, who exuded innocence.

That led right into his third impression, and that was that she was of limited sexual experience, if not a virgin. The way she tensed every time he 'accidentally' brushed against her was proof in and of itself. That shouldn't have aroused him as much as it did. Usually he avoided such virtue like the plague, preferring those with more experience to play with, but there was something unusual about this one. Something that he felt instantly drawn to.

She was studying him, he could tell. He could sense it. He actually felt her gaze rake over his arms and chest; knew when it settled in his lap, and she was treated to a glimpse of the physical effect her nearness was having on him. Of course, the slight catch in her breath was a pretty good indication, too. He felt sure that had he opened his eyes right then he would have seen that lovely flush across her cheeks again. It had been a long time since he'd been that close to such innocence.

Despite her obvious wariness, he found her easy to be around. How long had it been since he had been around someone who didn't want something from him? Not to mention, she smelled like sunshine. Such a nice change after the potent perfume he'd had to deal with for the first part of the trip.

It was adorable when he'd caught her staring at him, and strangely arousing. Ian wasn't a fool. He knew women shot him appreciative glances all the time. But this one was different. He had a feeling she didn't look at many men like she had been looking at him, and she certainly wasn't used to being caught at it. She had let her guard down, something else she probably didn't do very often. He shouldn't have gotten so much pleasure from her reaction, he knew, but he'd be lying if he said he hadn't enjoyed it.

Those final two hours of the trip had to be the most pleasant he had ever spent on a bus, he decided. Moving away from the blonde had been a brilliant move. She continued to cast suggestive glances back toward him, but he found it increasingly easy to ignore them. His new seat mate had drifted off herself some time ago. His right arm had become her pillow, not that he minded. Her cheek was soft and warm against his skin. Her breath was moist and smelled like peppermint. And she had the most arousing breathy little sighs that sent bolts of heat straight down between his legs. Unbidden images of her making those noises while curled up next to him naked in his bed didn't help. He gave himself a mental shake.

As if sensing his discomfort, she sighed softly, one arm curling tighter around his bicep. That made him smile. Since joining the service right out of high school, he'd fought against the bad guys, but somehow her simple trust --- even if it was given subconsciously --- made him feel like more of a hero than his last mission.

Ian glanced down at her hands where she held on to him. Small, with slim, pretty fingers. Nails, real ones, painted a pretty pearly white, filed to just beyond her fingertips in a graceful curve. No bands or gems on the left hand, always a good sign. On the right, however, a spiral of gold adorned her thumb. Looking closer, he saw that it was a delicate dragon, curling around her, its talons and tail gripping her protectively. It was quite beautiful, actually, and reminded him of a tattoo his younger brother, Kieran, had gotten several years earlier.

Ian felt a pang of sorrow when the bus pulled into the station. They would soon part ways. Maybe it was because he was coming home from a particularly nasty mission. Maybe it was because he was feeling especially restless these days, now that his brother Jake had found his *croie*, his soul mate. He didn't know what the reason was, didn't really care. What did matter to him, and what had him confused, was that for the past two hours he hadn't felt any of that, only peace. Maybe he could get her number before he left, try to hook up in a couple of days when he had some free time.

He wasn't sure what came over him, but he impulsively placed a kiss upon the top of her head before the vehicle came to a complete stop. The light fragrance of citrus and vanilla clung to the thin cotton hood, making him dream of pushing it back and burying his face in her hair, but there was no time.

Pulling back just as quickly, he feigned sleep again so she wouldn't feel embarrassed when she woke up and realized she had wrapped herself around his arm. Sure enough, she awoke within seconds and jerked away. Ian felt the sudden chill that accompanied the lack of her body against his.

He stretched, seeing it as the perfect excuse to

brush against her again. He was delighted when she didn't try to avoid the contact. Even more delighted when he realized she was getting off at this stop as well.

She stood and reached for the overhead compartment, stretching on her tiptoes and extending her reach. Ian grinned. Since he had only seen her sitting down, he hadn't realized she was quite so petite. It provided an excellent chance to play the chivalrous male.

"Here," he said, rising in a fluid movement. "Let me."

In the limited space of the bus, he was aware of her lips just a hair's breadth away from his chest. The top of her head barely reached his chin. He shook off the unexpectedly powerful urge to lower his arms and wrap them around her, tucking her close against him.

"Uh-oh," he said, so quietly that only she could hear him.

His little seat mate turned her attention away from his chest (had she just sniffed him?) and looked toward the older blonde waiting to catch him on the way out. He heard her take a deep breath, then straighten her shoulders and look up into his face.

"I would love to have dinner with you, thank you," she said rather loudly, surprising him.

Ian froze for a second until he realized what she was doing. Then he leaned down and whispered, "I think I love you."

chapter three

If only he knew how cruel those words were.

Lexi forced a smile, forced herself to remember that Ian had no idea who she was. He was just being charming. And she was no kid anymore, either. She was a grown, independent woman, fully capable of making her own way in the world. So why did she suddenly feel like that crushing girl she'd once been, so helpless and out of control?

Ian carried both of their bags off the bus, sticking close enough that she remained painfully aware of him. As her soft-sided suitcase came from the cargo bay beneath, she reached for it. Ian immediately took it from her hands.

"So where shall we eat?" he asked.

Lexi tugged at the suitcase, but Ian held on stubbornly. "We don't," she answered.

Ian frowned, looking confused. "Didn't you just say ---"

"Look," Lexi said, waving her hand toward the retreating blonde figure. "She's gone. You're safe now."

"But I really would like to have dinner with you."

Lexi almost believed him. Almost. She shook her head. Three days tops and she would be on her way back to Benton, Georgia. She couldn't afford to open old wounds that would take a lot longer than that to heal. "Sorry. After two days on that thing, all I can think about is a hot shower and a bed I can actually lie down in." She reached again for the suitcase and her pack, but he held tight.

"My lady," he said, breaking out that sexy grin again. "You have saved me from the evil witch. I must repay the favor. Dine with me. Please."

No woman was immune to that grin, including (especially) her. She couldn't help it, she grinned back, but inside, her heart ached. She had long ago accepted the fact that Ian Callaghan was nothing more than a fantasy, an impossible standard to which no other man could ever measure up. To agree to have dinner with him would make him seem too attainable, putting cracks in the carefully constructed walls she'd erected over the years. And afterward, when he left, it would hurt that much more. Even his lighthearted flirting was painful, a series of stinging reminders of what a playboy he was, had always been.

"Thanks, really, but no thanks."

This time when she reached for her luggage, he placed his hand over hers. That slight contact sent electric pulses right through her. Her lips parted, but somehow she managed to hold back the sigh that threatened to escape. If a simple touch of his hand could do this to her, what would it be like to be held in his arms? To be kissed by him? To lay naked beneath him?

That last thought nearly sent her over the edge, and she fought valiantly to regain some measure of self-control before she embarrassed both of them. She wasn't fourteen anymore, for God's sake. Her entire body stiffened and she pulled her hand away.

"All right," he said slowly, clearly not pleased with her response. "But at least allow me to get this for you." He looked around expectantly. "Is someone picking you up?"

"No." Of course he would think that she was rejecting him because of another man, Lexi thought. No one had probably ever turned him down before. The idea that she simply might not want to have dinner with him wouldn't have crossed his mind.

Coming to the realization that he was not going to relinquish his hold on her bag any time soon, she began to walk away. A moment later he followed, his long legs easily keeping pace with her, her suitcase held effortlessly in his strong grip.

"Need a ride, then?" Damn, he was persistent. But then she always knew he was. All of the Callaghan men were like that. They got what they wanted. Maybe a little rejection would be good for him.

"No."

The hotel she'd booked was only a few blocks from the bus station, and it was a beautiful evening. Despite the angst and awkwardness that came from being within touching distance of Ian Callaghan, she was enjoying the walk, especially after being cooped up on the bus for so long. The air was fresh and clean with a hint of honeysuckle and pine. She had forgotten how good it smelled. The fake fresheners and bottled scents never seemed to capture the natural sweetness of the real stuff. Lexi had travelled all over the world, but had yet to find some other place that affected her as deeply as her hometown.

Ian stayed agonizingly close, but was silent for the first block or so. She wasn't sure if he'd accepted her disinterest, or if he was just too thrown by her attitude to make sense of it all. He wasn't stupid, she knew that for certain. Most likely he was simply planning his next move.

They walked past a small Italian restaurant. The outdoor dining area was about half full, and the mouth-watering smells assaulted her full-force. Lexi's stomach growled loudly, enough for Ian to hear. He smirked. "So.... you're not hungry?"

"I didn't say that," she countered without breaking stride. "I said I didn't want to have dinner with you."

The smile fell away from his lips. "May I ask why?"

Because I am hopelessly, desperately in love

with you, and you will break my heart. "Look, ---"

"Ian," he provided helpfully. "Ian Callaghan." Yeah, as if she didn't know that.

"Ian. " She stopped, looking him up and down, stalling for time while she sought a suitable response, wishing her body would stop angling toward his like a divining rod. "I'm sorry. I didn't mean to be rude."

His eyebrow quirked up as she rubbed her forehead with her index and middle fingers, trying to stem off the headache that was starting. "I'm really tired, I smell like a bus, and I just really, *really* want to call it day."

* * *

Smelled like a bus? Hell, he thought she smelled like sunshine on a summer's day. If she smelled like this after two days on a Greyhound, he could only imagine what she would smell like fresh out of the shower. Like she would in about an hour or so, if she was serious about the top items on her to-do list.

It gave him ideas.

"Hey, no problem," he shrugged, turning slightly so she wouldn't see the wicked gleam in his eye.

She seemed a bit surprised --- and, dare he hope, disappointed? --- that he had given up so easily, but recovered quickly.

"Thanks for understanding, Ian."

"No problem," he repeated. "I get it."

Ian left her bags with her in the lobby of the Carlisle, the closest thing Pine Ridge had to a luxury hotel. He insisted on waiting near the door until he was sure she had a place to stay. Judging by the way she pursed those pretty pink lips together, she didn't really think that was necessary, but she must have read the determination in his eyes because she didn't waste any effort trying to dissuade him.

He offered to carry her bags to her room, but she declined, as he knew she would. It was so strange. He'd only just met her, didn't even know her name (her luggage tag read A. Kattapoulos), yet there was something very warm and familiar about her. No matter. If his plan panned out the way he hoped it would, he would soon know her much better.

"Thanks again for helping me out back there," he said, giving her one of his crooked smiles. More than one woman had admitted that they found his roguish grin sexy. He didn't see it, but hey, if it worked.

"My pleasure."

He waited until she took two steps away from him before he said, "What, no kiss?"

Her head whipped around to find him grinning from ear to ear, arms lifted in open invitation. She laughed, which is exactly what he'd intended.

Shaking her head, she turned and stepped onto the elevator. Ian slung his duffel over his shoulder and walked away, whistling.

Her laugh was like music, Ian thought as he walked the few remaining blocks to Jake's Irish Pub, owned and operated by his father and brothers. His step was light, his mind swimming with possibilities. She might have said no, but she didn't really mean it. Ian was an expert at reading a woman's body language, and he was confident that she had wanted to say yes.

Not for the first time, he wished he could have seen her eyes. It was kind of odd that she had kept her shades on, even at dusk. Maybe she had overly-sensitive eyes, he thought. He had a cousin-in-law like that.

In direct contrast to his mood, the atmosphere in the pub was unusually somber. His brothers were already there, talking in subdued tones. It brought the reason for his father's sudden request to return home earlier than planned back to him in a rush; a reason he had temporarily forgotten.

Brian O'Connell, a close friend of the family, had passed away suddenly the week before of a massive heart attack. The Callaghan boys would serve as pall bearers at the funeral tomorrow.

"Oi, Ian," said his brother Shane, clasping him on the back. "Glad you made it. Bus not too terrible, I hope?"

Ian shook his head. Not bad at all. At first he'd

been pretty pissed when his flight had been rerouted, forcing him to get a bus for the final six-hour leg home, but now, he was glad it had.

His older brother Jake poured him a beer as he grabbed a stool. Thankfully, his family had never been much for small talk or superfluous platitudes, so as soon as the initial greetings were over, Ian was left in relative peace. No one gushed over his safe arrival back home, nor did he expect them to.

Ian, along with his six brothers and his father, were part of an elite off-the-books team. Each of them had done time as SEALS, and some had black ops experience as well. They all had their special skills, and were called upon when needed (unofficially, of course). He felt their relief at his safe return in their handshakes and clasps on the back, saw it in their eyes. That was all he needed.

It felt good to be home. On paper, Jake was the official owner of the pub, but it belonged to all of them. For the most part, he and Jake ran the place, and all but the eldest, Kane, lived above the public area on the second and third floors of the nearly three hundred year old building, which dated back before the Civil War. Three centuries of Irish fighting men had lived and worked here, and as always, it gave him great comfort to be among them and their memories.

All around him, friends and family spoke respectfully of the funeral arrangements and the reception afterwards that was to be held at the pub.

Ian tried to listen, but his mind kept wandering back to the young woman he'd left at the Carlisle. She had captured his interest and then some. It had been a long time since any woman had warranted more than a second thought in his mind, beyond the obvious. The fact that he couldn't seem to think about anything *but* her was disconcerting.

A hot shower and a bed, she had said. He conjured up ideas of her in both, and found both extremely pleasing. Glancing at his wristwatch, he frowned. Nearly thirty minutes had passed since he'd left her. Was that all? It felt like longer than that.

Had she headed right into the shower the moment she got into her room, he wondered? Or maybe she took some time to unpack first and unwind a bit. Was she in the shower now?

He tipped his head back and let the Guinness glide down his throat as he considered the possibilities. How long was her hair? He'd only caught fleeting glimpses of shining gold peeking out from beneath that damn little hood. And what about her eyes? What color were they? It was probably his imagination, but he could have sworn he saw bright flashes through the dark lenses when she looked directly at him.

Her features --- at least the ones he'd been able to discern --- were decidedly feminine. Even the loose cotton hoodie couldn't completely conceal an ample chest; her faded Levis gave stunning testimony to a shapely behind that he just knew would feel amazing beneath his large palms. She was on the short side; the top of her head had barely reached his chin. A small flutter in his chest gave him pause as he imagined tucking her into him, sensing that despite their size differences, she would fit perfectly.

The flutter behind his rib cage grew into an insistent knocking. He looked around, certain that someone must surely have heard it, but everyone else seemed otherwise occupied. He checked his watch again. Yeah, enough time had passed. He'd made his appearance, said his hellos. After being out of country for a couple of weeks, no one would bat an eye if he didn't stick around tonight.

Downing the last of his beer, Ian excused himself and ran upstairs to get his own shower. Hell, he shaved while he was at it, too. She was worth it.

"Off again so soon?" his brother Jake said quietly, catching Ian as he tried to slip out the back without being noticed. "Anyone I know?"

Ian grinned. Jake knew him better than anyone. "Not even someone I know," he said cryptically. "Met her on the bus. Asked her to dinner, but she shot me down."

"A woman of class, then."

Ian snorted, but Jake was right. Despite the casual clothing and her choice of transportation, there was something about the woman that suggested she was well above the wild ones he usually went after.

"So you're going back... why?"

Ian shrugged. "I owe her." At Jake's questioning look he added, "She saved me from a very unpleasant woman on the trip."

"Mm-hm," Jake mumbled. "So to repay her for her kindness you're going to ignore her wishes and go after her anyway?"

"Yeah, something like that," Ian agreed happily as he strode out the door. "No good deed goes unpunished."

chapter four

In clean, worn blue jeans and a white shirt rolled up to the elbows, Ian stood outside room 333 of the Carlisle Hotel, registered to one Alexis Kattapoulos. He could hear the muted sounds of the local hard rock radio station through the door. That was unexpected. He would have guessed she was the easy listening type, but then again, he had thought the same thing about Jake's wife Taryn at first, and she turned out to be the biggest female head-banger he'd ever met.

He smiled. This was just getting better and better.

"Hang on," she called in response to his knock. He shifted his weight, feeling more like a seventeen year-old boy than a twenty-seven year old former SEAL. What was it about this woman that had him so off-kilter?

The look on her face was priceless when she opened the door. The look on his was probably even better.

"Ian!" she said, stepping back in surprise.

Ian might have responded had his brain not gone into sudden lockdown. His body, however, seemed more alert than ever, standing at attention for her and her alone (some parts decidedly more erect and eager to please than others).

Hair fell down below her ample breasts, now damp and curling into waves. He'd only caught a glimpse of the blonde strands before, but now he saw that her hair really wasn't blonde at all. It was made up of dark red, bronze, gold, and platinum, like some kind of living fire, wrapping her upper body in silken heat.

That wasn't the only difference. Instead of concealing jeans and a long-sleeved hoodie, she now wore low-rise Capri sweats, a cropped white tank, and, Lord help him, no bra. Her skin was unmarred, a perfect light bronze, glistening like brushed satin. A golden chain, so finely linked it looked like it could have been made by mythical elves, draped across her abdomen, resting lazily upon her lush hips.

If the sight of her wasn't enough, the scent of her nearly had him on his ass. Sweet, fresh, citrusy. Refreshing and warm at the same time. Suddenly his mouth was watering.

"Hey," he managed roughly, but just barely. "I, uh, thought maybe, …" Hell, he sounded like a moron, incapable of stringing a few words together to form a coherent sentence. Where had all of those smooth lines he'd been running through his mind gone? They'd probably rushed down into his groin along with all of his blood.

She didn't seem to notice his floundering (or if she did, she was too kind to say). Her surprised expression morphed into curiosity as her gaze landed on the bag he held limply in his hands. "Food?"

Shit, she was talking to him. At least he thought she was. He was having trouble breaking away from the hypnotizing sparkle of her eyes. Eyes that were like polished amber, fathoms deep, and *glowing*. This wasn't a girl. This was a freaking goddess. "Uh, yeah, I thought ---"

Taking pity on him, she gently relieved him of the bag and opened it up, leaning in to sniff the contents. The look on her face was one of such elation that Ian almost groaned out loud. "Oh my God! How did you know?"

How did he know? How did he know *what*? He couldn't even remember his own name.

"Burgers!" she was saying as she took the bag over to the small table in her room and began to unpack the contents. "Real, honest-to-goodness American beef!" Her grin grew even wider as she pulled out another package. "And fries! Good Lord, I hope they've been deep-fried in the real stuff…"

She pulled one out and put it between her lips. Ian swore that she orgasmed in that moment; the pure ecstasy on her face was so beautiful it made his cock throb.

"Oh, God, they are!"

She hadn't officially invited him in, but given her positive response to the simple take-out he'd brought, he figured she wouldn't mind too much. He stepped into the room, closing the door softly behind him.

"You haven't eaten, then?" he said with a smile as he tried to recover. She waved him into the chair across from her, shaking her head.

"No, I was just about to order room service." She took another bite and studied him carefully. "Are you psychic or something?"

He chuckled at her question. Psychic, no. One step away from spontaneously combusting, absolutely. "No, why?"

"Dragonfire burgers are only my most favorite meal in the world. Haven't had one in ages."

He shrugged nonchalantly, but inwardly he was doing fist pumps. "This isn't your first time in town, then."

While her attention was focused on the food, he looked casually around her room. He hid a grin when he spotted a paperback novel about Navy SEALs written by a well-known erotic author on the nightstand, right next to a velvety black bag. If his guess was right, and he was sure it was, that little bag contained a feminine tool geared toward self-pleasure. He forced his eyes away, shifting in his seat in a futile attempt to relieve some of the building pressure in his groin. On the bed was a notebook computer, displaying a generic start-up screen.

"No," she agreed in between bites, but she didn't elaborate. Instead, she closed her eyes in rapture, only to open them again slowly and fix them on him. "I'm sorry about before," she said. "But in my defense, I didn't realize you were talking Dragonfire's."

"You're feeling better now, I take it?"

"Much. Amazing what a hot shower and a bottle of body wash can do for a girl's attitude."

Ian's eyes flicked to the nightstand, and saw the instant blush adorn her cheeks. Oh yeah, he'd been right about that. And if there was a God she was thinking of him while she'd 'adjusted her attitude'.

They ate in silence. She finished about half of hers before giving it to him to finish, picking up an orange from the complimentary fruit basket (a gift of the hotel) and peeling it. He was already associating the sweet, citrusy scent with her.

"So... how long are you in town?" he asked, his voice rich and warm. While his body was still taut with awareness, she seemed to have put the rest of him at ease. No one had ever done that before. "I grew up here, I can show you around if you'd like."

She studied him carefully before answering. He had the vague impression she was disappointed by his words, but he couldn't imagine why. What he did know was that sadness had no place on that beautiful face.

Lexi pulled off a section of orange and offered it to him, taking one for herself. When she spoke, she did so slowly, as if choosing her words carefully. "That's very kind of you, Ian. But…"

"Thanks, but no thanks?" he guessed.

She seemed genuinely sorry. "I'm only here for a few days, and I'm afraid most of my time is already planned out for me."

"I see." He tried not to think too much about the rush of disappointment he felt at her words, because it made no sense whatsoever. He'd met this girl on a bus only a few hours earlier. Why should the thought of her leaving in a few days bother him so much? This was just supposed to be a one-time hook-up, right? A chance to satisfy his curiosity and move on.

Clearly he was having issues. Maybe his older brother Kane would let him hang up at the mountain cabin till he could get his shit together, because this whole unexpected connection was screwing with his mind.

* * *

Lexi watched his reaction. He seemed genuinely disappointed that she had turned him down again. Come tomorrow, he would understand, but for tonight, he was still clueless. Tonight, she was a mysterious woman he never thought he would be seeing again.

Her heart began to pound faster against the walls of her chest as she considered the possibilities. Dare she? There'd be hell to pay tomorrow, no doubt about it, but she was looking straight down the sights of a once-in-a-lifetime opportunity here.

"But... I am free tonight."

Ian's eyes snapped to hers, the deep blue instantly heating, becoming molten, liquid pools of blue fire. "What exactly did you have in mind?"

Lexi felt the heat rush into her cheeks. As many times as she had fine-tuned this fantasy in her mind, she was no smooth seductress. "I'm open for suggestions."

A slow, sexy grin began to curve his mouth. "Are you, now?" His voice was soft, low, infinitely dangerous for the effect it was having on her, stroking against nerves she didn't even know she had.

Lexi stood up, stuffing the remnants of their meal into the bag. Her hands shook as the implications of what she'd just offered him sunk in. Ian Callaghan was not a man to be played with lightly. Would she have the courage to back it up? And what if he rejected her?

Before she had a chance to fully analyze that, Ian was behind her. She could feel his warmth, his presence, as it wrapped around her. With a gentle motion he pushed her hair back over one shoulder, baring the back and side of her neck to him.

"Are you sure?" he whispered, his warm breath fluttering across her skin, making her shudder and giving her goose bumps. Her nipples hardened instantly; even the feel of the lightweight tank against them was sending bolts of sensation through her core and into her toes.

"I'll take good care of you," he promised.

It's now or never, Lexi, she told herself. She had dreamed about this. Fantasized about it her whole life. Well, at least since she started thinking about sex, anyway. Ian Callaghan had been her first love, though he never knew it. He had unwittingly ruined everything for her. There was no man smart enough, sexy enough, or gorgeous enough to make her forget the way she felt about him. Neither time nor distance had done anything to lessen the desire, either. On the contrary, it had only made her burn hotter. And if she didn't do something soon, the flames might just consume her from the inside out.

"Yes." The single word affirmation was more breath than voice. As she had rehearsed in her mind for years, she turned into him, placing her palm against his hard chest. Hesitating only a moment, she let it trail slowly southward, raking her nails lightly against him through the cotton fabric, until she turned her fingers downward and cupped the proof of his interest through his jeans.

* * *

Ah, fuck! His mind screamed as she placed her hand on him, catching him off guard. No subtle seduction there. He fought hard to regain some form of reasonable thought, which was nearly impossible with her small hand making light, rhythmic strokes up and down the length of him through his clothing.

He had planned on seducing her slowly, but it didn't look like that was the way it was going to play out. But hey, he'd been a SEAL, trained to make the most of any situation. He was nothing if not flexible.

He groaned, placing his hands on her shoulders and lowering his head for a kiss. He found her lips wet and waiting, softer than he could have imagined beneath his harder, more demanding ones. She instantly obeyed his unspoken request, opening for him.

Ian groaned again as he drank in the taste of her. So sweet, like oranges and vanilla. He deepened the kiss, sweeping her mouth with his tongue, fearing with sudden desperation that he would never be able to get enough.

As delicious as she was, his conscience poked at him. Things were moving swiftly, but this woman was no player. As much as he wanted her --- and holy hell, did he want her --- he still had some honor in him.

"Sweetheart," he said breathlessly, breaking the kiss to lean his forehead against hers and cup her flushed face. "Last chance to say no here."

Her hands snaked up around his neck. "I'm saying yes, Ian."

Yes! Ian did a mental fist-pump. Satisfied that he had given her ample opportunity to say no, thrilled that she hadn't, his hands pulled her closer to him. His earlier assessment had been spot on; her body molded to his perfectly, every soft dip and curve aligning themselves along his much harder planes.

His hands caressed her shoulders, her arms, her back. He couldn't touch her enough, and the layers of clothes between them quickly became irksome. Within seconds he was lifting the tank over her head, baring her upper body.

Ian sucked in a breath and sank back onto the bed. She was even lovelier than he'd imagined. He pulled Lexi between his legs to bury his face in her lush, full breasts. Her hand wound into his hair, holding him to her as she arched into him. Desperate for a taste, he nipped her delicate skin, then eased the sting with skilled licks that had her sagging against him.

Before long, he came to the realization that there was so much more he could be doing with his hands. And the way she was responding to him, he was going to put every one of them into action. With a swift tug he twisted and pulled her onto the bed. One hand slipped down her abdomen and beneath her low-riding pants. He hissed in unexpected pleasure as his fingers met bare, waxed flesh, soft and silky and moist.

"Ah, baby," he moaned against her breast. "You're so wet for me."

* * *

Only you, she amended in her mind. No man had ever elicited these kinds of feelings, the all-consuming desire that Ian did. Lexi moaned in response to the feel of his skilled fingers sliding along her slick folds, biting her lip as she lifted her hips to feel more of him.

"Easy," he cautioned, cupping her sex, but there was nothing *easy* about it. It was as complex as anything she had ever encountered. Every stroke, every kiss, every heated breath against her bare skin heightened her senses. Starbursts of sensation erupted from each point of contact, crushing any last vestiges of doubt or resistance. Lexi couldn't remember a time when she had desired anything quite so badly, and she wanted to savor every moment of it.

Ian was addictive. She had known it then, but not as well as she knew it now. Every caress, every lick, every nip was skillfully applied, inflaming her further. She gripped at his hard body, loving the feel of his corded muscles beneath her fingers. She drew his clean, male scent into her lungs with deep breaths, imprinting it there forever. She tasted his lips, salty and sweet and softer than she would have believed.

One long finger penetrated her and her entire body shuddered in response. He swore softly; it was music to her ears. Hopefully, it meant he was every bit as affected as she was. Forget slow and easy; the need that rose up within her needed more immediate satisfaction. They could try for slow and easy later, maybe, but not now. Hoping to convey that message, she ground herself against his hand and curled her fingernails into his upper arms.

His finger began moving rhythmically; before long he put his thumb to work as well, rubbing teasingly over her most sensitive spot. It felt so good, the way he worked her, but then she knew it would. It might have been their first time together, but Ian knew his way around a woman's body. He knew exactly where to press and exactly how hard, when to curl and when to flick.

"You're so tight, baby," he said breathlessly, running his finger around her entrance, stretching and testing. "You're going to make me work for this, aren't you?"

Her reply was a soft moan. As far as she was concerned, she was ready. She had never been more ready in her life. If he didn't get to it soon, the anticipation might just kill her.

His mouth trailed a line of teasing nips from her breasts, down along her ribs, onto her abdomen. Each one made her catch her breath, her stomach drawing in convulsively. She couldn't help it; her body was responding without any explicit command on her part. It seemed to encourage him further, as if eliciting such reactions pleased him.

Well, if he liked the way she reacted to his licks and caresses, he was probably really going to like what would she do when he finally got around to what she really needed --- that is, eliminating that awful, hollow ache between her thighs.

His tongue dipped into her navel, his teeth scraped her hips. She undulated beneath him, straining for more of his touch.

When his lips finally began their downward path, she was nearly frantic with need. Her hands clenched at his head, pulling at his hair as her nails raked against his scalp. It was such sweet agony, to be the focus of his attention this way. The fire he'd started deep in her core was raging, threatening to burn everything in its path to ash.

"Ian, please," she whispered in desperation.

"Soon, baby," he crooned as his fingers continued to work their magic, kissing his way southward.

Lexi couldn't breathe. Ian was kissing the soft, aching flesh between her thighs and it was at once the best and worst thing she had ever felt. With a tongue so skilled it should be considered a lethal weapon, he flicked against her, alternating between maddening, arch-inducing vibrator-speed flutters and long, languorous licks.

Half-lidded and heavy, his blue eyes turned as

dark as a midnight sky; he groaned as if she was the most delectable treat. When he began to rub himself against her leg and she felt how aroused he was, she knew she was in big, big trouble. Soon, if she had her way, that would be inside her, and she wasn't sure she would survive it.

She only knew she would die without it.

He managed to slip another finger inside her, simultaneously cursing and praising her tightness. Expertly he stretched and massaged her, turning the sting of each penetration into a fiery kiss of passion. She clenched around him as the pressure built, making him swear.

"Ah, baby, you're killing me," he murmured against her, his breath sending spasms across her lower half. "I can't --- I can't wait much longer..."

Then he began talking, more to himself than her. Through her haze she could barely hear him, his voice sending mind-numbing vibrations along her sensitive parts, her brain deciphering his words long seconds after he actually spoke them.

"Have to have you... soon... have to make you ready for me... so tight... I think... yes, *now*..."

Ian's fingers penetrated deep, curving and pressing into a spot within her that made colored stars burst behind her eyelids. At the same time, he sucked her into his mouth and tongued her mercilessly. Within seconds she was exploding, breaking into a thousand pieces, with only Ian's strong hands to hold her down, to keep her from scattering across time and space. She could hear him cursing as she seized uncontrollably, her body curling in on itself through the power of her orgasm.

chapter five

Ian ripped his clothes off in record time. He'd never seen a women come so powerfully. She had clamped down on his fingers like a vice; her thighs had squeezed around his head and shoulders as if her life depended on it. If he hadn't been holding her down she would have lifted clear off the bed. The mere thought of what it would feel like to be inside of her when that happened had moisture already beading along the top of his shaft, his groin tight and full.

He held her, kissed her through the crest, his muscles taut and tense beneath his skin. Desperate hunger coiled within him like a deadly serpent. Had he not known in his heart that he was capable of controlling it, he would have been terrified at the power building inside him.

Soon, very soon, he promised himself. Her orgasm would have loosened her, prepared her, but taking her the way he needed to would require finesse. He closed his eyes and took a deep breath in an effort to re-gather some of his self-control. He refused to lessen any of the passion he'd seen on her face with pain.

She, however, apparently had no intentions of just lying back and waiting for him to gather himself.

Ian grunted in surprise, opening his eyes to find her kneeling beside him, her slim fingers gripping him, her lips still swollen from his kisses, slightly parted and hovering above him. But it was her eyes, glowing amber and dazed with desire, that made his heart stutter. They looked at him with such longing, such pleading.

She licked her lips in anticipation, her hot breath skimming over his sensitive flesh. He swallowed hard and shook his head. He couldn't allow her to do this. He *couldn't*. He was too close; he wouldn't be able to hold himself back if she put those perfect lips to work on him.

Her face moved closer, the tip of her tongue peeked out, her eyes glued to his. He shook his head again, incapable of speech, mesmerized by the determined look in her eyes, his body on fire with the anticipation of how it would feel to have that sweet, sweet mouth on him.

Fire blazed in her eyes, flames of white hot heat flickering in defiance. She was going to have him, too. He saw it, *felt* it, a sixth sense that told him there would be no stopping now.

Her lids fluttered when her tongue licked the

bit of moisture there. She tasted it, rolled it in her mouth, testing it. Enthralled, his heart threatened to slam right through his chest. She swallowed. And then she smiled at him.

He watched as he disappeared into her mouth, then felt the persistent, hungry pull as she tried to draw more from him. Her tongue swirled around the sensitive spot just below the crest, her teeth lightly scraping against him. Ian prayed for the strength to hold on, just a little bit longer.

She closed her eyes, looking as if she was enjoying herself every bit as much as he was, which he knew was impossible. Every stroke, every lick, every suck sent him higher. Her nails raked against his legs, her palms and fingers swirled and pumped. In those moments, he was completely hers. Surrender had never felt so good.

Every second brought him closer to total annihilation. She was relentless, ever-changing, eager, hungry. As soon as he grew accustomed to her ministrations, she changed, blowing him further and further away from sanity. If there was any consolation, it was that she seemed to be losing control almost as quickly as he was. She was greedy, taking him as if she loved it, as if there was nothing more in this world that she could ask for than to have him in her mouth.

Ian knew he was close; it would be impossible to hold out much longer. She was just too damn good. "Ah, baby, you love it, don't you?"

She hummed in response, sending vibrations that had him wracking into spasms. He grabbed her head, knowing he had to push her away, knowing it would probably kill him to do so.

And then…time stopped. She looked at him, her amber eyes fierce and possessive. Her teeth raked against him in warning; her right hand cupped him and squeezed as she sucked him deeper into her mouth, her other hand pushing away the arm that would have separated her from him.

He growled in bliss and frustration, no longer pushing her away but pulling her closer, grabbing on to her head as if she was his lifeline. His hands tangled in her hair, flexing as the glorious patterns she was making with her lips and tongue continued until he was utterly spent. Only then did she release him, triumph in her eyes.

Ian grabbed her and pulled her to him, dropping back on the bed. She was going nowhere, not until he was able to think clearly again. Until then, he needed to hold her, to feel her.

Ian's mind was reeling, his body still thrumming from one of the most powerful orgasms he'd ever had. It wasn't the first time a woman had gone down on him. It wasn't the first time he'd released in a woman's mouth. It was, however, the first time he felt like part of his soul had been released in the process.

Who was this woman purring contentedly against his chest? Who was this quiet, innocent-looking female who had turned him down only hours before, only to transform into a wildcat right out of his fantasies? The way she had responded to him, her total surrender as he brought her to climax, followed closely by her eager but untrained aggression, assuming dominance and taking him better than a pro... it defied logic.

Of further concern was his body's response to her. He hadn't yet fully recovered and he was already hardening again. A slow, wicked grin spread across his face. He was just getting started.

Ian's hand slid down her back, his much longer arm easily able to slide past her deliciously rounded backside and stroke the petal-soft heaven between her thighs. So wet. So hot. Still so incredibly tight. He groaned.

"Warm-up time's over, baby," he growled, his voice soft and seductive. She whimpered, but it was a sound of hunger, not of fear.

He was going to have to get a little creative, he decided. If he forced himself into her, he would hurt her, and that was unacceptable. Rolling her gently onto her back, he placed tender kisses along her arms, her breasts, her hips, before kneeling in front of her.

Taking hold of her ankles, he crossed them and placed her feet against his chest, forcing her to bend at the knees so that she was almost in a reclining, Indian-style position. It opened her up to him, while allowing him the luxury of gazing upon her and affording her some control.

He tapped the tops of her feet as she watched him intensely. "Push if you're uncomfortable, all right?" He had every intention of going slow, of making it as pleasurable as possible, but it would not be easy.

Ian slowly slipped against her entrance. He rocked back and forth, tiny little movements that prepared her for him. Sweat beaded on his brow as she gripped him tightly, her hands on his biceps.

It felt so good. Too good. So good it drove thoughts of everything else from his mind. God help him, he was trying to do the right thing, but the perspiration dripping into his eyes was proof of just how difficult it was to hold back.

He leaned back to look at her, his heart aching at her sudden, vehement protest. "So pretty," he crooned, his voice rough. "Are you ready for me, baby?"

"Yes," she answered, her voice a low, sensual purr. "I need you, Ian."

"So much hunger," he rasped, awed by the way she looked at him when she spoke those simple but devastating words. He aligned his body with hers once again, then gripped her ankles. "Open for me, baby. Take me."

* * *

This was it. After years of dreaming, she would

finally know what it felt like to be taken by Ian Callaghan.

She appreciated his concern, but having her legs against his chest wouldn't allow the close contact she craved. Lexi spread her thighs, placing them on either side of his ribs as he came over her. His chest pressed against hers and she felt every delicious inch of his body. She wrapped her arms around his neck, buried her head in his throat, licking against the pulse point beneath his jaw. He tasted every bit as good as he smelled and looked – slightly salty and all male.

When he finally began to push inside her, she bit down on his shoulder to avoid crying out. Even with his preparation, it was a tight fit. He had to work his way in as she struggled to accommodate him. Sweat beaded his brow, and she could tell that he was trying to hold back, afraid of hurting her.

Even in the throes of passion, her bad boy was a gentleman. She wanted to tell him that it didn't matter; that she had wanted him so badly for so long that it could never be too fast, too hard, or too much. Not from him.

But she couldn't. Her breath was stolen completely as he slowly speared her, rendering her incapable of anything but the mewing whimpers that managed to escape.

With a final rock of his hips, he seated himself deeply inside her and stilled, giving her time to adjust. "It's okay, baby," he crooned in her ear.

"I've got you." He held her as if she was precious, as if this wasn't just sex for him, just like she'd dreamed. Except this wasn't a dream, and she knew better.

The sting quickly subsided, replaced by an incredible sense of fullness. She loosened her grip (but didn't let go), allowing him to rock gently against her. Pain was replaced by blinding pleasure. Each stroke heated her, burned her, soothed her like nothing else. His kisses were tender, though he never let her forget for one moment that he was in control.

That was all right; she was more than willing to surrender to him completely.

It was insane. Insane and perfect and better than she'd ever imagined it could be. Her only complaint was that it was *too* good. She wanted to draw it out, too make it last forever, but her body had other ideas. Her breathing grew ragged, her heart pounded, her nails dug into his flesh.

She was close, running headlong toward her peak but wanting desperately to take the long, scenic route there. She clenched around him, squeezing, pulling him in deeper until it was impossible to tell where he left off and she began.

"Protection?" he growled out through clenched teeth.

"Ian," she cried out in gasping breaths. "I'm on… I can't…"

And then her climax was on her, taking over

her body and soul until nothing else existed beyond the feel of Ian inside of her. Her muscles clamped down so tightly that he gasped; his entire body went tense and stiff before she felt the warmth bloom deep within her.

"Ah, baby," he panted. His extended thrusts became tiny strokes meant only to push into her more deeply. Lexi clung to him, silently coaxing him on, attempting to convey everything she felt without words.

Because there simply were none.

* * *

Spent, Ian collapsed. He was vaguely aware of her kissing his face, stroking his hair. It felt good, so good. She simply held him as his body shook and shuddered above hers, until he finally calmed.

He must have dozed off. When he woke his arms were filled with the most wonderful warm, soft flesh. The feeling of contentment was a new one for him; he had never stayed long enough to experience this before. Then again, he'd never had a woman like this before, either.

It had been stupid --- no, make that *beyond* stupid --- to engage in unprotected sex with a woman he'd met on a bus. Yet even now, he could not imagine it any differently. Yes, it was stupid, but the damage was done. No sense putting one on now, or for the next several times he planned on taking her.

Like now.

He nudged her, trying not to think too much about how his heart swelled at her sleepy smile or the way she welcomed him, denying him nothing.

chapter six

Ian woke up feeling more rested than he had in weeks, but with the unmistakable feeling that something was missing. He glanced around as memories of the previous night flooded back. He'd never had trouble with stamina before, but last night he'd surpassed even his own expectations, taking the woman repeatedly, coming harder each time.

Where was she now? He looked around the room, but he already knew she wasn't nearby. He didn't have to see her to feel her; his senses seemed to jump into über-mode when she was around. He mentally added that to the list of things he didn't want to analyze just yet.

He listened carefully, but heard nothing within the room or the en suite. A faint hint of vanilla and citrus hung in the air, mixing with the scents of a night filled with incredible sex.

Ian frowned. Waking up alone was not on his top ten list of things he'd most like to do this morning. He would have much rather preferred some more morning sex, followed by a hot, steamy shower together where he would soap up every inch of that luscious body he'd come to know so intimately, then maybe more sex. After all, he didn't have to be anywhere until…

Ian looked at the small digital clock on the bedside table and jolted upright. "Shit!" The glowing numbers told him it was 10:45. The viewing was already underway, going till 11:30, to be followed immediately by the Mass. His father would skin him alive if he was MIA.

He ran back to the Pub and took the stairs two at a time, grabbing a two-minute cold shower and donning his black suit. No time to shave, he thought, glad that he had chosen to do so right before heading over to the hotel the night before. At least he didn't look too bad. The dark circles under his eyes had disappeared, leaving him with the satisfied look of a man who had spent a good portion of the last twelve hours making a goddess scream out his name repeatedly in rapturous pleasure.

His thoughts were consumed with the woman as he made his way to the funeral parlor. Who was she? Why was she in town? And how the hell had she managed to sneak out of the room this morning without him hearing her? One thing was for certain: as soon as his obligations here were met, he was damn sure going to find some answers.

Glad for his SEAL training, he slipped among the shadows and into the back as if he'd been there for hours. The funeral home was packed with townspeople, and no one seemed to notice his late arrival. His brothers, however, had the same training he'd had and were more aware than most. He bore their accusatory glances stoically. It was their father he was most worried about.

Brian O'Connell had been a friend of the family's for as long as he could remember. He and Jack Callaghan had served in the special forces together, and had formed a bond that only those captured and tortured could ever truly understand. Out of respect for both his father and Brian, Ian forced himself to shove aside thoughts of last night to concentrate on the present.

"Glad you could make it," Kane's voice hissed in his ear. Damn, but his eldest brother was a sneaky bastard. No wonder they always called on Kane when stealth was key. "The old man's been looking for you. I hope she was worth it, bro."

Ian clenched his jaw but said nothing. Hell yes, she'd been worth it. If she'd been there when he'd woken up this morning, there was a damn good chance he wouldn't be here now. He'd be buried deep inside the sweetest, tightest, wettest…

"Ian." Jack Callaghan's voice sounded on his other side as Ian tried to keep his face neutral. Thankfully, his father didn't say anything about him being late; the uncharacteristically worried look on his face concerned something else. "I want you to stick close to Kayla and her mother today. Try to keep her from doing something... stupid."

Ian raised an eyebrow, but nodded. Kayla O'Connell was Brian's stepdaughter. Tall and model-like, stunningly beautiful, she drew a lot of male attention. Until fairly recently, she had been a bartender at the pub and a willing participant in some of the darker forays of sexual adventures with Jake and himself.

At least until Jake found his *croie* --- his soul mate --- in Taryn. Now Kayla looked to Ian, but he balked at a one-on-one. Jake had been the one she'd seriously pursued, and though Ian had been willing enough to be an occasional third, he wasn't interested in batting clean-up, for two reasons. First, she did nothing for him other than provide a physical release, which, really, was easy enough to come by. And second, even if he *had* found her desirable, he had too much pride to be anyone's second choice.

Thankfully, Kayla didn't come by the pub much anymore, except when she knew Taryn wasn't around. Taryn was fiercely protective of Jake (and Ian, oddly enough) and, unsurprisingly, had not taken to Kayla in the least. Taryn believed Kayla was a heartless, manipulating bitch (her words).

In all honesty, Ian had to agree. Jake wisely avoided her whenever possible, and the rest of the clan seemed content to do the same. The atmosphere around the pub post-Kayla was warmer and more welcoming all around.

Jack clasped his son on the shoulder. "Good man." He was gone before Ian could ask him to elucidate. Ian turned to ask Kane, but the big, sneaky bastard was gone too.

Ian threaded his way across the reception area toward the front, where Brian's immediate family sat accepting condolences from those paying their respects. From across the room, his brother Sean shot him a satisfied, cruel grin. *This*, it said clearly, *will teach you to be late.*

Kayla and her mother sat regally in hand-carved, richly-cushioned mahogany chairs, dressed the part in full black regalia. Ian offered his condolences to the widow as Kayla grasped his hand and pulled him down close to her. The reception room was packed; people milled about everywhere, taking up all available space. That wasn't surprising; Brian O'Connell had been a staple in the small, predominantly Irish community.

"I simply cannot believe *she* had the nerve to show up here," Kayla hissed into his ear venomously.

Ian looked up, having no idea whom she was talking about. He followed her glare to the other side of the room where he spotted his youngest brother, Kieran. Kieran was talking to someone, but Ian couldn't see who it was past his huge frame. The kid was built like a freaking Mack truck on steroids. But, judging by the protective stance

Kieran had assumed, Ian could guess who it was.

"Lexi's here?"

"The little bitch," Kayla spat. "Playing the poor long-lost daughter. Look at them over there. Grown men falling all over themselves like she's some kind of princess or something. It's *pathetic*. Where's she been for the past ten years, huh?" She paused, digging her claw-like nails into his forearm. "At least *you* have some sense."

Ian frowned. Lexi O'Connell was Brian's daughter from his first marriage. After his wife's death, Brian remarried and adopted then-teenager Kayla. Lexi was Kieran's age, several years younger than him, so that would put her at around twenty-four or so now. For a while, she and Kieran had been inseparable. Lexi had been a scrawny little thing, afraid of her own shadow, and Kieran's innate white-knight tendencies had him unofficially adopting her as the little sister he'd always wanted.

Ian had been in his senior year then, with plans to enlist immediately after graduation, but he could still remember how devastated his brother had been when Lexi left town unexpectedly. There had been a lot of speculation and nasty rumors, but he'd never heard the real story.

From what he remembered, Lexi was nothing like the self-centered bitch Kayla was describing. She'd been a tiny little thing, shy, quiet, always hiding behind Kieran when he'd drag her home with him after school. Being the center of attention was probably the last thing she wanted. Judging by the way Kieran was shielding her with his body and his brothers had arranged themselves protectively around her, he was willing to bet that not much had changed.

Another group of people stopped in front of them to pay their respects. With Kayla's attention diverted, Ian used the opportunity to glance back toward the corner again. He couldn't help feeling that this was somehow wrong. Brian's daughter should be sitting here before the casket, too. Surely she was grieving, even if she had been away for a while. After all, you never stopped loving your parents, did you? Didn't she deserve support and empathy from the people who had come to pay their last respects?

He'd heard there was a lot of bad blood between Kayla and Lexi. Now he understood the worry on his father's face and his request to keep Kayla in check. Given the chance, she'd cause a scene. Kayla loved to have the starring role in a good drama.

Kieran stepped to the side and all of the air whooshed out of Ian's lungs in one swoop at the sight of the familiar figure. The long, shimmering hair. The big, amber eyes. The full, womanly curves.

God help him.

Alexis Kattapoulos was Lexi O'Connell.

He'd spent the night having sex with his

brother's childhood best friend the night before she had to bury her father. His stomach roiled uncomfortably, and he was suddenly glad he hadn't had time for breakfast.

Misinterpreting his reaction, Kayla smiled cruelly. "I know. Ugly little bitch, isn't she?"

Irrational rage surged in his chest. Had Kayla been a man, Ian would have broken her jaw right then and there. He fought to regain his composure.

Alexis. *Lexi.* How could he have missed that? She looked like an angel, standing before the glass in the far back corner, the light from the window forming a nimbus around her hair, now smoothed and shiny, clasped loosely at the base of her neck with an antique-looking silver clip. She smiled at something Kieran said, but it was a sad smile. Kieran reached down and grabbed her hand. The gesture was one of friendship, Ian knew, but still a tightness formed in his chest. Against all reason, *he* wanted to be the one with her, even though he now knew just how wrong that would be.

As if sensing his gaze, she turned to him then and met his eyes. It only lasted a moment or two, but the look on her face was locked in his mind forever. *Now you know*, it said quietly, as if he could hear her speaking the words in his head.

Like pieces of a puzzle, things came together. Her initial attempts to keep her face and eyes hidden, afraid that he would recognize her. Her reluctance to go out to dinner with him. The look on her face when he offered to show her around.

It hadn't been disappointment he'd seen in her eyes; it was hurt. Because he didn't remember her. Because to him, she was just a girl he was trying to hook up with. He was such an idiot! How could he not have seen it?

But the most amazing thing of all? *She'd spent the night with him anyway,* giving him more pleasure than he could have imagined. More than he'd deserved.

Lexi turned away as Jack Callaghan took her arm and began to lead her toward the back exit, away from the masses gathering for the exodus to the church. Kayla grabbed his arm again as they were shuffled toward the limos. He caught a brief glimpse of gold silk getting into his father's Infinity before the door closed and they were whisked away.

Hell, he'd give anything to be in that car with her right now. To know what she was thinking. Did she hate him? Hate herself? If he could only talk to her, get her alone for a few minutes. Instead, he'd been relegated to ---

"If she thinks for one second that she's going to sit in the front pew with ---"

"Kayla, enough," Ian said firmly. Kayla looked stunned, unused to Ian speaking to her that way. "Don't cause a scene. This is neither the time nor the place."

Kayla narrowed her eyes, then licked her lips. "You're right, of course. It would make me look like the baddie, wouldn't it?"

Ian mentally rolled his eyes. He'd known Kayla was cold and self-centered, but even he was shocked by her total lack of propriety. "Yes," he agreed quietly. "It would."

During the Mass, Ian sat behind Kayla and her mother in the first pew. Lexi sat on the opposite side, toward the back of the church, between his father and Kieran. He was grateful that they were there for her, but he couldn't help the simmering resentment that it was them and not him. Then again, maybe this was how she wanted it. He certainly couldn't blame her.

How could he have not recognized her? Had he been that blinded by lust?

The answer was a resounding yes, he had been. It'd hit him hard and fast, and from the moment his eyes found her on that bus, he'd had to have her.

The lust was still there, and in spades, but no longer blinding, reduced to a torturous ache. Now that he knew, he could see the familiarity. She was still below average in height (Kieran always teased her about being "fun-sized"), she still had the same delicate, slightly exotic features, and the quiet, almost-stoic air. But in his defense, her slim girl's body now held the lush, full curves of a woman. Her hair was much longer, an intricate palette of fiery color. And her eyes, once rarely seen because they were usually downcast in shy reserve, were golden amber depths of passion.

Lexi stole glances at him throughout the service, he was sure of it, thanking God each time he felt the familiar prickling on the back of his neck. It meant… well, he wasn't sure what it meant exactly, but at least she was still looking; she wasn't ignoring him completely.

Other than a slight inclination of her head out of sheer politeness, she had not openly acknowledged his presence. Each time he'd glanced at her (and the times he had probably numbered in the hundreds over the course of the afternoon) she'd been looking elsewhere. If she had any reaction at all to seeing him with Kayla, she didn't show it. She stayed in the back, out of the limelight, allowing Kayla and her mother to play center stage throughout the service. He noted that she remained alone in the pew when the rest of them went up for Communion, looking even lonelier than he felt.

"Thanks, Uncle Jack," he heard her say after the Mass as they waited for the casket to be placed in the hearse, "but I really don't think it's a good idea. I'd just like to go back to my hotel." Ian managed to get within hearing distance while Kayla 'composed herself' in the ladies room, though as far as he could tell, she hadn't shed a single tear.

"This is not a time to be alone, Alexis," Jack said kindly, but firmly. "You belong with family, lass."

"I don't want any trouble." Lexi scanned the crowd, no doubt looking for Kayla. She took a half-step back, instinctively seeking the shadows of a marble column. Ian doubted she even realized she did it; hiding came naturally to her, and for some reason, that pissed him off.

"Of course you're coming," Kieran said adamantly, and for once, Ian agreed with him. Ian guessed that they were referring to the gathering immediately following the burial: a traditional Irish wake at the pub. The wake was an opportunity for the friends and family of Brian O'Connell to informally panegyrize him, to remember and eulogize and say their final farewells while sharing drink and song in his memory. It was a celebration of his life, laced in grief but more so in fondness, and hopefully one that would remind Lexi of better times and of the fine man her father had been.

As a bonus (albeit a selfish one on his part, perhaps), Ian also believed that anything that placed them in the same vicinity was a good thing. It would save him the effort of tracking her down later. Plus, he could keep an eye on her. Yes, his father and brothers seemed to be doing a great job of it, but she was looking smaller today. More fragile. And Ian felt somewhat responsible for that.

* * *

Lexi felt Ian's eyes on her again. His expression gave nothing away, but his crystal blue eyes were as intense as she'd ever seen them. Was he angry at her deception? Disgusted? Ashamed?

Other than the looks he was shooting her way, he hadn't spoken a word to her, nor had he given any indication that he wanted to. Lexi wouldn't have traded last night for anything, but she wished she could spare him the awkwardness now.

"He was your dad, Lex," Kieran was saying, his voice filled with compassion. "You have more reason to be there than anyone."

Lexi's breaking heart swelled. Kieran had always been her friend, her champion. She knew her abrupt departure all those years ago must have hurt him deeply, but, amazing man that he was, he didn't seem to harbor any resentment. He had been at her side all morning, offering his quiet support. Still her big brother, even after everything that happened.

Lexi shook her head. Kieran meant well, but Kayla and her step-mother had been shooting daggers at her all afternoon. While she didn't care in the least what either woman thought of her, she refused to dishonor her father's memory by causing a scene. It was because of her love for her father that she'd willingly left all those years ago.

"I shouldn't have come. This was a mistake."

"Don't let them get to you, Lex," Kieran said. "Patricia wouldn't dare say anything around Dad, and Ian will keep Kayla occupied."

Hearing her stepsister's name paired with Ian's opened up old wounds that had never completely healed. Through years of practice, she kept her expression neutral, betraying none of the pain those memories brought with them.

"They're still together, huh?" she asked casually.

Kieran shrugged, his voice laced with disapproval when he said, "You know Ian."

Yeah, she thought sadly, she did. She knew now what it was like to be held in his arms, loved by his body, brought to the heights of passion repeatedly and in such varied and creative ways. How could she ever fault Kayla, or any other woman for that matter, for doing everything she could to hold on to that?

The moment of silence that followed was heavy. Against her better judgment, she sought Ian out, finding him standing in the shadows of the alcove. Her eyes locked onto his.

Forgive me, Ian, she begged silently.

Kieran followed her gaze, his eyes narrowing. "Is that why you don't want to come, Lex? Because of Ian?"

Of course Kieran would think that. Even as kids he'd sensed her feelings for his older brother. He'd never embarrassed her by coming right out and saying anything, but he'd dropped enough hints, warning her away in his attempts to spare her a broken heart. Too bad she couldn't have listened.

Though Kieran's voice was tender as he spoke to her, his eyes blazed at Ian. Kieran was still her protector. Thank God he had no knowledge of what she and Ian had done last night; if he had, she would probably be mourning Ian's death right along with her father's.

Before she could answer, Kayla emerged from the restroom and demanded Ian's attention.

"Ian! Let's go, already." Kayla's voice rose over the respectful, muted conversations of those exiting the church. When Ian hesitated, Kayla followed his eyes, landing on her with barely concealed hate. Kayla pressed her body up against his side in a clearly possessive move. Ian clenched his jaw, but he didn't stop her. That told Lexi everything she needed to know.

Lexi lowered her eyes, accepting it for what it was. She had known the previous night was a once-in-a-lifetime thing, and had been mentally preparing herself for the stark reality of the morning after. Admittedly, she hadn't foreseen Kayla's blatant posturing, but that was her own fault, and ultimately, it changed nothing.

With one last lethal glance Ian's way, Kieran slipped his arm around her protectively and guided her toward the exit.

* * *

Ian stepped away from Kayla, refusing to meet her eyes. If he did, if he saw the malice and cruelty he instinctively knew were there, he wasn't sure he could maintain the charade. He was doing this for his father, no one else. Reluctantly, Ian led Kayla out to the black Lincoln that would take them to the cemetery, then to the pub.

If there was a hell on earth, Ian was in it. Several hours later, Kayla was drinking too much, getting louder and growing more obnoxious by the moment. Every time he tried to slip away she pulled him back again. If she made one more blatant reference to the need to be comforted, he was going to be physically ill. Thankfully, most of the crowd had left, leaving only family and a few close friends to witness it.

"Rough night, huh bro?" asked Jake, slipping him another beer. Kayla, satisfied that Ian was within grasping distance, turned to speak to someone else, giving him a few minutes of peace.

"You could say that," Ian admitted, raising the bottle to his lips and downing half of it in one swallow. "Throw a shot in there, would you?"

Jake raised an eyebrow but wisely said nothing, tipping the bottle of Connemara over the opening. "Not as bad as she has it, though," Jake said, nodding toward where Lexi was sequestered in the back of the room. Ian could think of nothing to say, so he remained silent.

"Do you remember her?" Jake prodded.

"Sort of." But the image Ian had in his mind of that young girl was nothing like the goddess he was stealing glances at now. The one surrounded by his family but looking so lost among them. He remembered a skinny, shy creature who always seemed to get lost in his brother's shadow, a wisp of a thing of whom Kieran was insanely protective. Definitely not the beautiful, sexy, curvaceous embodiment of his every fantasy come to life. Fantasies he now knew without a doubt were very real.

There was no indication of her wild passion now. Her hair was pulled back so that only the closest examination would have shown the streaks of vibrant colors. Her dress was simple, classic; dark but not black. No hat, no veil, no jewelry. Lexi wasn't here for show. If anything she was embarrassed by their attention. And in her face, Ian saw true grief at the loss of her father.

"You should," Jake said with enough admonishment in his voice to make Ian turn to him.

"Yeah? And why is that?"

Jake gave him a knowing smile, but it wasn't a friendly one. "She had it bad for you, bro. Used to drive the rest of us nuts. Especially Kieran."

Ian blinked, the only indication of his total bafflement. "She did?"

"Oh, hell yes," Jake confirmed. "Until the night she caught you and Kayla together, anyway."

The forgotten memory came back to him as if it had happened yesterday. He'd driven over to the school to pick Kieran and Lexi up after a basketball game, a condition of getting use of the family car for the night. Kayla had come out of the game first and spotted him, and asked for a ride, too. Next thing he knew, Kayla was in his lap and her hand was down his pants.

He still remembered the look on Lexi's face when she'd seen them, too; could still hear Kieran's curses ringing in his mind. Lexi had taken off running, Kieran tearing after her. Ian hadn't understood then, but he did now. He'd bet anything that Kayla had known of Lexi's crush, and had gone out of her way to hurt her.

Ian put his beer down and straightened, his eyes fixed on the far side of the bar. This had gone far enough. He'd done what he'd been asked to do. He needed to talk to Lexi. *Now*.

"Don't even think about it," Jake breathed in his ear. Jake had a knack for knowing what Ian was going to do before he did. It was a bit scary sometimes. "And get Kayla out of here before she causes another scene."

Why was Kayla suddenly his responsibility, Ian wanted to know? But he already knew the answer: because no one else wanted to deal with her. At one time, Jake had been the one to handle Kayla, but Jake wasn't about to risk the wrath of his new bride.

On the plus side, the sooner Ian got Kayla out of there, the sooner he could figure out how to get Lexi alone for a few minutes. His entire body tingled at the thought.

He grabbed his suit coat, reached for the keys, and turned to tell Kayla it was time to go. Except

Kayla was no longer where he'd left her. His stomach dropped when he saw her teetering over to where Lexi sat.

"Well, well, well," Kayla said, her voice carrying clearly throughout the bar. "If it isn't the little princess herself. Broke her daddy's heart and then came back to get her greedy little hands on her inheritance. Well you're not getting anything, sweetheart, you hear me?"

The bar grew silent, and all eyes turned in her direction. The tension in the room increased tenfold; Ian saw his brothers stiffen. Thankfully, Jack had left a bit earlier to drive Patricia home and wasn't there to witness Kayla's latest scene.

Lexi kept her face neutral, but Ian could *feel* how much Kayla's words were hurting her. He'd never been able to do that with anyone other than his brothers before, so that unexpected and intimate connection shook him a little.

Kieran shifted, positioning his body in front of Lexi's. Shane stood slowly, catching Jake's eye across the bar, but Lexi put her hand on his arm, stopping him from going any farther.

She looked so beautiful, Ian thought. The picture of class and composure, even in grief.

"I don't want anything, Kayla," she said, her voice calm and even, though weary.

"The hell you don't," Kayla sneered. "But then again, *I* got what you really wanted, didn't I?" She shot a look back at Ian, her smile laced with cruelty.

She might have been considered pretty on the outside, but her spitefulness made her ugly.

For the third time that day, Lexi's eyes met Ian's. In that moment, he would have given anything to change things, to take away the hurt he saw in her eyes. To hold her in his arms and feel the wonder of her heart beating against his. And it had nothing to do with sex.

But he couldn't. Damn it all, he couldn't. Not here. Not now. Not in front of his family. He'd embarrass Lexi, and that was the last thing she needed.

"For Christ's sake, get her the fuck out of here," Jake hissed in his ear.

The only thing Ian could do was put a stop to the flow of vile things still spewing from Kayla's mouth, so he would. He crossed the floor. "Time to go, Kayla," he said, hating what he was forced to do.

"See, princess?" Kayla taunted as she wrapped herself around Ian. "He wants *me*."

Ian had never been as tempted to strike a woman as he was in that moment, but his father had raised them better than that. Instead, he removed Kayla's hands and propelled her toward the door. But the look on Lexi's face was burned into his mind forever. The hurt, the betrayal in her eyes seared his heart.

It was the second time in his life she had given him that look. He would not survive a third.

chapter seven

"Stay with me," Kayla pouted as she tried to pull Ian into her house. "I don't want to be alone tonight."

He'd gotten her safely to her door, but that was as far as he was willing to go. Ian peeled her hands off of him. "No, Kayla."

"It's her, isn't it?" she spat, her eyes narrowed to slits. "Little Miss Perfect. You feel sorry for her, just like everyone else."

"You're drunk. Go to bed."

"Come with me."

"Good night, Kayla." Ian turned on his heel and walked away, ignoring any further pleas before he really lost his temper.

Ian rushed back to the pub, but Lexi had already left with Kieran. Ian felt like punching something. He needed to see her, even if it was only for a few minutes. He had to know she was all right, had to at least *try* to explain that none of what Kayla had said was true.

Clearly Lexi hadn't told anyone about their

time together last night, and given the day's events, that was probably a good thing. Tensions had been running high as it was, and she buried her father, for Christ's sake. If there had been any hint that he'd spent the night in her bed... well, he didn't even want to think of what Kayla would have done with that information, let alone his father and brothers.

Keeping their little secret off the radar made things more difficult, but not impossible. For now at least, discretion was paramount, for both of their sakes. But he *would* be visiting her soon.

They had a lot to discuss, and he had questions. *He* hadn't recognized *her* at first, but was the same true on her end? Had she known who he was all along? Or was that something that she realized afterwards? And why had she turned him down at first, only to surrender so completely to him later?

And how she had surrendered to him! Never had a woman taken him so well and given so much in return. Ian got an odd feeling in his chest every time he thought about it.

Was it possible that Lexi still had feelings for him, even after all these years? The more he thought about it, the more he believed that to be the case. It was in every touch, every word, every nuance of their time together. *That's* what had made the night so spectacular. His brief time with Lexi went beyond the lust and physical needs he was accustomed to. Plenty of women had said they cared for him, but he had never felt the pure concentrated power of the real thing before. Now he had, and he was afraid that nothing else would ever do.

Except he feared it might already be too late.

Ian bided his time while he waited for Kieran's return. He sat with his family, nursing his beer and half-listening to their conversations. His eyes glanced toward the door every few minutes. Once Kieran was back he would slip away and see her again.

"Give it up, Ian," Shane said finally, when everyone else had grown tired of his single-syllabled answers and gone to shoot darts. "Kier's not coming back tonight. Dad told him to stay with her, to make sure she was okay."

Ian turned to Shane, his gaze intense. Anyone else might have been intimidated, but Shane only smiled. "You haven't taken your eyes off that door since you got back," he explained.

Ian shrugged, containing his exhale. Shane was the equivalent of a human lie detector. It would do no good to deny it. The most he could hope for was to provide a little redirection, at least until he knew what the hell was going on.

"So what's her story? Lexi, I mean."

Shane grinned widely, and Ian knew he'd made the smart choice. Shane wouldn't have believed for a moment that Ian wasn't thinking about her. At least this way it sounded like a legitimate inquiry, as opposed to something a lover might ask. He would hit his beloved computers later and know everything there was to know about Lexi O'Connell, a.k.a. Alexis Kattapoulos, but Shane would have the interesting personal insights he couldn't get anywhere else.

"Yeah, I was wondering when you were going to ask. Saw you looking at her all day." At Ian's raised brow, he added, "But don't sweat it. You weren't alone. There wasn't a man there who wasn't checking her out for one reason or another."

So far, this conversation was not doing anything to settle his unease.

"Alexis O'Connell, only daughter of Brian and Adonia O'Connell," Shane began, slipping into subject analysis mode. In addition to being able to accurately sense people's emotions, Shane's mind was like a computer, storing images and data effortlessly. That made his input invaluable.

"Adonia?" Ian questioned. It was not a common name.

"She was Greek," Shane told him. "Brian met her on one of his tours in the Mediterranean." Ian nodded. That explained a lot, especially her daughter's goddess-like features.

"Adonia died when Lexi was only a few years old, leaving Brian to single-parent before it was socially acceptable. When Lexi hit junior high, Brian thought his daughter would benefit from having a woman around. Enter Patricia Jennings with her own daughter, Kayla. They married, and it was the classic Cinderella story." Shane grinned. "Guess who the ugly stepsister is?"

Ian bit the inside of his lip, something he only did when deep in thought. "Let me guess. The dad was clueless, right?"

Shane's expression grew more serious. His brows creased together and his eyes lost their teasing twinkle. "Not so much. According to Dad, he realized his mistake right away, but he'd already married Patricia, and he was a devout Catholic. Nothing short of a burning bush was going to make him renege on his vows."

"Not even concern for his daughter?" Ian found it hard to believe that a father could ignore that kind of behavior, especially with someone as innocent and loving as Lexi. Not to mention that old-generation Irish men were known for being extremely protective of their women and children.

A shadow fell over Shane's face. "There's a lot more to it than that," he said cryptically. Before Ian could ask what he meant, Shane continued. "You really don't remember anything about her, do you?" he asked, considering Ian thoughtfully. "Lexi would never put her father in that position - where he would have to choose one over the other. She did the next best thing. She started hanging around us. Instant big brothers." He grinned again. "Except for you, of course. We kept her far away from you."

"Yeah? And why is that?"

"For one thing, you only thought with your

dick back then. Christ, Ian, some things never change."

Ian scowled and shot him a withering look, but he knew it was true. There were some things he was not especially proud of.

"But for another," Shane continued, "Lexi had it bad for you, man. She couldn't be in the same room with you without starting to stutter and knocking things over. It was kind of embarrassing, really. Glad she's past that."

"Yeah," Ian said, his voice sounding strange even to his own ears. Shane shot him a suspicious glance.

"Hey, where were you last night anyway?" Shane asked suddenly. Too suddenly for Ian's comfort.

"With someone," he answered vaguely, but kept direct eye contact with Shane. Now was not the time for one of Shane's psychic bursts of insight. Ian's answers needed to be truthful without revealing the whole truth. He slammed his mental shields down around the images of Lexi now permanently burned into his brain. Images of her so adorable and shy on the bus; of her eyes lighting up with excitement at the burgers he'd brought her; her body flushed and hot and slick for him; the look on her face when she made love to him with her mouth and came apart in his arms...

"Well, *duh*," Shane said, interrupting Ian's recollections. "Whoever she was, she did a number on you. You've been walking around in a daze all day. Not like you, bro." He paused, sitting back and tapping his chin thoughtfully. "I know it wasn't Kayla."

Why did everyone assume he'd be with Kayla? And how did Shane know he wasn't?

"She came around looking for you," Shane answered, correctly guessing at least one of Ian's questions. "Got real pissy when we said we didn't know where you were."

"Whatever." Ian was tired of Kayla. Really, really tired. He had no desire to discuss her any more. "So why'd she leave?"

"'Cause no one else around here can stand her company for more than five minutes. And Taryn scares us, man."

What? It took him a moment to figure out who Shane was talking about. "No, you moron, not Kayla. Lexi. Why did Lexi blow town?"

A definite shadow passed over Shane's face this time. "Ah, right. Well, as time went on, things got worse over at the O'Connells. Lexi was happy with us, and that pissed Kayla off. Seems that Kayla had a bit of a crush on you, too. And Jake. Me and Sean. Mick. And ---"

Ian rolled his hand in a 'get on with it' gesture. "Yeah, yeah, I get it."

"Well, the story goes that Kayla must have gone whining to mommy about it because one day, Patricia decided that with Lexi 'maturing' it wasn't right for her to spend so much time with us, which, in retrospect, was probably a good thing, though none of us ever viewed her as anything more than a little sister. Brian apparently agreed, and told her she couldn't hang out with us anymore. Kieran got really pissed --- you know how close they were --- and talked to Dad. Dad tried to talk some sense into Brian, but he wouldn't listen. Lex ran away a couple of times, but we always found her and brought her home." Shane chuckled. "One time Kieran snuck her into his room to keep her from spending the night in the woods alone. Dad found out and nearly hit the roof."

Something ugly reared in Ian's chest. "Kieran and Lexi?"

"It wasn't like that, man. Not everyone's a whore like you." Ian scowled again, but Shane went on. "Kier was just trying to protect her, give her a safe place to crash. We all were."

Ian nodded, the pressure in his chest momentarily subsiding and then filling instead with something heavier.

"But that's not the whole story, is it?" Ian asked, the dread building in his gut.

"No. Something happened. And before you ask, I don't know what. But it was bad, real bad. Next thing we knew, Lexi was gone and no one would say anything. It wasn't even Brian that took her away; it was *Dad* that drove her to the airport and put her on a plane. That should tell you something."

"And you have no idea why?"

Shane shook his head. "There were rumors, of course. Some said Lexi got herself pregnant and went to some distant relatives to have the baby. Others say she finally snapped and threatened Kayla and her mom and Brian had to send her away to get help. But neither of those things are true," Shane said emphatically. "No way, not Lex. She was protecting someone, and I'd bet my left nut it was one of us, probably Kieran."

Shane drained the last of his beer and stood. "I've never seen anyone take the abuse she did and not fight back. She'd just get all quiet and go off by herself. Used to drive Kier crazy, but there's no way she went postal, not her. And as far as the pregnancy thing went, well, Lexi was a good girl, you know? Not to mention we would have beat the shit out of anyone who dared to change that." He shot Ian a pointed glance. "That's another reason we tried to keep her away from you. Dad would've been pissed if we killed one of our own."

Ian had the distinct impression that Shane was warning him that they still would. He'd been right in assuming his father and brothers would not take kindly to the knowledge of what had happened between him and Lexi. Apparently those old protective instincts were very much alive and well amongst the Callaghan clan. So he did the only thing he could for the moment: he ignored it.

Shane's face grew somber. "I do know that

right before she disappeared, Lexi started missing a lot of school. I overheard Kieran telling Dad that he'd seen some cuts and bruises on her that didn't look right. Dad went to Brian again, told him he had to do something. Shortly after that, Lexi was gone. Apparently Kieran was the only one she told; the rest of us didn't find out till later."

"The official story was that Brian had sent her to stay with some distant relatives of his late wife's. Wouldn't tell anyone exactly where, but Dad knew. She'd legally changed her name to her mother's maiden name: Kattapoulos. He's kept tabs on her all these years, sending her birthday cards and shit. That's how he knew where to contact her about Brian's death when no one else did."

Shane paused, letting all that sink in. "Dad said she didn't want to come back for the funeral, but he talked her into it. Told her it was the right thing to do, that she'd regret it later if she didn't pay her final respects, blah, blah, blah. But now, after seeing what happened today and tonight, I'm wondering if maybe she was right." He shook his head. "She doesn't deserve to be treated like that, you know?"

chapter eight

By the time midnight rolled around, Ian conceded that Shane had been right; Kieran wasn't coming back tonight. The only reason Ian was able to sit tight and refrain from showing up at her door was because deep down, he knew that Kieran would take good care of her. Better than he would, in fact. Because if Ian was there with her now, he wouldn't be providing her with a brotherly shoulder to cry on. He'd be buried deep inside her, making her forget her own name and every bad thing that had ever happened to her, and that probably wasn't what she needed.

Instead, Ian went upstairs and fired up the bank of electronic devices that took up an entire wall in his room and went to work. Sitting at his computer, his fingers began to fly across the keyboard. Gathering intel was his specialty, and he had lots of questions. If he couldn't openly fish for the answers, he'd find out for himself.

He paused, briefly remembering how he had accused his brother Jake of being a creeper when he'd asked Ian to look into Taryn's background. Jake had disagreed, arguing that his gut told him that Taryn needed their help, therefore justifying the request. This wasn't exactly the same situation, but it was close enough that Ian figured he could rationalize his actions as well.

It was his wholly irrational, clawing need to know more about her that was harder to justify.

After several years of compiling dossiers on radicals, terrorists, and assorted persons of interest, pulling together a bio for an average citizen was child's play for Ian, especially since most of the information was a matter of public record. People really had no idea just how much of their private lives were out there, sitting on servers or clouds, just waiting to be read by anyone with a basic understanding of digital security and code decryption. If they did, they would probably never shop online or join another social media site again.

Ian started with the little bit he'd learned from Shane and went from there. After leaving Pine Ridge, Lexi moved to a small town along the southeastern coast where she stayed with two unmarried aunts, sisters of her mother. She attended a private school there, graduating with high honors. Was on the swim team, set a few records for the school. Was shy, kept to herself. She dated very little, spending nearly all of her free time working at a local restaurant after school and on weekends.

Lexi did not attend a traditional college, opting

to pursue a career in the culinary arts instead. Here she excelled, far surpassing expectations. Cooking, it seemed, was her métier. She spent time apprenticing in some of the best restaurants in Europe under some of the finest chefs before returning home to work full time as master chef at the Celtic Goddess. The restaurant had done so well under her hand --- specializing in a unique blend of Irish and Greek cuisine --- that two additional locations opened based specifically on her customized menu.

There was no record of any serious love interests, but she was often photographed in the company of Aidan Harrison, the CEO of the Celtic Goddess. Ian made a mental note to do a complete work-up on him later, just pulling up the basics for now. Harrison was twenty-six, unmarried, wealthy, and considered very eligible, at least according to the society page references that popped up in Ian's searches.

Ian glared at the picture that came up at the grand opening of his last restaurant: Aidan Harrison with his arm around Lexi. They were smiling at each other, looking very comfortable together. That same photo had thrown the social elite gossip mill into a frenzy, predicting that Alexis Kattapoulos would soon become Mrs. Aidan Harrison, breaking the hearts of those who had hoped to capture the eye of the young multi-millionaire.

Like hell, thought Ian as his fingers began to fly

once again, pausing only briefly to register the intensity with which that thought had bulleted into his mind. He had no claim on her. So why did the thought of her marrying another man feel as if someone was slicing him in half?

Was it even an issue, or pure media hype? Lexi wore no ring upon her finger. She had travelled to Pine Ridge alone. Wouldn't a serious lover accompany her on such a personal journey? Want to be there for her, with her?

More importantly, would Lexi have given herself so completely to him if there had been someone else?

No, the more he thought about it, the less sense it made.

Closing down the image, Ian rubbed his eyes and checked the clock. Five a.m. *Shit*. He'd been up all night, and Kieran still hadn't returned. He hoped Lexi's night had been more restful than his had been.

So what had he learned about her? Nothing he couldn't have already guessed. She kept to herself, worked hard, and was one hell of a chef. He snorted. His conversation with Shane had proven much more enlightening.

Ian sat back in his chair, running both hands through his hair. For the first time in a very long time, he had absolutely no idea what to do. He knew what he *should* do. He should let it go. Let *her* go. He should keep his head down, his nose clean, and stay away from Lexi until she went back to Benton, Georgia, and resumed her life.

His gut churned at the notion. His head began to pound and his chest grew tight. There was not a chance he was going to allow *that* to happen, not until he understood what had happened between them. He might not be old, but he sure as hell knew the kind of connection he'd felt with Lexi didn't happen often.

And when had he ever done what he was supposed to anyway?

No matter how he looked at it, he kept coming back to the same question: *Why?* After all this time, why would she suddenly give herself to him without telling him who she was? Why did she let him believe he was just an incredibly lucky bastard?

On some level, he had assumed she knew what she was doing. That the innocence, the exploration, the novelty in her touch and discovery was deliberate, but now he knew better. The more he thought about it, the more he was driven to the same conclusion, one that both thrilled and terrified him at the same time: Lexi still had a thing for him.

Catching some sleep after *that* little revelation just wasn't going to happen. Instead he showered, shaved, dressed, and was waiting downstairs in the old kitchen, his third cup of coffee in hand, when Kieran came in. *With Lexi*. Kieran was still wearing the same clothes he'd left in the night before, and Ian was pleased to see that he obviously hadn't showered. It made the possibility of any intimate contact less likely, not that Ian believed they had done anything other than talk through the night. If he had, he sure as hell wouldn't have spent the night in front of his computer screens, twiddling his virtual thumbs.

Despite the slight hint of dark shadows beneath her eyes, Lexi looked radiant in a pair of simple slacks and a soft tan blouse that made her eyes sparkle. Part of her hair was secured with a clip, allowing some of the many-colored streaks to show through, like ribbons of silken flames. Even casually dressed as she was, she threatened to take his breath away.

"Good morning," Ian said quietly. He sat at the massive, scarred table with his feet propped up on a chair and the morning newspaper spread out in front of him. If asked, he wouldn't have been able to recall a single story or column, though he'd been staring at the same page for an hour.

Kieran's arm went protectively around Lexi as he narrowed his eyes Ian's way. Ian could understand his suspicion; he was *not* typically an early riser. Then Kieran's expression eased, and Ian guessed that Kieran was putting the pieces together (incorrectly). Kieran probably assumed that after escorting Kayla from the bar, Ian had spent the night with her and had only just returned himself.

The thought that Lexi might be coming to the same conclusion clawed at his gut, but it was neither the time nor the place to set either of them straight.

"Good morning," Lexi responded, her voice calm and polite, which chafed. There was nothing to indicate that it was anything more than a pleasant, mannerly greeting. The natural musical lilt of her voice might just as well have been directed toward the man at the counter in Dunkin Donuts or the woman vacuuming the hallways at her hotel. Her facial expression held nothing more than mild interest. Other than looking a bit tired, she was as beautiful and fresh and distant as ever.

"Would you like some coffee?" Ian waved his hand toward the fresh pot he'd just brewed. His question was directed at both of them, but his eyes didn't stray from Lexi.

"Had some," Kieran answered brusquely.

"Actually," said Lexi, turning to Kieran, "I think I could use another cup." Her head inclined toward Ian, though her hand rested lightly on Kieran's arm. Ian recognized it for what it was --- a comforting gesture intended to calm his over-protective little brother (since Kieran was approximately the size of a rather large bear, the term 'little' referred only to the fact that he was the youngest of the brothers).

"It's full octane, right?"

Ian grinned. "It is."

Kieran scowled at Ian over Lexi's head as she moved toward the machine, a warning, clear and simple. *Mess with her*, it said, *and there will be consequences.*

Ian kept his face carefully neutral; raising Kieran's hackles would only complicate things at this point, and things were already quite complicated enough.

"I'll stay with you till Dad comes down." Kieran spoke quietly, but loud enough for Ian to hear.

Lexi smiled at Kieran, a smile filled with so much affection that a pang of jealousy speared through Ian's chest. He wanted her to look at him like that. When she wasn't screaming his name in climax, that was.

"It's all right, Kier. I'll be fine. "I've already made you late."

Kieran clearly had his doubts about leaving her alone with him, but with a few more soothing words from Lexi, he reluctantly headed upstairs. Ian didn't miss the second warning look – this one even more pronounced - that Kieran flashed his way.

"Care to sit down?" Ian asked casually, keeping a tight lid on the turbulence he felt within. Damn, it was hard to sit there, pretending to be polite strangers, when all he wanted to do was crush her in his arms, carry her upstairs, and spend the rest of the day picking up where they had left off in her hotel room.

"Thanks."

Ian removed his legs from the chair and Lexi

sat down across from him. She sipped at her coffee, both hands clutching the mug. Her eyes were focused on the coffee, but Ian's were on her. Several long moments passed before either of them spoke.

"You knew, didn't you?" Ian asked, his voice so quiet someone a few feet away wouldn't have heard, even in the silence of the closed pub.

Lexi exhaled without looking up, her shoulders slumped slightly as if she had been expecting the question. "Who you were? Of course I did."

"Why didn't you say anything?"

She didn't answer right away, taking a sip of her coffee and swirling the liquid inside the mug, looking into it as if it was a crystal ball that held all of the answers. "If I had told you who I was, would you have come back to my room?"

"Hell, no!" he said emphatically, running his hand through his hair.

She smiled into her mug, a sad smile. "Exactly."

He hadn't expected that. "Why, Lexi?" His voice had reduced to a whisper.

Her finger wiped slowly at the drip of coffee running just below the rim. "I guess I needed to know."

"Needed to know what?"

This time she looked right into his eyes, and he was nearly blown away by the amount of raw emotion he saw there. "Whether or not I was living in a dream world," she answered. "If the reality could even come close to the years of fantasy."

Ian was floored. She'd been fantasizing for years? About him? God help him, his central nervous system just about shut down. At that moment, he was grateful his autonomic systems were perfectly capable of functioning without any explicit direction from his brain, because if they weren't, he'd already be dead.

"And what did you come up with?" Hell, was that his voice? That rough, raspy tone that sounded as though little to no air was making its way through his closed throat? He felt as if his entire future hung in the air between them as he waited for her answer.

"Ah, there you are." Jack Callaghan's booming voice resonated through the kitchen as he entered from the private staircase, interrupting their little Q & A session. "Hope I didn't keep you waiting too long."

"Not at all," Lexi said, her face instantly returning to the calm, pleasant mask she presented to the world. Shane was right. She had a core of solid steel, and he was one of the lucky few to have seen beyond it. "Ian was kind enough to keep me company."

Jack shot a glance at his son, one that spoke volumes. In it, Ian could see both warning and promise, eerily similar to the one Kieran had given him only moments before. Given the opportunity, he was pretty sure he could have vocalized his father's thoughts at that moment in one simple statement: *Hurt her*, they said, *and I'll have your arse*. Since Jack Callaghan was not one to utter idle threats, Ian knew he was walking a thin, dangerous line.

"The pleasure was all mine," said Ian casually, rising. He took her cup, letting his fingers brush lightly against hers in the process. One brief look promised her that they would finish their discussion later, before he wished them both a good morning and disappeared into the stairway.

chapter nine

Jack Callaghan was a well-known and respected staple in the Pine Ridge community. For all intents and purposes, he was a retired serviceman who travelled occasionally and tended bar with his sons. It was true enough; he did do those things. But no one was fool enough to believe that was *all* he did. The closest anyone ever came to the complete truth was a vague realization that they didn't really want to know.

Jack and his boys held respectable jobs in the community, though occasionally one or more of them would disappear, often for weeks or months at a time. They were fine, upstanding, law-abiding citizens, yet most people regarded them with a sense of wariness that bordered on awe. They knew instinctively that the Callaghans were the good guys, and most were content with that knowledge. There was no refuting the nearly non-existent crime rate in the area, either, not all of which could be attributed to the Pine Ridge PD.

It was precisely for these reasons that Jack

accompanied Lexi to the official reading of her father's last will and testament. Jack had always had a soft spot in his heart for Lexi, ever since Kieran dragged her home one day like a stray kitten. Back then, for a little while at least, Lexi became the daughter he and his wife had always wanted but never had.

As much as it had pained him to see her go all those years ago, he knew it was probably for the best. Now that she was back, however briefly, he would do everything he could to ensure that she got a fair shake. He had no doubt Patricia O'Connell and her daughter would not be particularly magnanimous, as evidenced by their deplorable conduct during the previous day's events.

Poor Brian was probably turning over in his grave.

Jack held her small hand in his as they sat across from Patricia and Kayla in the understated elegance of the lawyer's office. The dark, polished wood desk and bookshelves complimented the antique-style brass fixtures and supple leather seating, creating an atmosphere that fostered a sense of professionalism and trust.

On the outside, Lexi looked as calm and unruffled as ever, but he knew better. He could feel her hand trembling in his, her pulse beating fast beneath his fingertips. He gave her a reassuring squeeze.

As things went, the reading was relatively

straight forward. Nearly all of Brian O'Connell's assets went to Patricia as his surviving spouse. Both she and her daughter seemed to take pleasure in the fact that he hadn't left much more than a small stipend to Lexi. Of course, thought Jack, they had no idea that Brian had Jack set up a fund in Lexi's name years ago and had been making regular deposits. The result was a substantial amount to which no one else was privy. And if Jack had been adding a little himself here and there, well, he saw no harm in that. The result was a nice nest egg that, in reality, surpassed the amount willed to Patricia and Kayla.

Lexi, however, didn't know that. Jack's admiration for her grew with each passing moment as the solicitor ticked off the items one by one. Not once did she give any indication that the terms of the will bothered her. Her expression was thoughtful, her posture composed. Had it been the other way around, Jack was sure that the women facing them would not be conducting themselves with such grace. Lexi was Brian's daughter, all right. Beautiful, like her mother, but strong, like her father.

Jack's theories were tested shortly thereafter, and, as usual, he had been dead on. The lawyer waited until the end to drop the bombshell: Brian O'Connell had stipulated in his will that a small house and property on the outskirts of town was to go to his only daughter, Alexis, in the hopes that one day she would return to her roots.

For a few moments no one said anything, the silence both heavy and practically tangible. Lexi seemed just as shocked as the rest of them. Her eyes widened and her mouth parted in surprise, offering the biggest reaction he'd seen from her thus far. Then Patricia started sobbing and Kayla's face turned purple with rage. The lawyer did his best, reminding them that they had the much larger house and property in town, several vehicles, and hefty sums in bank accounts, stocks, and insurance. Unfortunately, his assurances did little to appease them.

"It's all right, Mother," Kayla said, patting her hand. "Surely she's not going to keep it." Kayla shot a challenging glance over Lexi's way.

Lexi stiffened beside him. "And why not?"

"I would think that would be obvious."

"Enlighten me."

Kayla sat up straighter, setting her shoulders. "You have no reason to stay, of course," she said with a cold smile, daring Lexi to disagree. "There's nothing for you here."

It was a blatant display of pettiness and malice. "The hell she doesn't!" he said forcefully. Lexi squeezed his hand. He looked at her in surprise. She was giving *him* reassurance. Had the situation not deteriorated so quickly he might have smiled.

"You know what, Kayla? I'm not really sure that's true," Lexi said slowly. "Being back in Pine

Ridge these past few days, well, it's made me realize how much I miss it. The clean, fresh mountain air. The dramatic change in seasons. And the people. Everyone has been so kind and supportive." She gave Jack a warm smile. "Especially Uncle Jack and the boys. They've been wonderful."

The atmosphere in the room grew noticeably chillier. "I beg your pardon?" Patricia's sobs became sniffles.

Lexi stood, squaring her shoulders. It was a slight movement, very graceful, but powerful. "You heard me. I don't think I'll let you run me out of town again just yet." Turning to the lawyer, she said, "Mr. Williamson, have we finished?"

The solicitor's eyes shined with approval and respect. "We have."

"Then I thank you for all of your efforts. I'll be in touch." Then Lexi swept out of the office with the dignity and grace of royalty.

As they took their leave, Jack heard Patricia and Kayla arguing in earnest with the solicitor, but in a cool voice hinting of impatience, he explained that there was nothing he could do. Jack, however, was walking tall with a huge grin on his still-handsome face and pride radiating from every pore in his body.

"Alexis, lass," he said as he beamed at her, "I am going to treat you to the best steak dinner money can buy."

* * *

Lexi's head was spinning, the band of panic tightening around her chest. It was a good thing that Jack Callaghan was the old-fashioned, chivalrous type. He thought nothing unusual about the way she clung to his arm as he escorted her back to the pub. He appeared to like it actually, patting her hand and telling her how proud he was in that heart-warming, old-country accent of his.

What had she just done? Jack Callaghan was beaming at her like she'd just won the Nobel Prize, yet her legs felt so wobbly she wasn't sure she could take the next step without his support. Luckily, Jack was too riled up to notice. Or if he did, he was too kind to say anything.

She'd let her anger get the better of her. She blamed it on her inherently volatile Irish temper, the one she usually kept hidden beneath layers of discipline. The one over which she thought she'd mastered control years ago.

Apparently coming back to Pine Ridge was affecting her good judgment, beginning with her first night. She'd given her body to a man who didn't even know who she was in a desperate, once-in-a-lifetime opportunity moment. And not just once. Heaven help her, just thinking of all the things she had done to him, that she'd let him do to her --- had her body temperature rising several degrees, her skin tingling, and a twinge of residual soreness that reminded her of just how inexperienced she'd been.

The hell with good judgment. She couldn't --- wouldn't --- regret their time together. No matter what. Ian had been magnificent. At once tender and fierce. Maybe it was just her imagination, but she would swear it had been more than sex, even for him. For one glorious night she'd felt desired. Treasured. *Loved*.

She gave herself a mental shake. *Don't go there. Don't even think about it.*

But *this* fell on the opposite end of the poor judgment spectrum. This wasn't filling her with the same warm and fuzzy. Instead, cold dread slithered through her belly, instantly quelling the good feelings that memories of her time with Ian had brought forth. Now she had effectively drawn a line in the sand with her stepmother over a house she didn't want in a place she didn't want to be. What was wrong with her?

Her life was in Benton now. Her stable, lucrative, uncomplicated life with a definite schedule: Wake up at five. Have a light breakfast. Exercise in her building's exclusive fitness center (an hour in the pool, a few light weights). Shower and dress. Walk to the restaurant. Have lunch with Aidan. Work till ten or so. Walk home, shadowed by the escort Aidan always dispatched but didn't think she knew about. Shower again. Read a few chapters. Sleep and dream about Ian.

Boring, maybe. But it *worked* for her. She was successful and content. She had a job she loved and the opportunity to help others. The Benton County Shelter had become her second home on Sundays, when Aidan physically banned her from entering the restaurant. Her life was simple, and she liked that.

Another bonus? Nobody *there* wanted her head on a platter, at least not that she knew of. Why complicate things?

Pine Ridge might be where she started, but Kayla was right. There was nothing here for her anymore.

At least that's what she tried to tell herself, but even she felt the lie. There was plenty here. History. Friendship. Support. Incredibly hot burning passion.

Inexorably mixed in were hatred, pettiness, jealousy, and, she was pretty sure, the certainty of a broken heart. She'd already had enough of all that to last her a lifetime. No, to live here would take more strength, more courage than she had. There would be too much drama, throwing her already-fragile, chemically-balanced life into a tailspin.

Lexi didn't need a steak dinner. She needed a good stiff drink. Several of them. The fact that she didn't drink was completely irrelevant.

With that in mind, she gratefully accepted the finely-aged Irish whiskey Jack poured for her in celebration when they returned to the pub. She sat quietly, letting the alcohol slide down the back of her throat like silken fire, as Jack regaled Jake, his wife Taryn, and Ian --- the only ones in the Pub at that hour --- with a condensed version of what had occurred. Jake looked almost as proud as Jack did, and Taryn seemed genuinely excited. Lexi had met her at the funeral and had instantly taken to the woman. Had she remained in Pine Ridge, she felt sure she and Taryn would have been good friends.

Ian's face was unreadable. She could feel the intensity of his devastating blue eyes on her, as if he was trying to work out a particularly difficult puzzle. This morning's brief encounter had left the waters murky at best. She didn't have a clue what he was thinking, and that was tying her up in knots even more.

Was he angry with her for not telling him who she was and why she was in town? Maybe. The "Hell, no" she got in response to her earlier question stung more than she'd cared to admit, but she'd deserved it. She was playing a dangerous game with a man way out of her league. What did she expect?

Well, if he was angry, he was hiding it pretty well. Everything about him suggested intensity, but not necessarily umbrage. Then again, he wasn't exactly fist-pumping at the idea of having her around any longer than necessary.

Of course he's not happy about it, she told herself as she lifted the glass to her lips, acutely aware of Ian's penetrating gaze and completely unaware that Jake had refilled her glass. Twice. *He doesn't want you sticking around. You were supposed to be a one-time thing, remember? Not to mention the fact that --- oh yeah --- he's got a long time thing with Kayla.*

Lexi winced when pain shot through her stomach at that last thought (or was that the shot she'd just chugged?). Ian's watchful gaze narrowed. She could understand why he would not be quite as pleased as the rest of them. Still, it hurt. Somewhere deep down some tiny little part of her still held out hope that he might actually want her to stay, even if it was completely out of the question.

chapter ten

Despite her protests, Jack insisted on driving Lexi over to look at the property. All she really wanted to do was head back to the hotel and soak in a hot tub for a day or two until she returned to her senses and could make a rational, practical decision based on something other than pure emotion. But after standing up and giving the whiskey a chance to circulate, she had a lovely, warm buzz going and didn't have the heart to tell him no.

What would she do with a house, she mused on the way over? Houses required maintenance, upkeep. Who would do all that? She liked her apartment. When something broke, she called Aidan and it would be fixed right away. Beyond changing a light bulb or jiggling the handle of the toilet when it ran, her knowledge of home repairs was non-existent.

As they drove farther out of town, it dawned on her that it wasn't just a house, but a house that most likely had property associated with it (she blamed the whiskey for the slow uptake). What about mowing the lawn and trimming shrubs and that sort of thing? Outside of the kitchen, she stayed far away from anything that included a motor and sharp blades, or, Heaven forbid, both. She shivered just thinking about it.

But it would be nice, a tiny voice in her head said, to plant your own flowers and have a nice little herb garden, wouldn't it? She shushed the voice away, earning a curious glance from Jack.

The property was located about ten miles past the outskirts of town. She hadn't even noticed the turn-off, well-concealed as it was by massive trees and mountain laurel in full bloom. A strong sense of déjà vu came over her as they wound their way along the long, overgrown drive.

The feeling grew stronger as the ancient-looking stone cottage came into view, and it had nothing to do with the Irish whiskey. She couldn't quite put her finger on it; the place seemed so familiar, and yet somehow different, if that made any sense.

The trees seemed bigger than they should have been. The overgrown gardens should have been neatly tended and weed-free. Blossoming vines grew unchecked over stone that had once glistened in the sunlight, and the slate roof was badly in need of repair. Without looking, Lexi somehow knew that if she walked around the exterior, she would find a huge flat-stone patio in the back. And beyond that, a creek that bisected near the edge of the property, forming a tiny island in the middle, perfect for childhood adventures.

Without conscious effort, her mind transformed the reality of the property's present state into long-forgotten images. Visions of bright yellow and white flowers appeared, blossoming around the wrap-around porch. There had been roses once, too, but after she'd gotten tangled in them, they'd been ripped out and replaced with less thorny selections. Baskets had hung from the roof of the porch, spilling blooms downward like soft-petaled waterfalls. Dark reddish-brown shutters, painted to match the hues of the natural stone, framed windows opened wide to capture the summer breeze. The picture of a gallon of sun tea on the wide, southerly facing kitchen sill and a basketful of ripe peaches from the small orchard on the right was too clear, too detailed to be just a dream.

"You probably don't remember," Jack said, watching her reaction carefully, "but this was your Grandmother's place. Your dad's mama. It was where you and your mom used to stay when your father and I got called out."

Jack took the keys from her trembling hands and opened the door for her. Memories flooded back in earnest.

"I remember!" she murmured, retracing the steps she had taken years ago. Off to the left was a huge sitting room, where her grandmother would rock back and forth while she played on the floor.

To the right was a kitchen, a massive room that had once held a wooden table the size of a car and a fireplace so big she could walk into it. Farther back were the bedrooms; she remembered the three of them used to fit quite nicely on the enormous poster bed in the largest one. There was a bathroom, too. One with a big claw-foot tub that she'd needed a wooden box to reach. By today's standards, the house was small and ancient. But to Lexi, it was quite possibly the most perfect thing she'd ever seen.

* * *

They spent several hours at the house, moving from room to room, discovering sections that Lexi didn't remember as well. They explored the ten secluded acres. The orchard was barely recognizable now, thought the creek's path had changed very little over the years. They found a few outbuildings, too, including a cold cellar with its own still-flowing spring, and a smokehouse. Even with the poor shape the house and grounds were in, the small estate had tremendous value.

Jack, a man of few words, said little, finding enjoyment in the beautiful afternoon and the pleasure of Lexi's company. He stayed close, watching as Lexi went from room to room, her face filled with wonder. Damn if it didn't do his old heart good to see her smile again. In all his years, he'd never come across a lonelier soul, or a woman who deserved it less. Even after all this time, the look in her eyes the day he'd driven her out of town still haunted him.

It was therefore with much sadness he saw Lexi's joy fade as the sun began to set. They sat together on the southernmost border, on a small ledge that overlooked the entire valley, now bathed in a soft, amber glow that matched her eyes. The view alone made the property priceless.

"This has been wonderful," Lexi said, her eyes moist as she gazed out at the sunset.

"Aye, that it has," Jack said simply, but the wonder he'd glimpsed hadn't been in the house or the grounds. It had been in the eyes and heart and mind of a girl who had, at least for a few hours, remembered how to dream.

"Thanks, Uncle Jack, for bringing me here."

"My pleasure, lass."

"I can't keep it."

Jack remained silent, watching the spark of light he'd seen in her eyes all afternoon as it began to dull. "It's not habitable," she said.

"No," Jack agreed, slowly. "But it could be with a bit of work. She's structurally sound."

"A bit?" Lexi asked doubtfully. "Uncle Jack, you said yourself the wiring was shot, the plumbing needs a complete overhaul, ..." She went on and on as he let her get it all out, somewhat surprised and impressed that she had registered and retained all that information. With every reason she listed, her exuberance continued to wane.

In his opinion, Lexi needed this house. She wanted it; she just didn't believe she could have it.

"I wouldn't even know where to start," she concluded, blowing out a breath, deflating before his eyes.

"You speak as if you had to do it all alone, lass."

Her eyes flickered with hope for a moment, but then she shook her head. "I'm sorry, Uncle Jack, but I just don't belong here anymore." The sadness in her eyes was heart-wrenching.

"Bullshite. You've got family here."

Lexi snorted softly, a cross between a choked sob and a laugh. "Surely you're not talking about Patricia and Kayla?"

"Of course not."

Lexi looked genuinely baffled.

"Now you are just being insulting, lass," he huffed.

Realization dawned on her face; her eyes widened and her cheeks grew red. "I didn't mean -"

"I know what you meant. But family doesn't always have to be blood." He took her hand in his, and looked at it intensely while he gathered his thoughts. "As long as we're around, you will always have family here, do you hear what I am saying, Alexis?"

She nodded, averting her eyes, but not before

he saw the telltale sheen of moisture in them.

"That's a good lass. We will talk about this more tonight over dinner and then you can sleep on it. All right?"

* * *

Lexi picked at her dinner under Kieran's watchful eye, but only because Kieran threatened to force-feed her if she didn't eat something. Part of her itched to call his bluff. The other part of her though, the realistic part, knew him well enough to know that he would make good on his threat, and wouldn't that just be a barrel of fun?

For the most part, she remained silent as Jack brought Kieran up to speed on the day's events. While listening intently, and managing to put away more than she could eat in a week, Kieran apparently tired of her playing with her food. He reached over and cut her steak into small, bite-sized pieces.

"Eat," he commanded, as if she wasn't a grown woman perfectly capable of taking care of herself. Without thinking, she stuck her tongue out at him. His eyes blazed (all of the Callaghans had that strange optical power), then the corners of his mouth twitched.

"Oh, that's real mature, Lex."

She couldn't help it. She smiled, too. Then she started to laugh. Kieran had always been able to do that. To push her buttons until she was ready to throttle him, then say or do something that made her laugh and forgive him instantly.

"Goof," she muttered. He pointed at her plate. She sighed, spearing a carrot instead (purely out of spite) and brought it to her lips.

The food was delicious, but to say she was feeling a bit off-balance would have been putting it mildly. Within intervals as short as five minutes she'd swing from childlike enthusiasm to adult-like pessimism and back again. Throw in a decided lack of sleep, the loss of her father, the stress of Patricia's appeal against the will, and the whole mess with Ian and she didn't know which way was up. Taking on the added responsibility of home-ownership was more than she was capable of handling at that moment.

While her logical mind created a list of the reasons why it was a bad idea, the idealistic, romantic part of her --- the same one that had been pining for Ian all these years --- tuned it out. The cottage and the land were perfect. Everything she could ever want. Contrary to what her realistic side said, it wasn't a broken down cottage on neglected acreage. It was a castle straight out of a fairytale, situated smack-dab in the middle of enchanted ground.

"Can't wait to see it," Kieran said as Jack spoke of their afternoon. "Sounds awesome."

"It needs some work," Jack admitted, and

began to run down the substantial renovations required to make it livable.

Just like that, Lexi's fantasy took a decided nosedive into reality once again. He meant well, she knew he did, but he didn't understand, and she couldn't expect him to. The kind man she called her Uncle Jack spoke as if she really was a part of their family, but she wasn't.

She *was* alone. Had been for a very long time. She preferred it that way, actually. Except for Aidan. Aidan knew all of her secrets (well, most of them, anyway) and kept the monsters at bay. If he was here now, he would be the first one to tell her that she was in over her head.

Which was yet another reason why she should be getting the hell out of Dodge and not looking back.

"We're heading back up tomorrow," Jack was saying, avoiding the sudden look of surprise Lexi shot him. "Johnny's coming to take a look."

"Who's Johnny?" Lexi asked, not quite sure she wanted to know.

"Our cousin," Kieran explained. "He owns a huge construction business across the way in Birch Falls. Does mainly big stuff, but he's into restorations and renovations now, too. There's nobody better."

"I really don't think that's a good idea."

"Calm down, lass," Jack soothed. "Johnny can give us a good idea of what's what, and you'll need that, no matter what you decide to do."

He was right, of course, and she would have realized that if she wasn't riding such an emotional roller coaster. She needed to get a grip. Thanks to her father, she was the current owner of the place, whether she wanted to be or not. Having it appraised was the smart thing to do. Even if she wasn't going to keep it, she should have an idea of its worth.

She nodded. It was the responsible thing to do. And she'd be lying if she said some part of her didn't want to go up there again, at least once more.

Things only got worse when they stopped back at the pub after dinner. Jake, it seemed, had spread the word to the others, and they all wanted to help. By the end of the evening she'd grown tired of trying to rein them in; they weren't really listening to her anyway. Eventually she'd given up, sitting quietly off to the side, nursing her clear soda, until Kieran finally noticed her eyes drifting shut and took pity on her.

Back in her hotel room, Lexi flopped down on the bed, her head still spinning as she tried to process it all. So much was happening so fast; she felt as if she was being swept away in a current of events over which she had no control. She was running on empty and she knew it. Before long, the past two days finally took their toll on her and she dozed off.

She wasn't overly surprised when she woke up

to find Ian sitting at the small table in her room, watching her as she slept. Somehow, even in slumber, she had sensed his presence. Of course, that might have been because she'd been dreaming of him. Again. Except in this dream, Ian had been making love to her when Kayla suddenly appeared, laughing hysterically and leading Ian away from her by a collar while Lexi tried desperately to hold onto him.

She didn't need a psych degree to figure *that* one out.

She glanced at the clock, noting that it was just after midnight.

"Do you make a habit of breaking into people's rooms?" she asked sleepily, forcing herself to sit up and pin him with as fierce a glare as she could muster. Damn him, he looked good, even in the middle of the night, even with the sound of Kayla's cackle still echoing in her head.

chapter eleven

Ian studied her carefully. He'd been watching her sleep, intrigued by her dreams. At first it was erotic as hell. She was tossing under the sheet, uttering those soft little sighs and moans he now associated with very specific areas of her body. But then something changed. Her whispered cries grew anguished, her expression pained, her hands clawing in some nightmarish struggle as she murmured his name.

He was on the verge of waking her, the need to protect her, even in her dreams, strong. But she'd awoken on her own, and the look in her eyes when she spotted him tore at his heart. Whatever she'd been dreaming, it had shaken her. Hoping she might confide in him, or at the very least take some comfort from him, he waited silently.

"Well?" she demanded. "Do you?"

She was not going to share her dream with him. He wouldn't push, this time. If it happened again, all bets were off.

"I'm afraid that's classified information," he

said, opting for an attempt to lighten the mood. "I could tell you, but then I'd have to kill you."

For one brief moment, he thought he saw her lips quirk, but it was gone before it had a chance to take hold. "Ian, why are you here?"

"I was worried about you."

"Don't be. I'm a big girl."

"You don't have a problem with Kieran looking out for you."

"Kieran is my friend."

"Maybe I want to be your friend too, Lexi."

Lexi snorted, padding to the bathroom and closing the door behind her. With each step she seemed to recover a bit more, and Ian forced himself not to stalk across the room and pull her into his arms. He would refrain for as long as he could, allowing her to regain her footing. He was still learning about her, and he had a feeling there was a lot to learn. It would be worth it, though. That, he knew.

In the meantime, he appreciated the view, the curve of her lovely behind hidden beneath the hem of her plain white cotton V-neck T, the one that nearly went down to her knees.

With a start, he realized the shirt looked familiar. It was *his*. He must have left it here that first night in his mad scramble to get to the viewing. The corners of his mouth curved upward. She was wearing his shirt?

Ian felt like thumping his chest. Something

about Lexi called to the primal male in him more than most. Around her he felt more protective, more possessive, more aggressive than usual.

His eyes remained riveted on the bathroom door. Had she always been this enchanting? Her sleep-tussled hair. The sexy, drowsy look. That lush, curvy body that made his cock hard, his mouth water, and his hands itch to touch her. Oh yeah. He wouldn't mind waking up next to that. Which, frankly, scared the hell out of him. But he was trained to ignore fear and go in anyway.

The toilet flushed and the shower went on. *Torturous vixen.* She was doing it just to drive him crazy with the thought of her under the hot spray, naked and wet. He clenched and unclenched his fists, promising himself he would behave. Frankly, he was surprised she hadn't kicked his ass out right away. He was grateful for it, but surprised. Most women would have been less receptive and more hostile, given the circumstances.

He sighed. Lexi might be out of his sight, but her intoxicating scent still filled the room. It made him restless. He needed a distraction until she tired of punishing him.

Ian scanned the room; his eyes fell on the laptop next to the bed. A little recon, perhaps.

"So who's Aidan?" he asked innocently when she emerged from the bathroom a full thirty minutes later. He was propped up on her bed, legs extended, her notebook computer open and in his lap (which had the added benefit of covering what had become a natural state in her presence).

Steam billowed out into the room. Her hair was wrapped atop her head turban-style; another towel was wrapped around her body, hiding the more delicious parts. That was probably a good thing. If they were as flushed and pink as the skin she *was* showing, he would be hard pressed not to lick and kiss every inch before it cooled.

The expression on her face was unreadable when she realized he was still there. Obviously she knew nothing about the infinite patience of SEALs and how long they would wait to accomplish an objective.

"What do you think you're doing?" Lexi crossed the room and snapped the laptop closed. The aroma of freshly washed, warm, soft woman hit him full on. God help him.

"Checking your email." Ian was unrepentant, speaking in a tone that suggested he had every right to go through her personal things.

He frowned, noticing the marks on her body. Marks he had left in the throes of passion. Had he been that rough with her? He hadn't meant to be. He reached up to touch one along the back of her shoulder, but she quickly moved away, stepping out of his reach.

Her eyes narrowed, all traces of whatever had spooked her gone. "And you thought I would be okay with that *why*?"

He gave her a roguish grin and put up his hands in a gesture of surrender. "It's your fault. You left me out here all alone. You were practically begging me to find something to keep myself busy. I guess I could have followed you into the shower instead. That certainly would have been more fun, though far less informative."

An instant flush appeared above the towel, rising up the slim column of her neck and into her face. Ian spotted the lovely coloring and felt himself harden even more. She placed her laptop on the other side of the room and opened her suitcase, searching for something to wear. Ian frowned. He liked seeing her in his shirt. He unbuttoned the one he was wearing and held it out to her.

"He certainly sends you a lot of email."

"Who?" she asked, eyeing his shirt as if she just might take it. He approved of her glances at his chest, too, and the way it seemed to drive the thought of any other man out of her mind.

"*Aidan.*"

"Not that it's any of your business, but Aidan is my …. boss."

Ian shrugged, as if the information meant nothing to him, but her hesitation bothered him. A lot. Of course by now he knew everything there was to know about Aidan Harrison, including the fact that he didn't want him anywhere near Lexi again. Ever.

Ian wasn't quite sure how he was going to

swing that one, considering that she was the head chef of Harrison's most successful restaurant chain, but he would figure out something. So far he had fearlessness and resourcefulness going for him. Why not a little cleverness as well?

Lexi stared hard into the small closet. "You went through my stuff?" she accused in disbelief.

Ian shrugged again, his eyes mischievous. He'd deliberately left things in different positions, wondering if she would notice. She did. "I was bored."

She was sexy when she was riled. Her chest heaved, her eyes glowed, and her perfect skin turned the most beautiful shade of peachy pink. Her eyes went from him to the Salienne Dulcette erotic romance novel on the bed next to him and she scowled. *Beautiful*.

"So why won't you sleep with him?"

"Excuse me?"

"Your *boss*, Aidan. Why won't you sleep with him? Is he ugly or something? Old? Great big warts and age spots? Maybe he has a tiny little --- " Ian held up his thumb and index finger about an inch apart from each other.

* * *

"For your information, Aidan is young, gorgeous and *very* sexy. Not to mention extremely wealthy and brilliant." Which was all true, but it didn't matter, not to her. *Because Aidan was not Ian.* But Ian didn't have to know that. "And what makes you think I'm *not* sleeping with him?"

Ian flashed a smile, showing nearly every one of his perfect white teeth. "Because if you *were* sleeping with him, he wouldn't dare let you out of his sight and anywhere near the likes of someone like *me*. He'd be here right now, pleasuring you, ravaging your perfect body over and over again until you were too exhausted to even scream his name."

Her breath caught. Warm, moist heat pooled between her thighs. Her breasts grew instantly full and heavy, aching for his hands to cradle them. Then Ian was behind her, sending exciting little shudders up and down her spine.

"At least that's what I'd be doing," he added softly, releasing her hair from the towel, gently pulling the damp strands through his fingers. "If I was sleeping with you."

His fingers skimmed the tops of her shoulders, feathered down her arms. Despite the warmth of the room goose bumps began forming along her skin. She shuddered, her nipples growing harder, nerves firing from the tips of her toes to the base of her skull. Even the slight rasp of the terry towel had her practically moaning with need. How did he do that? How could he render her totally helpless with a few whispered words and a gentle caress?

Lexi fought for self-control as her traitorous

body wanted nothing except to melt into him. "Ian," she moaned, hating the desperation she heard in her voice. The stark, raw hunger that consumed her whenever he touched her, spoke to her, looked at her.

Everyone said it had been a crush. Puppy love. But she knew better. Ian Callaghan was the only man she would ever want; the only man she would ever love. Her feelings had only grown stronger with time and distance, to the point where they were terrifying. There was nothing she would not do for him if he asked it of her. She could never tell him no.

Had Ian felt the same, it would have been a match made in and blessed by Heaven itself. Two people so desperately in love could be nothing less, the stuff of ageless legends.

Lexi had been drawn to Ian from the very first time she'd seen him. Over time, she began to realize that what she felt for him was not an infatuation, not a silly crush. It was so much stronger than that, so much deeper than anything she'd ever felt before. So much so that she'd never been able to give herself to another. The only man she had ever wanted, ever needed, could seduce her with his voice, his touch, his very presence. And therein lay the problem.

Unbidden, Kayla's voice echoed in her head. *But then again, I got what you really wanted, didn't I? See princess? He wants me.*

Visions began slamming into her, one after the other as Kayla's words repeated over and over in a vicious loop: Ian beside Kayla in front of the casket. By her side in the church. At the cemetery. Kayla's arms wrapped around him as he practically carried her out of the wake.

In each one, Ian was exactly where a man should be for a woman he cared about. Part of her wanted to believe that Ian's actions were those of a man comforting a friend of the family's in her time of need, but none of the others had shown such support.

Only Ian.

And that entire day, Ian had said not one word to her. He had gone out of his way to avoid her, in fact.

Oh, she'd felt him glancing over at her occasionally. Surely it had been quite a shock when he realized who she was. She couldn't blame him for being angry, for pretending not to know her under the circumstances. She hadn't been honest with him, and she sure as hell would have been upset had their places been reversed. But that didn't explain why he was here now, running the pads of his sinfully skilled fingers up and down her arms and giving her chills while a fire burned in her core.

The way he touched her, with so much tenderness and passion, made her doubt her theories. Had he not been at Kayla's side all that day, Lexi might actually believe Ian felt something for her. But he had been. She'd witnessed the two of them together with her own eyes. Even Kieran had confirmed that they were still together when she'd asked. And ten years was a long time. There were plenty of marriages that didn't last that long.

But God, she loved him so much it hurt. Ian desired her, that much she could tell easily from the shaft of pure steel pressing into her back. But was it enough? Could she be his secret mistress, the one he came to under cloak of darkness to fulfill her fantasies, only to have him leave again in the morning to return to another? A crushing band tightened around her chest making it difficult to breathe, because part of her screamed *Yes!*

Yet another part of her, the part that had taken her to Benton and saw her through the daily struggles of her life, simply said, *No*. Not in the desperate, clawing voice of the other, but calmly, objectively.

She knew which voice she should be listening to.

"Is that how you are with Kayla then?" Somehow the words made it past the closure in her throat, even as her heart reached up to pull them back down.

Ian's hands stilled. She felt him tense, felt the power accumulating around him like an encroaching darkness.

"No." The word was clipped. Sharp. Like a falling axe.

She stepped out of his arms. It was one of the hardest things she'd ever done.

Ian ran his hand through his hair, leaving some parts sticking out at odd angles. The look on his face was pained. "Lexi, you need to understand ---"

She broke him off immediately. "Don't worry, Ian. I won't tell on you." Her voice was hollow and removed, speaking from her mind and not from her heart. It sounded as wrong as it felt.

"Though it is strangely tempting. I imagine it would drive Kayla over the edge to know that you slept with *me*, of all people."

His pained expression gave way to disbelief. "Is that why you did it? Revenge? You thought you'd hurt her, like she hurt you?"

"Of course not," she snapped, insulted that he would think her capable of such a thing. "How could I possibly know you two would still be together after ten years?"

Ian winced. Lexi hated saying anything that hurt him, but sometimes the truth was painful. She tried to soften the blow a little. "What happened between us had absolutely nothing to do with her."

"And what exactly happened between us, Lexi?" he asked quietly. "Please. Explain it to me."

Everything drained out of her then. All of the fight, all of the anger, leaving nothing but a soul-deep ache in its place. What was she fighting for anyway? She was in town for what, a few days? Kayla lived here, and had both a past and a present with Ian. How could she hope to compete with that?

"Fulfillment of a young, foolish girl's fantasy," she said, sounding weary as she sat down on the edge of the bed. "I'm sorry, Ian. I should have told you who I was before…" The words trailed off, unnecessary.

"Why didn't you?" he asked, repeating the same question he'd asked only that morning. Had it really only been this morning? It felt like half of a lifetime had passed between then and now.

"Because I …" She drew in a shaky breath, unable to look at him and feeling more ashamed by the moment. She couldn't answer him, not truthfully, because to do so would be to bare her soul, to open a hole into her heart so big it would suck whatever little remained of her down into it.

"I'm so sorry." She whispered the words, trying valiantly not to cry and embarrass herself further. She was failing miserably. Huge crystalline drops trailed down her face onto her lap, absorbing immediately into the towel, but not before he'd seen them. Her shoulders were hunched in, her arms wrapped around herself protectively.

Ian took a step toward her, but she held up her hand. If he came near her, touched her, she would tell him the truth. All of it. She needed to retain some shred of dignity, no matter how thin of a thread it might be. "You should go."

"*Please*." She begged, her voice thick with tears.

Lexi kept her gaze downward, knowing that if she looked at him she wouldn't be able to remain strong. After several long moments, he picked up his shirt and walked quietly to the door.

"You're wrong, Lexi," he said quietly. "Me and Kayla, it's not what you think. It's just... not."

"You mean you didn't sleep with her?"

His lips thinned, but he didn't deny it. "Lexi..."

"Go."

Ian opened the door and was gone, and Lexi gave in to the tears.

chapter twelve

It had not been a good day. After Ian left, Lexi cried alone in her room until there were no more tears left, falling into an exhausted sleep sometime right before dawn. Then Aidan called, worried that she hadn't responded to his emails or texts. As soon as he'd heard her voice, he'd known immediately that something was wrong, and she'd spent the next hour convincing him not to drop everything and fly up in his private plane.

Jack had come for her in the late morning. The concern was evident in his eyes as he insisted on taking her out to lunch, commenting that she looked too tired, too pale. It was true enough. The drama of returning to Pine Ridge was definitely taking its toll, though she had only herself to blame. She had learned a long time ago that life wasn't so much about what happened to you as how you dealt with it.

Yes, Ian had pursued her, but she could have said no and refused to sleep with him. Hell, she'd had no problem turning away everyone else.

And yes, Kayla had made things unpleasant for her, but what was new about that? Kayla had spent nearly every moment of their childhood together doing that, and she'd learned to deal with it. To this day she had no idea why Kayla despised her as much as she did, but things didn't always make sense, did they?

It just proved that the move to Georgia had been the best thing that could have happened to her. Thankfully, her father had realized that even when she hadn't been able to see it. Lexi had grown up, grown stronger, made something of herself, but Kayla hadn't changed at all. She was still the petty, vain, insecure girl she'd been ten years ago, and in a way, Lexi couldn't help but feel sorry for her.

The trip back to her grandmother's house? Well, that had just been poor judgment on her part.

Even with an unsettled stomach from forcing down a meal she didn't want, the short trip had been pleasant enough. She'd forgotten how much she loved the mountains. The cool, clean air. The deep greens and turquoises against a crystal blue sky. The smell of damp earth and pine needles mixing with honeysuckle and mimosa and mountain laurel. No matter how far she travelled, no matter how long she stayed away, this would always feel like home to her.

That nice, cozy feeling hadn't lasted long, though. The moment the house came into view so did several vehicles. Jack had conveniently neglected to mention that the others had come earlier. Jake and Taryn were there, holding hands as they appeared along the side of the house. Judging by the flushed look on Taryn's face and Jake's mussed hair, Lexi guessed they'd found a little magic of their own. Shane and Sean were on the roof, checking out the view, and Lexi was amazed the thing was able to hold their combined weight in its current state.

Kieran appeared in the doorway with a man who had to be the cousin, Johnny. Lexi sucked in a breath when she saw him; he was huge, like all the Callaghan men, with layers of rippling muscle that would have had professional body builders weeping in envy. His long, multi-hued golden hair was tied neatly at the back of his neck by a leather chord. And even from so far away, Lexi could see his green eyes clearly. He was gorgeous, yes, but so were all of the men in this family. What floored her was that he was the spitting image of the guy featured on the cover of her latest Salienne Dulcette novel.

"Lex!" shouted Kieran with a huge smile as he jogged out to the car. "This is Johnny Connelly. Johnny, meet Lex."

Lexi accepted his hand. It swallowed hers, the roughened callouses telling her that he maintained a hands-on role in his business, which elevated him immediately in her eyes. His smile, like his eyes, was warm and genuine.

"Nice to meet you, Lexi," Johnny said. "Hey, Uncle Jack! Thanks for calling me out on this one. This place is incredible. Kieran has been walking me through it."

The roar of a motorcycle announced yet another arrival. Lexi stiffened when she heard Ian's voice behind her and approaching quickly.

"Johnny! Been awhile, man." Ian greeted his cousin with a firm handshake and a genuine smile.

"Ian. Glad to see you made it back in one piece. Heard it was a tough one."

Ian shrugged, brushing it off, but Lexi had seen the brief moment of darkness in his eyes, and it sent an unwelcome jolt of fear through her. She had known all of them had (or had planned to) enter the service right out of school; it was a family thing. She didn't like to think about that, though.

"How's Stace?"

Johnny's green eyes practically glowed at the mention of his wife. "Hanging in there. The baby's giving her a bit of a hard time, but you know Stace. She won't ever admit it."

Ian grinned. "Yeah. She's as stubborn as you."

Johnny chuckled. "Maybe even more so." Turning to Lexi, he said, "So, you inherited this place from your grandmother?"

Lexi nodded. "I used to come here when I was little. I'd forgotten all about it until yesterday."

"Kieran told me your father just passed. I'm sorry about that."

She thanked him for the kind sentiments. "So tell me, what do you think?"

Johnny smiled. "I like her. No bullshit, just straight to the point --- ah, sorry, Uncle Jack," he added as the older man gave him a disapproving glance. "So, Lexi, are you looking to fix the place up for yourself or put it on the market?"

"I'll most likely be putting it on the market," she said, ignoring the laser-like precision of several pairs of luminous blue eyes boring into her. "My home is in Georgia now."

Johnny nodded. "Kieran told me. You're some kind of master chef or something, right?"

Lexi reddened. "Kieran exaggerates," she said, shooting him a look. "But I do cook for a restaurant."

Kieran snorted. "Yeah. The Celtic Goddess. The entire menu is her creation."

Lexi cringed. She hated that name, but Aidan had insisted.

"No shit!" Johnny said, shooting another apologetic glance at Jack. "My wife loves that place! We hit it whenever we're in Boston or Chicago. Never been to the one down south, though. Stace is always saying she wishes they'd open up one around here."

"You travel a lot then?" Lexi asked, attempting to divert the attention away from herself.

"Yeah, Stace is an author, has to do these book things, you know. Gets us out of town a couple of times a year, but we haven't been doing much lately because of the baby. She's due any day now. It's our first."

His green eyes glowed with pride and excitement, and something else: fear. Instinctively, Lexi sensed that he was a lot more worried than he let on. She'd seen enough worry and fear in others' eyes her whole life to recognize it instantly.

"What's her favorite dish?"

"The pasta with the steak and olives."

Lexi smiled. "That's one of my favorites, too. Tell you what. If it's okay with Uncle Jack, I'll use his kitchen this afternoon and make some for her."

Johnny beamed. "She would love that."

"Then consider it done. Now about this house…"

"It's a great house," Johnny told her. "Foundation is good, solid. Structure is sound. Can't remember when the last time was I came across stone like this," he said approvingly. "Or saw a cellar with an honest-to-God cold spring. It needs some work, but nothing too major. Mostly cosmetic stuff. Biggest thing is the roof, you'll want that replaced as soon as possible. Most of it these guys can handle," he said, indicating the men who'd gathered around, "but I'll oversee the reno personally if you agree."

Lexi thanked him.

"Hey," Johnny said with a grin, "Kieran says you're family."

"I'll see you Saturday," Johnny called back a short while later, getting into his truck. "And bring Lexi," he added with a smile and a knowing laugh. "Stacey's going to kill me if she finds out I met her and didn't introduce them."

"What's on Saturday?" Lexi asked, turning to Kieran.

"The county fair. Official site of the annual Callaghan/Connelly family reunion."

"Oh." She bit her lip. She would be gone by then, but there was no need to bring that up now. The last thing she needed was for them all to gang up on her at once. She just didn't have the strength.

Lexi wandered around the house again while she waited for the others. They seemed to understand her desire to be alone, but she also knew she was always within sight of one of them. She'd forgotten what it felt like to be the focus of so much attention, so much worry. It was comforting, in a way, yet somewhat suffocating.

Having Ian there made it even more uncomfortable. Kieran mentioned something about a security system, and that was Ian's area of expertise. It was hard to concentrate, knowing he was in the next room or just down the hallway. Despite herself, she sought him out, hoping to catch him in her peripheral vision, or to turn suddenly and find him there, watching her. So far, she'd only managed occasional glimpses of him now and then. She should have been glad he was avoiding her, but felt oddly disappointed, too.

Still, she felt his presence keenly. And as the afternoon went on, the weight of the tension between them increased. The pressure in the air around her grew heavier until it as if a storm was bearing down on them. Thankfully, no one else seemed to be aware of it.

Escaping outdoors had its own perils as well, even though it seemed like a good idea at the time. The yard was overgrown; the path around the once lovingly-tended gardens was now a haphazard collection of barely-visible, disjointed stones.

Lexi meandered around the area, fondly recalling the beauty she had seen there so long ago. Her eyes widened in excitement when she saw the huge clump of black raspberries near the far end of the yard. It had been ages, but she remembered how sweet and juicy they tasted right off the bush.

"LEXI!" Kieran's roar was so loud and so unexpected she yelped in surprise and stumbled, her shirt catching on the thorns. Within seconds she felt herself being hauled backward forcibly out into the open while Kieran frantically disentangled her from the brambles.

"Are you crazy?" Kieran hissed, searching her arms and legs for cuts.

The others were moving quickly, brought forth by Kieran's yell. Not surprisingly, Ian was the first to reach them. Lexi saw the question burning in his intense blue eyes and felt her cheeks grow scarlet in embarrassment.

"Let me go," she demanded, slapping at Kieran's arms until he released her. Feeling more humiliated than ever, she shot Kieran a look fierce enough to make him take a step back, then stormed away.

"What was that all about?" she heard Ian ask behind her. *Please don't tell him*, Lexi silently begged.

"Nothing that concerns you," Kieran barked in response. "Just stay away from her, Ian."

Thank God for Taryn. After catching the tail end of the drama, she stepped up and offered to take Lexi back to the pub for a little girl time.

Lexi liked Taryn; she really did. She felt an instant kinship with Jake's new bride, and that in itself was an unexpected bonus. Lexi rarely felt connected to anyone, but the few she did were a small group, and almost exclusively male. To find a woman she genuinely liked and felt semi-comfortable around was rare. As a matter of fact, she would be hard-pressed to come up with another example. The fact that Taryn had rescued her without asking any questions only reinforced her initial opinion.

The afternoon took a definite upturn when they picked up some groceries and went back to the pub kitchens. Taryn was bold and wickedly funny, her irreverence for the world around her refreshingly pleasant.

"You and Jake," Lexi commented, as she sliced the veggies, her hands moving fast and accurately, cutting the ingredients into perfect, consistent pieces. "You guys are the real thing."

Taryn pounded the steak into paper-thin strips like Lexi had shown her. "What do you mean?"

"Soul mates." Lexi scooped the veggies into a frying pan and splashed them with extra virgin olive oil before turning to the piles of fresh herbs. She did so effortlessly, her hands working independently of everything else, without having to think about it. "I mean, the way you look at each other. It's like the stuff they write about, you know? When Jake looks at you, it's like you're the center of his whole world."

"You mean like how Ian looks at you?"

The knife hit the cutting board hard, the sound discordant with the perfect rhythm she'd had going. Lexi cursed, immediately wrapping a towel around her hand.

"Oh, Jesus, I'm sorry," Taryn exclaimed, her eyes going wide.

"Don't worry about it," Lexi said, keeping her voice calm. "Got any super glue around here?"

Taryn looked confused. "Super glue?" She glanced down at Lexi's hand, where blood was already soaking through the towel at an alarming rate. "Oh, shit … yeah, hang on."

Taryn ran to the other side of the kitchen and threw open a drawer, tossing things out of the way till she found what she was looking for.

"Good," said Lexi, cursing herself for letting this happen. "Give it to me." Taryn watched in horrified fascination as Lexi pulled off the cap with her teeth and poured the stuff over the cut. "I'll call 911," Taryn said, reaching for the phone.

"NO!" Lexi yelled. "It's okay, trust me. I've got this."

Two more towels and half a bottle of super glue later, the bleeding had almost stopped.

"That's not normal," Taryn said, looking a little shaken, though not as much as Lexi would have expected.

"No," Lexi agreed. "But it's okay, really. It's not the first time this has happened, and it won't be the last. Watch this for me, will you? Don't let this burn." Remaining calm, Lexi went over to her bag and pulled out a preloaded syringe. Taryn watched as she injected herself directly above the wrist.

"I need to sit down for a few. I'll talk you through the rest."

"Are you sure? Maybe we should forget about dinner."

"I'm sure." Lexi's tone left no question. She looked right into Taryn's eyes. "*I'm sure.*" Taryn nodded, looking far less certain.

Lexi grimaced as the industrial-strength clotting agent burned like fire through her veins. After a few minutes, she forced herself to get up and move around, knowing if she didn't keep her circulation moving, there was the danger of a serious clot forming.

"You're doing great," Lexi said a little while later, peering over Taryn's shoulder. "Call me if you ever want to work as a chef."

"Lex, I'm really sorry. I didn't mean to upset you."

"It's okay, Taryn. Really. No big. But listen, I have to go, okay? Let that simmer for another few minutes then take it off the heat, and you're good to go."

"Wait, I'll drive you back to your hotel."

"No, I need to walk it, but thanks. And Taryn? I'd really appreciate it if we kept this between us." Without another word, Lexi picked up her bag and made her exit, keeping her head high and a smile pasted on her face until she got outside.

chapter thirteen

When she got back to the hotel, Lexi changed out of her bloodied clothes, gave herself a quick clean-up, wrapped up her hand in waterproof tape, and headed for the pool. The cool, soothing water felt good, and if she was lucky, she would be able to swim herself into enough of an exhaustive state that she might get a few hours of sleep. She should have known better.

Lexi sliced through the water with such precision she barely made a sound. Stroke after stroke, lap after lap. Swimming had always been a good outlet for her, one of the few athletic events in which she could actually participate. No physical contact with others, no balls or sticks or blades. No one expected her to excel at it.

Like the way Ian looks at you? Taryn's words echoed in her head over and over again, right along with the image of Taryn's horrified expression at the sight of all the blood. She pulled harder, faster, cutting through the water as if she could outpace them. The chemicals rushed through her veins, the familiar burning in her nose and throat and ears as her body absorbed them, until little by little, she started to feel normal again. Until she started thinking clearly again.

In the water, she felt weightless, invincible. It soothed and calmed her, held her while she worked out her demons. Kieran used to tease her that Poseidon was one of her ancestors. Sometimes, especially in times of great stress when the water was her only comfort, she wondered if there was a tiny grain of truth in there somewhere.

Kieran was watching her now, just like he used to when they were in junior high. For more than an hour she'd caught the sight of his big body sitting off to the side at every flip-turn, waiting patiently. She wasn't surprised. He knew her well enough to know a pool would be the first place she'd flee to when things got to be too much. She would swim until her lungs burned and her muscles deadened, then he'd pull her out of the water and make her tell him what was bothering her anyway.

Right on schedule, she saw him crouched along the far end. In the midst of her flip turn, he reached in and wrapped his hand around her ankle before she pushed off. When she whipped around to protest, he simply plucked her out of the pool.

Lexi just went with it, had known it was coming, though she was somewhat surprised at the ease with which he had done it. After all, she wasn't a skinny kid anymore. Then again, Kieran was the size of a rather large bear these days.

While she appreciated that he had come, her mind was already made up. She was leaving Pine Ridge tomorrow and not looking back. She was going to place a call to the lawyer's office first thing in the morning and ask him to draw up whatever papers were necessary to sign the house over to Jack Callaghan. He could do with it whatever he wanted.

"What the hell were you thinking, Lex?" Kieran asked. His voice was far too quiet, far too controlled to be good. Oh, he was angry. *Really* angry. Taryn must have told him what happened. While Taryn hadn't understood the severity of Lexi's mishap, Kieran certainly would, and did, if the fury in his eyes was any indication.

"Put me down, Kieran," Lexi said resignedly. "I'm not your new bath toy."

Normally Kieran would have grinned and shot a smart-ass comment right back at her, but he didn't. His face was somber, his eyes deep and probing. He didn't even seem to notice that she was dripping all over him. Lexi felt the unwelcome stares of a few curious onlookers. Not wanting to give them anything more to gawk at, she said, "Seriously, Kier, let me down. You're giving me a major wedgie, and that perv over there is getting a little too much enjoyment out of it."

Kieran's eyes flashed to the far side of the pool where a man was sitting, towel in lap, watching the scene with great interest. With a warning look and a low level growl from Kieran, the man suddenly gathered his things and left in a hurry.

"If I let you down, will you walk quietly back to your room with me?"

"No."

"Doesn't give me much incentive, then, does it?" Kieran said, taking the choice from her and hefting Lexi one-handedly over his shoulder. Quickly grabbing a towel, he draped it over her rear end. Ignoring the stares of anyone they passed, Kieran took the steps toward the third floor.

She sighed heavily, letting him carry her. There wasn't really much she could do about it anyway. Very little could stop Kieran when he was in one of his overprotective snits. The best thing to do was to just go with it and wait it out until he started thinking like a rational human being again.

It was yet another reason why she needed to leave. It would be better for everyone. As long as she was around, Kieran would feel the need to protect her. He deserved better than that. They all did.

Kieran wouldn't want to hear that, though. He'd try to convince her that she belonged here, but he'd be wrong. She should never have come back, never should have put herself in a position to be around them again. It was time for her to return to her familiar, steady job in her private, solitary apartment, interacting on an impersonal and as-needed basis with those around her. It worked for her, and God knew, it had to be better for them, too.

Arguing the evening away with Kieran didn't fit into her plans. Somehow she needed to find the strength to get through the rest of the day with as little strife as possible until she boarded the Greyhound tomorrow.

He dropped her unceremoniously on the bed, then began pacing in front of her. "Jesus, Lex. What the hell happened?"

"Don't start with me, Kier," she warned, walking away from him. "I just don't have the strength."

"Good. That means you're not going to give me a hard time."

Lexi didn't respond, instead grabbing a few things from her suitcase and disappearing into the bathroom. She re-emerged a few minutes later, scrubbing at her hair with a towel and wearing something he was sure to recognize: his old football jersey from high school. It hung down to her knees.

"Jesus!" he said when he saw it. "You still have that?!" His face lit up like a kid's on Christmas morning.

"Of course," she said, glad that he seemed to be breathing easier. "I have it with me always. This shirt has travelled the world, Kieran. At least twice." She laughed, giving him a good look up and down. "Bet you didn't know you've been sleeping with me all this time, huh."

"Jesus Christ, Lex," he sputtered, turning beet red. "That is wrong on so many levels. You know that, don't you?"

She laughed softly and punched him in the arm. It was like hitting a brick wall. "Yeah, I know. But you should see the look on your face right now."

"Not funny, Lex. You know you're like my little sister, right?"

"I'm older than you," she reminded him.

"By what, a month?"

"Doesn't matter. Still older. Respect your elders, and all that."

His smile faded somewhat when he saw her extract a small kit from her makeup bag. "Still have to do that, huh?"

She gave him a reassuring smile as she filled the syringe. Kieran was one of the few who knew her dark secret. "Yeah. Sucks, right?" She pushed the plunger to clear the syringe of air, then turned away from him and slid the needle into the fleshy part of her thigh. "You'd think with all the things they could do today I wouldn't have to."

He picked up the empty vial, frowning when he saw the dosage. "It's worse, isn't it?"

Lexi plucked the vial from his hand, tossing it back into her bag. She never left empties behind.

"You worry too much." It *was* worse, but he didn't need to know that.

"What happened at the pub, Lex?"

"Taryn didn't tell you?"

Kieran shook his head. "No. She just said you weren't feeling well and came back to the hotel to lay down for a while. But I knew better." His tone was serious, his expression earnest. She knew he was thinking about all the times she'd needed his help when they were younger. Honestly, she didn't know what she would have done without him. He pointed to the wrap around her hand. "Come on, let's see."

"It's nothing. A little cut, that's all."

"Damn it, Lex. A little cut can *kill* you."

"Don't you think I know that?" she snapped, her voice rising. "Don't you think I live with that knowledge every fucking day of my life? I know what I am."

At her uncharacteristic use of vulgar language, Kieran stopped dead in his tracks. He swept his hand through his hair, messing it up and reminding her of the awkward fourteen year-old he had once been. The worry, the pain in his eyes was killing her. "Damn it, Lex. I'm sorry."

She nodded, but couldn't help the tears that fell. She was becoming such a cry baby.

"Ah, hell, don't cry," he said, going to his knees in front of her. "Please don't cry."

"I'm all right," she sniffled, trying to wave him away. "It's just been a tough couple of days."

Kieran ignored her protest and pulled her into his arms anyway. "God, you're such a brute," she mumbled into his chest. "Let me go."

"Make me," he said softly, holding her head to his chest and rocking. She didn't bother. He was twice her size, twice her weight, and she had the feeling he needed this even more than she did.

"Kieran." Her voice was soft, compelling. The kind of voice that calmed him almost instantly. The one that had stayed his anger more times in school than she could count. If not for her, he probably would have been expelled. Everyone always assumed that he had been the one looking out for her, but it had worked both ways. If she hadn't encouraged him to pursue martial arts, to learn the skill and discipline he needed, who knows what kind of trouble his explosive temper might have gotten him into.

He sat on the bed so she could reach his head, a silent permission for her to stroke his hair next. She did. He leaned into it and closed his eyes.

"I'm a grown woman."

"So? That means I have to stop caring about you?"

"No, of course not. But you can't protect me anymore."

He sighed. "Maybe not all the time. But right here? Right now? Yes, I can."

Lexi had been so caught up in her own problems she forgot that she wasn't the only one who would be leaving soon. Kieran, like each of his brothers before him, had enlisted right after high-school with the dream of becoming a Navy SEAL.

That was a minimum six-year commitment, she knew, since it was all he ever talked about. It was a gift of fate that he had not been actively deployed when her father passed away, so that he could be here with her now.

A few moments passed in silence before she asked, "How much time do you have left?"

"Not much. A year and a half, two years, tops. One more round of training, one more deployment."

"Then what?"

He gave her a crooked grin. "I'd tell you, but then I'd have to kill you."

"Hmmm. I think I've heard that before. Do all of you have that stitched on your pillows or something?"

"Yep. And you know what's on the flip side? *Take care of your own.*"

"I'm not one of you, Kier."

"Bullshit. And as long as you are in Pine Ridge, you are just going to have to deal with that."

Lexi knew he believed that. But he would have to face the truth sooner or later.

"Well then we won't have a problem much longer."

Kieran looked at her then. He blinked once. Twice. "You're leaving?"

She walked away, toward the window. Outside it was still light, though the sun was well below the buildings. Cloud cover made it darker than it would normally be at that time of day. A storm was brewing, and down below, she could see the streetlights just starting to come to life, people walking on the sidewalks. Some were alone. Some were holding hands or walking their dogs. So much normalcy. And here she was, always looking on from a distance. Always separate. Always apart. Never belonging.

"Yes."

"When?"

"Soon."

She let him mull that over for a few moments. "I thought you'd stick around a little longer at least. What about your grandmother's house?"

"I don't belong here."

His eyes told her he didn't believe that for one second. "You'll always belong here. It's part of who you are, where you come from. And you've got people here who love you, who'll take care of you."

"Maybe I don't want anyone to take care of me anymore, Kieran," she said, her eyes flashing. "Maybe I don't want to be anybody's burden. Maybe I just want to be left alone to live my own life without everyone feeling the need to interfere."

Lexi regretted the words the moment they were out of her mouth and she saw Kieran's face harden. She'd hurt him. Deeply. "Kieran, I'm sorry. I didn't mean that."

He held up his hand and stood, cutting off whatever she was going to say. "Fine. You know what? Go. Run away again. You're really good at that. And I promise I won't *interfere* anymore."

"That's harsh, Kier."

He stood up, making the room seem much smaller. "No, Lexi. What's harsh is you not giving a damn that people care about you. You think you have to do everything on your own, like some freaking martyr, leaving the rest of us feeling like we don't even matter enough for you to care."

"Kieran, that's not it at all."

"Save it. I'm outta here."

Yep. This day just kept getting better and better.

Chapter Fourteen

The faint glow of flickering candlelight both relieved and terrified him at the same time. Relieved, because he'd found her. Terrified, because she'd come all the way out here by herself and hadn't told anyone. Pine Ridge wasn't exactly a hotbed of criminal activity, but a young, beautiful, vulnerable woman like Lexi out here, alone? Ian had seen enough evil to know that even here, in this sleepy mountain valley, there was no such thing as "safe".

Keeping his distance from her at the house that afternoon had been more difficult than he'd ever imagined. To be so close and not speak with her, touch her, kiss her; it had nearly driven him mad. At least he got to see her, though. To know that she was all right. To hope that some small opportunity would present itself to rectify the misunderstanding between them.

Lexi was under the impression that he and Kayla had something serious between them. That was something he had to change, and soon, because he was quickly coming to realize that there was only one woman with which he wanted a future. She, and everyone else for that matter, were going to have to come to grips with it.

She'd looked so lost that afternoon. Oh, she'd smiled and said all the right things at the right times, but when she thought no one was watching, he saw the anguish, the sadness. Maybe he recognized it so easily because he was miserable himself and was putting up the same kind of front. One thing was clear, though. Neither one of them could keep it up for very long.

As difficult as it had been to keep his distance from her at the house, it had been even more so when she'd left suddenly with Taryn. Something had gone down, and Kieran wasn't talking. Kieran was overprotective, they all knew that. But to freak out because Lexi was picking berries? There had to be more to it than that.

What did Kieran know that the rest of them didn't?

When he'd finally returned to the pub, Lexi was gone and Taryn had been upset. Like Kieran, Taryn refused to say why. That excuse that Lexi just wasn't feeling well was a load of total bullshit, but Jake had warned him off loud and clear when he pressed Taryn for more info. A short time later, Kieran had taken off like a bat out of hell, looking both angry and worried, presumably to see Lexi.

It was enough to send chills down Ian's spine.

Kieran was only gone for about two hours. When he did return, he looked even worse than when he'd left. Ian overheard his clipped answers when Taryn cornered him. Yes, he'd found Lexi. Yes, she was safely at her hotel. Kieran refused to say anything else. Instead, he grabbed his keys and tore off on his Harley the way he always did when he was upset and needed some space.

Ian wasted no time heading out after that, leaving Jake and Taryn to tend the bar. He didn't care who saw him, either; he was beyond that. All he knew was that he needed to see Lexi with his own eyes. Needed to know that she was okay.

It had been a shock to find her room empty, her bed completely untouched. After checking the few eateries still open at that time of night, Ian went to the only other place he could imagine her going. No matter what she said, Ian could tell she truly loved her grandmother's house.

His approach was silent out of habit, but he wouldn't have wanted to startle her anyway. He made a sweep around the perimeter, stopping briefly at the patch of raspberry bushes. The sweep was more for his benefit than hers. No one had probably stepped foot on this property for years, but you never knew. Ian had learned a long time ago not to trust in the innate goodness of human nature; he'd seen too much of the other side. Maybe that was one of the things that drew him to her so strongly. Lexi had a goodness, an innocence about her that was completely outside his own reality.

* * *

Lexi was in the kitchen of the old stone cottage, sitting in the large bow window seat, looking out at the moon. Her knees were drawn up to her chin, her arms wrapped loosely around her legs as she leaned against the panes, her mind millions of miles away. Several candles burned on the counters, bathing the room in a dim, warm glow.

It seemed a fitting way to spend her last night in Pine Ridge. Tomorrow she'd be gone, and she would not be coming back. Things had come full circle, in a way. It seemed appropriate that one of her last memories of this place should be the same as some of her first.

How she had loved sitting here when she was little. Back then, her grandmother had stitched a soft cushion for her, perfectly contoured to the window seat. Here she would perch for hours, reading, drawing, playing games while her Greek mother and Irish grandmother cooked or baked or quilted. It always smelled so good when they made their homemade bread, pies, and cakes. She smiled to herself. Maybe that's where her love of cooking had begun.

Her heart ached. How she wished they were still here. They would know what to do.

She began singing softly, the same melody her

grandmother used to sing to her all those years ago. Lexi didn't understand all of the words, but she didn't have to. Even back then she knew her grandmother was singing of something very special.

Once Lexi had asked her mother about the song, and her mother simply said that it was the song her husband used to sing to her back in Ireland, before they moved to the States. It was haunting, and filled with so much love that just singing it made her feel like her grandmother was right there in the room with her again. As she sang, she felt a familiar presence, and despite the torrent of emotions roiling within her, everything calmed.

* * *

Ian watched her from the doorway, listening in silence as the long-forgotten melody filled his heart and soul. Lexi had a beautiful voice, low and lilting, perfect for singing ancient Irish lullabies. And he could envision it so clearly: Lexi sitting in that very window, singing their child to sleep as he looked on silently…

His heart began to hammer in his chest. The image was so clear, so perfectly defined, he had to blink several times before he convinced himself it wasn't real.

"My grandmother used to have the most beautiful lilies right outside this window," Lexi said quietly, breaking into his vision. "Bright yellow ones, and white ones with streaks of pink in the middle. I could stare at them for hours sometimes, daydreaming that instead of flowers they were fierce dragons, and I was a fairy princess, stuck in her tower, waiting for my prince to come and rescue me."

It took him a moment to realize she was talking to him. She continued to gaze out the window, still and unmoving. Ian was sure he hadn't made any noise, yet she had known he was there.

"Come sit with me," she said, patting the area beside her.

Ian crossed the room silently, sitting beside her in the huge seat. He held his hand out to her. Lexi smiled at the handful of juicy black raspberries cradled in his palm, then looked directly into his eyes. In that moment, Ian felt like he had given her the moon.

He reached for her hand and gently rolled the berries into her palm, frowning when he saw the tight bandage covering it. She took one raspberry and lifted it to his lips before taking one for herself, repeating the gesture until they were all gone. It was all done without a word, without a touch, but it was one of the most intimate things he'd ever shared with anyone.

"I miss them so much," she said finally, looking out the window once again.

Ian knew how it felt to lose his mother at an early age, but he'd always had his father and brothers around him. He couldn't imagine what it would have been like without them. Wishing he had words that could help, but knowing he didn't, he gently put his arms around her.

Thankfully, she didn't resist. She curled into him like a kitten against his chest. He closed his eyes, letting the warmth of her body soak into him. A sense of peace, of rightness settled over him as he rested his chin on the top of her head and breathed in that familiar orange and honey scent.

"Why did you come here, Ian?" she asked several minutes later, breaking the silence.

"I was worried about you," he answered honestly, though there was so much more to it than that.

"Why?"

He'd been wondering the same thing himself, and he wasn't sure she wanted to hear his theories, especially after his earlier vision still had him a bit shaken. "You shouldn't be out here all alone," he said finally. It was the truth. Sort of.

"I'm used to being alone, Ian," she said against his collarbone, sounding weary. There was no anger, no malice in her words, just simple truth.

"Not anymore," he answered.

* * *

It felt so good to be in his arms, she could almost believe him. She'd dreamed of hearing him say things like that for years. But he was talking about right now, and in her dreams, he'd been talking about forever.

That was the great thing about dreams. They were yours and no one else's, custom-fitted to what you wanted most.

Dare she hope? No. She might be tired, but she wasn't a fool. There were a million reasons why she could never have the kind of relationship she wanted with Ian; wishing for the impossible held nothing but the promise of heartbreak.

As if her heart wasn't already broken.

She briefly considered bringing up Kayla again. That would definitely put a damper on things, but she couldn't bring herself to do so. It felt too good to be close to him like this to waste it on silly things like pride or a broken heart.

His hands caressed her arms so tenderly, his chest was so warm and solid against her back. His scent, clean and male and dark, filled her with a sense of completeness and made her feel safe. What was wrong with pretending for just a little while? To sit here in the dark, feeling the thrum of his heart. To live her dream for just a few minutes more.

"Tell me about them." His voice, low and hypnotic, vibrated against her.

Lexi wasn't a woman who liked to talk about herself, but she was suddenly sharing childhood memories with him. Doing so felt natural. She told

Ian things she'd never even told Kieran or Aidan. Being here, in this house, brought back so many memories she had long since forgotten.

"I'm sorry," she said apologetically as she realized that she'd been going on for a long time. "I don't know what came over me." She sniffed and started to pull away. "Bet you're sorry you asked, huh?"

"On the contrary," he said, keeping his arms loose but refusing to let her go, "I can't remember when I've enjoyed an evening quite so much." His eyes glittered. "With the possible exception of our dinner together, that is."

Lexi blushed. It wasn't the dinner he had enjoyed so much, but she couldn't blame him for that. She'd be a hypocrite of the highest order if she did.

"But I think we should get you back to your hotel," he said. "You can't sleep here. It'll be dawn soon, and you need some rest."

Lexi sighed and nodded. He was right. She'd talked for hours, reliving her past. Now she felt drained.

Ian helped her blow out the candles and lock up, walking her out to his truck. Much to her surprise and pleasure, he held her hand the entire time, almost as if he was afraid to let go.

"Are you going to tell me about this?" Ian asked, tapping her wrapped hand lightly.

Lexi hesitated only a second or two before

answering. "Nothing to tell. I got distracted while slicing and cut myself. You'd think a chef would know better, huh."

* * *

It wasn't the whole story, he was certain of it, but she was already pulling away from him, and he wouldn't allow that to happen again. He'd find out the truth soon enough. Kieran was not as invincible as he pretended to be. In the meantime, Lexi was well enough, and more importantly, with him. He was not going to screw that up by pushing her unnecessarily.

"No more sneaking out?" he asked as he took her key and inserted it into the hotel room door.

She stiffened. "I wasn't sneaking," she said defensively.

"You didn't tell Kieran what you were going to do."

"Was I supposed to?"

Ian chuckled. "You know he would never have let you go over there by yourself."

"First of all, Kieran left before I even decided to go. Secondly, I don't need his permission. I am a grown woman. And I told you, I'm used to being alone."

"And I told you," he said authoritatively, stepping into her room behind her and sliding the deadbolt lock in place. "You're not alone anymore."

Golden-amber eyes flashed up at him. Dare he hope that he wasn't imagining the desire in those depths?

Her tongue peeked out as she licked along those perfect pink lips. "Does that mean you want to stay?"

"I'm not leaving." It was a statement, spoken without arrogance, but daring her to contradict him. For the first time in his life, he felt connected to a woman. Really connected. The things she'd shared with him, whether she knew it or not, had captured his heart. He'd felt her pouring into him, lighting him from the inside out with her trust. He didn't want that closeness to end. It couldn't. Not yet.

Her eyes widened just a little as he took off his shoes. Then they widened a little more as he began to remove his shirt, his pants. They were like saucers by the time he slid beneath the cool sheets of her bed, naked.

"Come on," he said, patting the bed beside him. "Or are you going to make me get out of bed and undress you myself?"

She bit her bottom lip, shifting her weight ever so slightly as she considered her options. He could have told her not to bother. Self-denial was no match for the hunger, the want he saw in her eyes. But perhaps a little assurance might help her come to terms with it.

"I won't do anything you don't want me to," he said quietly. "But I need to feel your body against mine. Just for a little while. Please, Lexi."

It wasn't a lie. He needed the contact. He wasn't quite sure what he would do if she refused; he wouldn't let himself even think about that.

Thankfully, she didn't. His eyes burned with intensity as she removed her clothing piece by piece. He held up the covers for her as she slid in beside him. He sighed in relief as she slipped into his arms and the ache was replaced by her soft, silken warmth.

"You never answered my question," he said softly, wishing he could capture the feel of her against him and hold onto it forever.

"What question?" she asked, her breath feathering across his neck as her hair cascaded over his arm.

"Did the reality come close to the fantasy?"

Ian felt her entire body tense, heard the sharp intake of breath. He flexed his arm and pulled her closer, just in case she had any misconceptions that he might allow her to pull away from him. Within moments, though, her body relaxed, and a stream of air brushed along his skin as she exhaled.

"No," she said honestly, but so quietly even his acute hearing could barely pick it up. His heart stopped, pausing for a second as the pressure built in his chest. "It didn't. The reality was better than anything I could have dreamed up."

The floodgates opened in his soul and everything poured out in a rush, only to be filled again with her light and warmth. Along with the blinding truth he must have been an idiot not to see before.

Everything in him stilled. No. It wasn't possible. He couldn't have been her first. But the more he thought about it, the more he realized it probably was. With startling clarity he recalled her impossible tightness, the sound of her cries and the feel of her nails digging into his back when he first penetrated her.

He should have heeded his first instincts. On the bus it had taken him all of about two seconds to form the opinion that she was a virgin, or at least someone of extremely limited experience. But then, in her hotel room, that theory was blown right out of the water when she put her hand on him so boldly. No innocent, he reasoned, could have held such complete power over him from such a simple caress.

"Why didn't you tell me, Lexi?" he asked, stroking her back, once he was able to speak again. "Why didn't you tell me you were a virgin?"

"I wasn't."

It didn't feel like a total lie, but it wasn't quite the truth, either. It took him a few moments to put the pieces together. No, maybe she hadn't been a virgin in the true sense of the word. But she *was* innocent. He closed his eyes, sure that he was right. He didn't know the details, wasn't sure he even wanted to. But he knew with every fiber of his being that he was the first --- the only --- *man* she'd ever been intimate with.

"I was your first, wasn't I?"

She tensed again and tried to pull away, but Ian held her tight.

"Was it that obvious? Was I that awful?"

Ian slipped a finger under her chin and lifted her face to look at him, not sure whether he wanted to crush her in his arms or throttle her for even thinking such a thing. He swore that if he wasn't already head over heels in love with her he would have been in that moment. Her eyes were big, so filled with worry and uncertainty that it blew him away. How could she ever believe that, even for a moment?

"No," he said gently. "You were that *good.* I've never felt anything like it, never." And that was the God's honest truth. He'd never had anyone respond to him with such pure, honest emotion. Innocent, yet wanting. "But I wish you would have told me. I would have been gentler. I know I must have hurt you."

The thought that he had hurt her cut ribbons through his gut. He pictured the marks he'd left on her body and felt a fresh wave of guilty pain.

"You didn't hurt me."

"Liar," he chastised, kissing her forehead.

"Okay, maybe it hurt a little," she admitted, drawing small circles on his chest with her fingers. "But I was afraid if I told you, you'd stop."

He almost snorted. She believed he could have stopped? Obviously she had more faith in his self-control than he did. Well, he probably could have stopped, but it would have killed him. Or caused permanent damage at the very least. He told her as much.

"I'm sorry, Ian," she said, and he wished she would stop apologizing. "Are you upset with me?"

She had to stop looking at him with those big doe eyes or he was going to kiss her until she lost consciousness. Then again, he might just do that anyway, but he needed to taste her. Soon.

Could he ever be upset with her when she looked at him like that? No, not seriously, but Ian was not a fool. The slightly wicked part of him pointed out the glaring possibilities that the right response might elicit.

"A little," he fibbed, wishing his voice wasn't quite so husky. Then he felt her melt into him, and almost felt bad for misleading her. Yes, he was upset, but only because he couldn't bear the thought of hurting her. But he knew that's not how she understood it.

"Can I make it up to you?" Lexi's voice was far too seductive to belong to a woman who had been innocent only a few days ago. Either she was a really fast learner or he brought it out in her. He preferred to think it was the latter.

Ian appeared to consider her question, but he already had a plan in mind. She would regret leaving him alone in her room while she took that extended shower yesterday. He had made good use of the time.

chapter fifteen

"Yes, you can. Read to me." Lexi's head lifted from his shoulder. He fought to hold in a grin as he handed her the Salienne Dulcette novel from the nightstand. Her eyes narrowed suspiciously.

"Start on page 129, if you don't mind," he said.

For a moment he wasn't sure she'd comply, but he saw the instant her eyes changed from surprised to excited and aroused. Ian pulled her onto him, letting the proof of his own desire press into her lower belly. Her weight felt good, comforting. As long as she was touching him, he could control himself. If she pulled away, all bets were off.

She opened the book against his chest, and looked at him questioningly.

"Go on," he encouraged, his hands strategically placed along her well-rounded hips. She took a deep breath --- he loved the way her breasts pressed into him as she did --- and began to read.

He was easily the biggest man she

had ever seen, sinfully adorned with smooth bronze flesh and rippling layers of muscle, one atop the other until it formed a relief that would take hours, days, years to learn intimately. She trembled at the sight of him, at the hungry look in his eyes, as she sat on the bed in her prim little white nightgown.

"On your knees," he growled, removing his belt with one fluid, erotic movement. The leather snapped in the air, making her flinch, but he didn't mistake the look in her eyes for fear. It was arousal, pure and potent.

When she made no move to obey, he grabbed her, flipping her onto her stomach. With one hand spanning her back he held her down easily, even as she wriggled against him. His other hand slipped beneath the hem of her gown, his hands rough and calloused, rasping along the back of her thighs, sending bolts of pleasure right into her core. Despite herself, she cried out.

The panties she wore were torn viciously from her with no regard for their worth, only the barest brush of his fingers against her swollen sex when she craved so much more. He smirked as he raised his hand and landed heavy, the resounding crack loud in the quiet room. But his smirk vanished and his eyes darkened when he beheld the rush of wetness running down her thighs from his little caress. This was supposed to be a night of seductive torture as he readied her for him, but he soon realized that he was the one in danger of being tortured.

"Lift your ass to me," he growled, harsher and huskier than before as his cock strained against the limits of his jeans.

"No."

The simple denial, spoken with obvious effort, had the first droplets of cum pearling along his swollen head. She was going to be the death of him, surely.

"I said, lift your ass to me."

A shiver ran the length of her spine before she once again answered, "No."

Holding her upper back firmly against the mattress, his other arm snaked beneath her hips and pulled roughly upward. Before she could react, he dove between her legs, pulling her over him to straddle his face. Every effort against him was futile; he held her locked in place, his arms as strong as his resolve.

She tried to withhold her cries, but it was impossible with his wicked mouth, tongue and teeth on her. He devoured her as if he was a starving man and she was a king's banquet. Long slow licks, teasing nips; he sucked her between his lips and then dipped his tongue into her hot entrance. He moaned, loudly, as if in great pain as she spilled even more for him.

"Son of a bitch," he muttered as the pressure built within her. He could feel it, sense it, and it angered him. It was too fast, too easy. She could not climax yet; he would not allow it. He had clearly underestimated her need for him; she'd hidden it well.

But there was no hiding from him now, not when the truth was there in his mouth, on his tongue. He continued to hold her with one iron hand while he released himself and worked his jeans below his hips with the other. Damn her. She was making him burn hotter than the sun.

When she began to clench around him he withdrew. A string of foul oaths spewed from her lips, so bold and explicit he could not believe they had come from her sweet mouth. He would have laughed had it not been for the pain nearly ripping him apart. To think that he could reduce her to such a primitive, visceral level made him drunk with power. Within seconds he held his engorged shaft at her entrance, hating himself for being so weak.

With one tremendous thrust he impaled her, making her scream so loudly the windows rattled. It was sheer ecstasy, pure and simple. He'd never felt anything like it. For a moment he just held himself inside her, certain that he had just died and had gone to heaven. But after the initial shock, she began to clench around him, a wave of ripples up and down his cock, demanding his undivided attention.

He pulled out and thrust into her again, so hard and deep that his balls slapped against her, his grip on her hips unbreakable. She wasn't fighting him anymore. She was crying, pleading, begging him to take her harder, faster, to ease her pain. Sweat poured down his back as he lost himself in her, gave her everything, withheld nothing. The bed's headboard banged against the wall with the force of his thrusts, yet she begged for more until she tightened around him, strangling his cock tighter than any fist.

She began to come, squeezing him so hard he saw stars. He pulled out and shoved himself into her again, finally releasing his last thread of control as he began to empty inside her. He penetrated her over and over again, each stroke milking more seed from him until black rimmed the edges of his sight, and still he came. His cum filled her, dripped from her, coated her already slick folds, coating him as well. He rolled his hips with the final jet of seed, losing himself to the blackness as he gathered her seizing body in his arms...

* * *

Lexi stopped reading, her heart pounding like a jackhammer against his chest. Ian's blue eyes were glowing. "Is that what you fantasize about, Lexi?"

She moved the book aside and rubbed herself against him so he could feel her desire. She dipped her head and licked his throat, eliciting a low growl that rumbled through his chest and into hers.

She was beyond coy games, beyond lies. "Yes."

"With me? Tell me you dreamed of me doing this to you, Lexi, while you played with your little toy."

He knew about her toy? Yes, of course he did. She let her teeth scrape across his skin. "*Only* you. Ever."

His eyes were as intense as she had ever seen them. Darkened to a midnight blue, they were still so clear, so flawless, like the finest sapphires. He rolled her onto her back. "I'm going to take you like that," he told her, his voice thick with lust.

"You can try." Her skin was flushed, her nipples pebbled, the ache of anticipation riding her hard. She smirked at him, basking in the intoxicating sense of power at having a man like Ian look at her like that.

"God*damn,* baby," he growled, flipping her onto her stomach with one smooth move. She caught the end of the bed and with surprising strength, pulled away from him. He growled, no words this time, grabbed her by the hips, and hauled her back.

"Raise your ass to me." His voice was rough, commanding, demanding obedience.

"No." She pushed her hips into the mattress. How many women had dared to deny him? If the deep-throated growls of warning were any indication, not many.

He brought his hand up and smacked her on the ass, not exactly painful but enough to leave his hand print. She pushed her face into the pillow and screamed, but she raised her hips just a little as he kissed and licked the sting away. If this is what defiance got her, she vowed to do a lot more of it.

"More," he commanded. She shook her head back and forth, still lodged in the pillow. Another smack, this time on the other cheek. She cried out again and lifted enough for him to gain purchase beneath her. His mouth found her sex and he buried himself deep, immediately causing her vision to blur with the sheer intensity of it. Lips, teeth, and tongue set to work on what had to be the most glorious form of punishment there was.

"Ian, please," she pleaded as he took her to the edge over and over again, pulling back just before she came each time, building her need to a fever pitch. "Please, please, please, Ian. Have mercy."

* * *

When her cries became so desperate he could no longer bear them, he positioned himself behind her and began to enter her. Unlike the man in the story, he would go slow. He would never intentionally hurt her again, no matter how out of his head with lust he was.

But Lexi had other ideas. The moment he began to move she thrust back against him, taking him all at once. He cursed as she cried out into the pillow, feeling the shockwaves as her sheath fought the brutal and sudden penetration.

He held her still as he came over her, pressing her back to his chest. One arm reached beneath her, crossing over her breasts and grabbing on to her opposite shoulder, locking her into place. "Easy, baby," he whispered in her ear. "Easy."

His other hand found her sensitive nub and began to caress it until the pain turned into pleasure again and he felt her inner muscles begin to work him from the inside. Only then did he begin to move, slowly at first, then increasingly faster and harder as her body grew accustomed to him.

When she came, she came so hard that he was forced to hold her up, gripping her hips while he pistoned into her harder and faster, the slap of flesh a fast, furious tempo. Ian was lost, no longer a civilized, disciplined man, but a brutal, primal beast. He gripped her tightly, needing to feel every possible inch of her against him. When his own release was imminent, he held her hips and curled his pelvis, driving deeper and harder, scraping against her most sensitive spots, forcing a second, fierce climax, rocketing his release right into her cervix.

Like the man in the book, darkness tinged his vision as sweat burned his eyes. He collapsed to the side, holding Lexi tightly against him, but remained joined with her. Gasping desperately for breath, he tried to make sense out of what just happened.

"Are you all right?" he choked out, suddenly fearing that he might have hurt her in his temporary loss of control.

She turned her head back to him, and the look in her eyes annihilated him. They were glowing, *glowing*, with pure, unconditional love. He squeezed her tighter, fighting back the urge to sob. *She loved him.* He knew it, felt it as certainly as he'd ever felt anything in his life. And if there had been any doubt, he knew in that moment that he loved her too.

Their coupling had been so intense, so profound, that had she not been on birth control, they would certainly have created a child. The thought saddened him a little; he would love to see her grow round with his child. It was something they would have to discuss. Right after he asked her to marry him. He considered proposing right then and there, but thought better of it. He wanted to do this right. Really right. Candlelight. Roses. The most stunning ring he could find.

"She's good, isn't she?" Lexi said sleepily a while later, Ian's body spooned protectively around hers, still buried deep inside her as he lazily contemplated different methods of proposal.

"Who?" He could probably figure it out, but why expend the effort?

"Salienne Dulcette. The way she writes."

"Mmm-hmm," he agreed, too relaxed and spent to say much of anything else. She'd wiped him out, pulled everything from him. His body was spent, and substantial parts of his mind were out of commission. She held it all now. His body. His heart. His soul.

"I love her stuff. I have every one of her books," Lexi continued.

"Do you?" Ian said, a spark of interest igniting. This was promising. Definitely information he could use.

"Yes. Dozens of them."

Ian's semi grew harder within her, though he could barely believe it. Given the force with which he'd just come, he shouldn't be stirring again for hours.

"Dozens?"

"Mmmm-hmm."

Damn. He was going to have to start taking vitamins.

chapter sixteen

Dawn came far too quickly. He struggled to find a viable reason to separate himself from the heavenly goddess beside him; she fit against him so well, and her skin was incredibly soft and warm.

His dark, male musk mixed with her more delicate feminine scent, eliciting images of deep forests with shafts of sunlight peeking through; gentle breezes, moist earth, and pristine air.

And she made those whisper-light sounds in her sleep that wrapped around his heart and squeezed.

Lexi shifted slightly, snuggling into him as she slept. Never would he have believed that such a small gesture could bring him so much happiness. Two nights spent in her bed was enough to know he didn't want to go back to sleeping alone. Before Lexi, he'd never had the desire to stay with anyone. And even if he had, he would not have fallen into such a contented, dreamless sleep.

As wonderful as it was, it confused him. Sex, he understood. But this? It made no sense whatsoever. He *craved* Lexi like he had never craved anyone before. It wasn't just the sex, though that was admittedly fantastic. Just the feel of her against him was a balm to his soul. Her smile lit him up from the inside. The soft lilt of her voice calmed him. And when she looked at him with so much love in her eyes, he felt like Superman.

Was this what love felt like? Was this what Jake felt every time he looked at Taryn?

Ian buried his face in Lexi's hair and inhaled, for no other reason than because he could. She answered his soft moan with one of her own. Even in sleep, her response was immediate.

"Lexi," he breathed, half in awe, half in a hunger he failed to comprehend. It seemed no matter how many times he made love to her it only made him more desperate to have her again. With every moment he spent with her, that feeling grew stronger.

Eyes still closed, but no longer asleep, Lexi moved on top of him, feeling her way. Once again, Ian marveled at the perfect fit of her soft, lush curves to his. The new position allowed his hands followed the natural slope from her breasts in to her small waist, flaring back out again to fill his palms with her delectable behind.

Without a word, she lifted up just enough to position herself properly, then began an achingly slow descent to take him into her. She was incredibly wet, still slick from their night of passion. There was deep, and then there was this.

She opened her eyes then, the burning amber filled with enough raw desire to make his heart stutter, and began to move against him. She went slowly at first, acclimating herself to the new position, the different way they fit together. He hoped it was as pleasurable for her as it was for him.

* * *

Ian spoke to her without words: low growls of encouragement; deep, dark moans of pleasure that accelerated her burning need. His hands held her, guided her to new and exciting sensations until she could no longer hold onto her control. Her eyes closed, her head fell back, and Lexi totally gave herself over to her needs.

God, she loved this. The power she had! To be the one in control was amazing. She could set the pace; slow down to feel each part of him sliding inside her, or speed up to set flames to her inner nerve endings. She could angle her hips, adjust the depth, and explore every possible way of feeling him inside her.

She found that if she rolled her hips and curled against him with each stroke it felt like heaven. When she extended the curl into a full body undulation, her sensitive nipples scraped against his hard chest, firing even more sensations into her core.

And he loved it. He surrendered himself to her, letting her use him, begging her to, whispering such naughty things that she had to fight to make it last.

But she couldn't hold out forever, and Ian must have instinctively known she was nearing her limits. He wrapped his arms around her and pulled her down to him, thrusting upward. She cried out, fighting her release all the way, until one hand landed heavy on her backside, the sting shooting right up into her core. Ian's fingers smoothed the sting away, the soft caress tender and possessive.

It was at once the most terrifying and most exciting thing she'd ever felt.

"Oh God, Ian," she cried. "I'm not going to survive this."

"Yes, you will, baby," he crooned. "You will, and you will love every second of it."

"Ian!" she screamed as the first wave began to crest. Ian held her tightly as he continued to pound into her from below. His hands clutched her hips, angling her to maximize her pleasure.

"Ah, baby, I can't... hold... on..." His upward thrusts became harder, more urgent. Lexi tumbled over the edge, taking him with her.

* * *

Lexi collapsed on his chest, fighting for breath amidst soft keening sounds. His arms wrapped around her protectively. Lexi was his. And he would never let her go.

He had pushed her, he knew, but if he believed for one second she really didn't want what he offered, he would have stopped. He could happily spend the rest of his life pleasing her in ways that didn't make her uncomfortable.

When her breathing returned to normal, Ian reluctantly left the haven of her body, smiling when she pouted. She was soft and limp in his arms, offering no resistance whatsoever. With great care, he lifted her in his arms and carried her into the bathroom. Her arms snaked around his neck as she simply let him take her wherever he would, do whatever he wanted.

She had no idea what she did to him, Ian thought as he ran the soapy cloth along her body, the now-familiar scents of orange and vanilla and honey filling the steamy shower. Lexi leaned against him, humming every now and then when he caressed an especially sensitive spot. He growled in response when she used some of the lather to stroke him clean as well.

"You are going to be the death of me, Lexi," Ian said huskily, taking the soap from her hands. There was no way he should be getting aroused again so quickly, but the moment she touched him and began those gentle, light strokes, his cock defied him.

The look in her eyes almost had him handing

the soap right back to her. "You don't like it?" She glanced doubtfully at his rapidly hardening shaft.

"I like it too much," he said honestly, pulling her to him. "And there are other things I want to do with you today."

Lexi raised an eyebrow as if she found that hard to believe, the hint of a smile on her face. "I know," he chuckled. "I can hardly believe it myself."

"So you don't want me to do this anymore?" she asked innocently, reaching down and cupping him between his legs, rolling lightly with her fingers. Ian closed his eyes and prayed for the strength to say no. All he could manage was a groan.

"Well, all right then," she said as she reached around him with her other hand and turned the faucet all the way to the left. The water went almost instantly from hot to icy cold against his back.

"Wicked vixen," he hissed, turning so that she took the brunt of it. She squealed and wriggled against him, but he held her fast. When he dipped his head and took her mouth, the icy water was forgotten.

"God*damn*, baby," Ian said breathlessly moments later when he finally remembered to turn off the water. Lexi's back was like ice, and she didn't even seem to notice. She looked up at him with those half-glazed eyes, and his heart lurched. No one had *ever* looked at him like that - like he was everything to her. The very idea that he could affect a woman so thoroughly was both sobering and intoxicating, and Ian realized in that moment that it was a once-in-a-lifetime gift. A gift he would do well to treasure, because he couldn't bear the thought of her ever looking at another man the way she was looking at him.

"Come on, baby," he said huskily, grabbing a towel. "I've got plans for you."

* * *

Ian's words finally seemed to register. She licked her lips, trying to clear her mind (which was not an easy thing to do while he was on his knees), deftly maneuvering a thick, fluffy towel along her inner thighs. "Ian, I can't."

He finished drying her legs, rising with smooth, masculine grace to take care of her back. "Don't worry about Kieran. I'll take care of him."

"No, no, it's not that. I'm … I'm leaving today."

Ian's hands stilled. "What did you say?"

Lexi stepped away, taking the towel from his hands and wrapping it around her torso. "I'm leaving. Going back to Benton."

"What about …" Ian paused, his face looking pained. "What about the house?"

"I'm giving it to Uncle Jack. He can do what he wants with it."

"Why, Lexi? Why are you doing this?"

Lexi bit her lip. Ian seemed a lot more upset than she thought he'd be. She'd figured Kieran would take it the hardest, but he would understand. But Ian...he couldn't possibly know, could he? Dare she tell him the truth? She'd never been very good at lying, and regardless of the situation, she didn't want to lie to Ian. "Because..."

Ian stood unnaturally still, his face expressionless, though his blue eyes blazed with so much intensity she actually began to feel weak in the knees. Ian had power over her that no man should have. She had to turn away before she forgot every reason why she had to go.

"Because that's where my life is. My job. My apartment. My..." She hesitated, not sure she wanted to finish the thought. What else was there for her, really? Her elderly aunts were well taken care of in an exclusive nursing home and didn't even recognize her anymore. She had no close friends, with the possible exception of...

"Aidan."

Lexi's head whipped up. Dear Lord, Ian couldn't possibly be reading her thoughts now, too, could he? "What?"

"Your *boss*. Aidan."

His tone was strange. There, in those fire-and-ice blue eyes was something Lexi never expected to see when he looked at her: jealousy. Her heart squeezed.

"Yes," she said slowly, drawing out the word as her brows knitted in puzzlement. "Aidan is there. But what does that have to do with anything?"

He blinked, as if he hadn't expected her to ask him that. "You care for him."

"Of course I care for him. I've known him for years. So?" She crossed her arms over her chest, still confused by Ian's reaction.

"He's in love with you."

The words nearly stole the breath from her. Her lips parted, her eyes widened in surprise. Forgetting her defiant stance, she let her arms drop. "You're insane."

Ian didn't blink. She felt the heat of his gaze acutely. So much power. Too much. Ian Callaghan had been controlling her life for years, and he didn't even know it. But somehow he believed he knew enough to suggest that Aidan, a man he had never met, was in love with her.

Lexi considered this for a few moments before her eyes narrowed suspiciously. "And you know this how?"

Ian stiffened, hesitating only briefly. "He sends you a lot of emails."

The corners of her mouth twitched. "Hmmm. Email proliferation. You're right. How could I have missed the signs? Gee, I guess the guys at Amazon and Barnes and Noble really have a hard-on for me, then."

Ian's eyes glittered warningly. "You're

mocking me."

"Yes, I am," she agreed. "Because you're being ridiculous! And besides, why do you care?"

White fire flamed in his blue eyes; she had to make a conscious effort not to take a step back.

"Why do I care? Have you not been with me these last couple of hours or so?" He ran his hand through his hair, taking two steps left, two steps right and then back again, as if he couldn't make up his mind in which direction he wanted to go. Lexi watched him intently, the ripple of muscles from shoulder to ankle hypnotic. Thank God he had draped a towel around his hips, or she couldn't be held responsible for her actions.

At his words, a tiny spark of hope flared within her, but she kept it carefully contained. "What about Kayla?"

"What about Kayla?!?" he exploded, making her flinch backward.

"Well..." Lexi began, caught off guard by Ian's vehement reaction, "you guys are, like, together, right?"

Ian shot a look of disbelief at her, one that told her she, of all people, should know better. "Why does everyone assume that Kayla and I..." He shook his head as if trying to make sense of it all and resuming his pacing. "Honestly, Lexi, do you think if Kayla and I had anything between us I could have been with you?"

Lexi was stunned. "You're not?"

"Fuck, no!" Ian shouted. "Yeah, okay, we hooked up a few times, but it was just...." He seemed to be getting more frustrated with each passing second. "It was stupid. It meant nothing."

"But I thought you two were…"

"Yeah," he laughed bitterly. "You and everyone else. I wonder who's spreading those rumors, hmm?"

"But you were with her at the funeral, Ian," she pointed out. "I was there, remember? You didn't leave her side, not once."

"As a special favor to my father," he explained. "Because he was afraid she would try to do something to *you*. I wasn't there to comfort Kayla, Lexi," he said, his voice softening. "I was there to protect *you*."

Thoughts were whirling around in Lexi's mind so fast she had trouble making sense of them. "But you said you had sex with her."

"Yes, that's true, I did. Usually when Jake wasn't available or needed a third."

"Jake?"

"Yeah." He could tell Lexi was shocked, but he refused to lie to her. "Look, Lexi, the only time Kayla was ever interested in me was…" he paused, his expression going eerily blank. "…when you were around. *Son of a bitch*."

Lexi gasped. She knew her stepsister hated her, but she was still taken aback by the lengths Kayla would go to make her life miserable. She didn't doubt for a moment that Ian was telling the truth. Anger radiated from him in waves, his beautiful body tense, his expression hard.

With a compelling need to soothe him, Lexi went to him as he stood by the window, gazing out. Wrapping her arms around him, she laid her head on his back. "I'm sorry, Ian."

chapter seventeen

"Please don't leave."

"Ian - " she began, starting to pull away.

Ian turned, capturing her in his arms. "Surely you can take a few more days, can't you? I bet you haven't had a vacation in years."

Lord, but it was tempting. Not to mention that pressing her cheek against that satin-over-steel chest of his made it hard to think logically.

And this weekend is the big county fair," he continued. "Tell me you don't miss that."

She did miss the fair. It had always been one of her favorite events of the year. Ian's hand moved up and down the length of her back, giving her the strangest urge to purr.

"And you could spend a little more time at the house, you know, before you get rid of it."

She would like that. There were still several areas she wanted to explore, both inside and out. From what she remembered, her grandmother had secret cubbies all over the place. Lexi had hidden treasures in them when she was little: jacks, glass marbles, shiny beads. How cool would it be to rediscover a few of them?

"Come on, Lex. A few days are all I'm asking for. I'll make it worth your while."

She looked up at him, at the sexiest half-smile she'd ever seen, and thoughts of carnival rides, funnel cakes, and childhood treasures were instantly swept away. Didn't he know that when he looked at her like that, he made it impossible to deny him?

"You will, huh?" Her heart melted, and was now laying in a molten pool somewhere around his feet.

"Yeah," he said, his voice husky. She felt him stirring beneath the towel. Felt the now-familiar tingling between her thighs. *Focus, Lexi, focus.*

"I only planned to stay a few days. I don't have enough clothes." *Or meds.*

"What you're wearing looks fine to me," he said, eyeing the towel as if he was determining the fastest way to remove it.

"I'll just wear this to the fair then, shall I?"

Ian's face darkened. "Good point. I'll buy you some new ones. Preferably long, concealing, loose fitting clothes fit for wearing in public."

Lexi chuckled, but the idea of spending a few more days in town was appealing. Additional opportunities to explore more of her fantasies with Ian --- even more so.

She hadn't taken a vacation since... well, never. Aidan wouldn't begrudge her a few days, right? Hell, he'd probably cheer. He was forever trying to talk her into taking some time off.

Her meds were a problem, though. She always brought a little more than she needed, but she hadn't planned on staying a whole week, and had already doubled-up for that mishap at the pub. Unfortunately, it wasn't the kind of stuff she could waltz into the local CVS and pick up. Maybe if she stretched out the doses, took a little less each time, and didn't try to cook for anyone over the course of the next few days, she could make it.

* * *

She was so close, he could sense it. She wanted to stay; she just needed the proper incentive.

Ian turned, pulling her into his arms. If he had a few more days, he'd be able to make her see that leaving him was not an option. Lexi couldn't just leave. She couldn't give him a gift like that and then take it away. She couldn't rip out his heart and take it with her.

He was not above playing upon happy childhood memories to keep her around until he could convince her to stay permanently. Hell, there was nothing he wouldn't do for her.

"Is there anything I could do to persuade you?" he asked softly, his hands reaching under the lower hem of the towel to cup her delicious backside. She moaned softly.

"I want a ride on your motorcycle," she hummed, petting his chest. "The big Harley. And no granny-speed either. I want full-throttle, back mountain roads."

It sounded dangerous, but he was confident she would be safe enough with him. His bike was like an extension of himself, perfectly customized for him specifically, thanks to his highly skilled cousin-in-law, Kyle.

Ian cocked an eyebrow at her. "Done. Is that all?"

Her eyes glittered mischievously. "A moonlight swim at the lake. Dragonfire burgers and beer mandatory. Swimsuits optional."

Oh yeah, he was so there. He nodded once. "Anything else?"

Lexi's fingers stilled and she looked away. "I want more nights like last night, Ian." Her voice was so quiet he could barely hear her.

Ian tried to swallow and found he couldn't. His blue eyes darkened to glistening sapphires as every one of his systems nearly ground to a halt. Unable to speak, he simply nodded.

"Every night," she whispered, her breath hot against the skin of his chest.

Sweet Jesus in Heaven, she really was going to kill him.

"Deal," he rasped past the closure in his throat.

Ian gave Lexi some privacy to call her boss. Well, sort of. He moved to the bathroom under the pretense of shaving, but he was listening intently to every word.

"Yes, Aidan, I'm fine... No, no I'm feeling much better, thanks... No, no need to do that, really... Yes, just through the weekend. There's this big county fair, and I haven't been to one since I was a kid..."

Lexi went on to tell Aidan about the house and what Johnny had said about the renovations. Ian noticed she didn't say a word about him.

"Lex, do you mind if I use the complimentary toothbrush?" he asked as he poked his head out of the bathroom, making sure his deep male voice carried easily.

Lexi shot him a look and tried to slap her hand over the phone but it was too late. "Aidan? Yes... no... no, I'm fine." She sighed, shooting Ian an annoyed look. He grinned back at her, unrepentant.

"Ian.... Yes, Ian Callaghan... No, you're thinking of Kieran... No, that was Shane, or Sean --- I always did have a hard time telling them apart... Yes, there are quite a few of them... Now really, Aidan, I think you're overreacting a bit..."

* * *

By the time she finally managed to hang up the phone she was beyond flustered.

"What the hell was that about?" she demanded, pushing open the cracked bathroom door to find Ian leaning over the vanity, wiping the last of the shaving cream from his face. Oh, and he was buck naked. Her eyes followed the rippling muscles downward, past the hardened ridges, along the very distinct masculine "V", a soft sigh escaping before she could stop it. She forced her eyes back up, only to find Ian grinning in smug male satisfaction.

"What?" he asked innocently, but his eyes gave him away.

"You did that on purpose."

"What's your point?" Ian turned to grab a hand towel, bending slightly and giving her a lovely view of his perfectly toned backside in the process. Years later, Lexi would still not understand exactly what had come over her. All she recalled was a sudden, compelling, undeniable urge to do what she did next. She drew her palm back, and…. *SMACK!*

She pulled back almost immediately, her hand stinging, watching in horrified fascination as a perfect red imprint of her hand appeared on his bare flank.

Ian stilled.

He rose to his full height very, very slowly. Lexi swore she could see every one of his myriad of muscles rippling and flexing, growing larger before her eyes. She took a step back. Then another. By the time Ian began to turn around, she was sprinting full-tilt across the room.

In the span of a split-second, she calculated that she would make it to the door faster if she hurdled across the queen-size bed rather than try to skirt around it. She never got the chance. With no warning, without even a sound to give him away, he snatched her out of mid-air. She landed on the bed and was instantly pinned by a naked, lethal male.

"You *spanked* me," he growled, holding both of her hands above her head in one of his while his other hand made short work of the bath towel still wrapped around her.

Lexi summoned every bit of courage she had. "You deserved it."

Ian pressed himself between her legs. *God, was he really that big before?* Fresh, hot wetness poured from her center.

"Why? Because I want every man to know that you're mine?"

If Lexi had any sense at all she would have told him off, but she couldn't bring herself to do so. Not when she wanted him so badly. She'd had a glimpse of his darker nature; it was one of the things that drew her to him and thrilled her to no end. Against her wishes, her nipples hardened, shooting bolts of fiery sensation into her core every time he shifted.

"Yes."

Ian's eyes darkened further. "But you *are* mine, Lexi."

"For how long, Ian? A few days? What happens when the week is over?" She knew it was a mistake the moment the words were out of her mouth. Ian's expression grew even darker as he lowered his face until it hovered a hair's breadth above hers. Lexi held her breath to keep from whimpering. Did he reveal this side of himself to anyone else?

His eyes burned a stunning blue that made her every nerve sizzle in response. It was like looking up into the summer night sky, long after the sun went down but before everything turned black, when only the brightest stars were visible, mesmerizing and bewitching and making you believe that your every wish could come true.

When Ian lowered his head and captured her lips with his, all thoughts of token resistance immediately fled. Her body softened and melted beneath his. Her lips parted. Her hands twined around his neck, fingers tangled in his hair. One kiss and she was helpless before him.

"Damn you," she murmured, but her voice was too husky with passion to put any force behind it. Ian's hand slid up the outside of her thigh as he ground his hips against her, his other hand holding her firmly in place. His arousal pulsed against her inner thigh, seeking entrance.

* * *

One check with his fingers assured him what he already knew: Lexi was wet and ready for him. A couple of quick, swirling penetrations with his fingers were all he could manage before his hunger overwhelmed him.

Looking directly into her eyes, he impaled her in one solid, swift stroke. Her eyes glazed over, and he knew she was just as lost as he. It was fast. It was hard. Primal. He forced her to look into his eyes as he took her so she would have no doubt to whom she belonged.

"You are mine," he growled above the hunger that consumed him. She cried out as he thrust deep, branding her inside and out. "Say it!" he commanded, withdrawing to the tip only to slam forcefully into her again.

She gasped and clutched at his shoulders.

"Who is inside you now, Lexi?"

A soul-deep sound tore out of her chest, a visceral keening that wrenched his heart.

"Say it!" he ordered again, his fingers holding her tightly in place. It was low of him, he knew, to force her to admit the truth this way, when he held such complete and utter sway over her. An abuse of power, perhaps, but it was the only time those impenetrable shields of hers were completely down, the only way she would ever confess the truth to him, and he needed to hear it almost as much as she needed to say it.

"You!" she cried out as he ruthlessly took total possession of her mind, body, and spirit. "Yours, always yours… only yours… oh, God, *Ian*!" She cried out in climax, clenching around him with more force than he'd ever felt. With a final thrust he buried himself at the entrance of her womb and emptied inside her.

For a few timeless, precious moments, he held her as she sobbed against his chest. He'd done it. He'd stripped her down to her bare soul, made her reveal what he had suspected all along. There would be no more pretending, no more walls between them.

"Sweet Lexi," Ian said against her ear as he withdrew, his voice raw. "My sweet Lexi. Remember that no matter where we go today, no matter who we see, that it is *me* inside of you."

chapter eighteen

Something changed in Ian after that. He became centered. Focused. He had a goal now, knew exactly what he wanted. He wanted Lexi. Not for a night. Not for a week. Forever. And he had the next four days to convince her of that.

She loved him, he knew that much. He saw it when she looked at him. Felt it in every touch. Heard it in every word she spoke to him. But she was scared, and he couldn't blame her. When it was just the two of them, she was open and loving. Around anyone else, she tended to get very quiet, very subdued, hiding away her thoughts and keeping to the shadows. It tugged at something deep inside. He was beginning to realize why Kieran was so fiercely protective of her.

"You okay?" Ian asked, catching Lexi's hand.

"Yeah." She glanced into the front door of the pub and looked back at him uncertainly.

On impulsive Ian pulled her to him, the need to comfort her overwhelming. "Are you sure?" he asked, kissing the top of her head before releasing her. She'd been quieter than usual at breakfast, and it had him worried. She nodded, but the way she nibbled her bottom lip gave her away.

"It'll be okay, baby," he said, smoothing her hair. "Do you trust me?"

She looked at him with those big amber eyes and nodded again, sending a rush of warmth through him.

Jake was restocking the shelves when they walked in.

"Lex," Jake greeted with a friendly smile for Lexi and a quick glance toward Ian. If he was surprised to see the two of them arrive together, he hid it well.

"Taryn's putting on a fresh pot of coffee in the kitchen. I know she's worried about you. Think you can go in and talk to her for a bit?"

Lexi nodded quietly, offering a small, shy smile as she left the two men alone. Ian didn't take his eyes off of her until she disappeared into the next room. Jake's voice dropped down low to avoid being overheard.

"Tell me you are not doing what I think you are," Jake said, his voice laced with concern.

There was no good way to respond to that, so Ian didn't. He didn't have to. All he had to do was look into his brother's eyes and Jake understood. Along with understanding was empathy, because less than a year before, Jake had had the same tortured look in his eyes.

Jake blew out a breath. "I sure hope you know what you're doing, Ian."

"Not a fucking clue," Ian responded, echoing the words Jake said to him all those months ago. It was honest, at least, even if he couldn't admit it to anyone but Jake. When Taryn came into their lives, Jake fell hard and fast. Ian hadn't understood it then, but he sure as hell did now.

Jake whistled softly. "So it's like that, is it?"

"Yeah. Exactly like that."

Jake held out his hand. "Welcome to the club, man. Hits you like a freight train, doesn't it?"

Ian took his hand and smiled. Oh, yeah. Jake got it.

"You have your work cut out for you though. It's not going to be easy."

Ian snorted. When had things ever been easy? In the end it didn't really matter. Lexi was his *croie*, his heart. He accepted that now, and all he could do was move forward with it. But he had a feeling Jake was referring to something a bit more specific.

"Tell me."

Jake placed both hands on the bar and leaned closer. "Kieran went over to Lexi's hotel this morning. Apparently they got into it last night, and he's been crawling the walls ever since. When he finds out she's not there, he is *not* going to be a happy boy. When he finds out she's with *you*, he's going to go completely batshit."

"I'd never hurt her, Jake," Ian said quietly.

"Yeah, I get that. But I don't think Kieran is going to be quite as understanding. He remembers, even if you don't." When Ian's eyes flashed, Jake put up his hands. "Hey, I know you were clueless then, so I'm not laying blame here. I'm just saying."

Had he been clueless then? Ian wasn't so sure. Last night, when Lexi was snuggled against him and he dozed contentedly, flashes of those golden amber eyes came back to him, eyes that had speared through him a dozen years earlier when Kieran first brought her home. Eyes that he would see in his dreams when he was away on missions and wasn't sure he would make it home again. Eyes he had attributed to his guardian angel, that he now knew belonged to a real woman, the one who would always haunt his thoughts and bring him home again. *Lexi's eyes.*

"Yeah." He hadn't told anyone about that, not even Jake, and he wasn't about to then. Those insights were too personal, too damn deep, and he was just beginning to comprehend what his subconscious had known all along: that Lexi was *The One*. Maybe some instinctual part of him had recognized it way back then, but they had been so young, and anything between them would have been impossible. No wonder he'd locked it away and buried it beneath a decade of denial.

"I'm heading upstairs for a few. Keep an eye on her, would you?"

Jake nodded. "She'll be in with Taryn for a

while yet I'd bet, but yeah, I got it." Feeling more at ease knowing that Jake had his back, Ian ran up to their private living quarters to change and grab a few items.

* * *

Ian was still upstairs when Kieran's bike roared up out front a short while later. Within seconds, the youngest Callaghan was blowing through the door, resembling a massive, dark storm cloud.

Lexi and Taryn came from the back; their light laughter ceased the moment they caught the stormy expression on Kieran's face.

"Uh-oh," murmured Taryn.

"Kieran," Lexi called softly. At the sound of her voice Kieran turned, the dark expression morphing instantly into relief.

"Lexi! I thought I missed you!" In a few long strides he crossed the floor and Lexi disappeared in a thorough embrace.

"I've decided to stay out the week," she said, her words muffled against his chest as she laughingly extricated herself. Then she closed her hand into a fist and punched him solidly on the arm. It hurt her more than it did him, she was sure.

"What was that for?"

"For believing for one second I would leave without saying good-bye, no matter how much you pissed me off."

His eyes softened then. "Sorry, Lex. After last night…"

"I know," she said, patting the area where she'd smacked him. "I'm sorry, too, Kier."

"You still know how to scare the shit out of me, you know that?"

The sound of a throat clearing had them both looking toward the bar, where Ian now stood beside Jake. There was no mistaking the look on Ian's face. It screamed possession.

Kieran pulled Lexi tightly against him and glared over the top of her head at Ian, his message clear.

"Ah, shit…" murmured Jake, pushing Taryn safely behind him.

Kieran's jaw clenched; his muscled arms rippled with barely restrained anger. Ian straightened himself to his full height and faced him head on, his body in a battle-ready stance.

The two men faced off, clearly on the verge of blows. But before anything happened, Lexi placed her hand on Kieran's arm. "Kieran," she said quietly.

He looked down, reading the truth in her eyes. "Oh, fuck no."

Across the room, Ian tensed further. Jake discreetly put a hand on his shoulder, warning him to stay put.

Kieran's tone was one of total disbelief. "What the hell were you thinking, Lex?"

She was silent for a few moments, trying to think of words that could explain what she herself didn't quite understand. When she finally spoke, her voice was quiet but level. "I'm not thinking, Kier. I'm *living*."

"But Lex ... Ian? Really?"

"Leave her alone," Ian said, stepping forward.

Kieran stiffened immediately, tension rippling through his body. He pushed Lexi behind him, his body a massive shield. "Why don't you fuck off?"

Ian's eyes glittered, silvery specs against a darkening blue. "She's not a child, Kieran. Stop treating her like one."

Kieran looked down at Lexi, disbelief etched in every feature. "You didn't tell him, did you? He doesn't know."

"Know what?" Ian demanded.

If it was possible, Kieran grew even larger in his barely controlled rage. "You have no clue what you're messing with, Ian. She's not one of your whores."

Ian would have launched himself at Kieran at that point had Lexi not spoken up and shocked them all. "Yes, Kier," she said clearly. "That's exactly what I am. At least for the next few days."

Taryn gasped audibly, her hand flying to her mouth. Beyond that, you could have heard a pin drop in the heavy silence. The men were shell-shocked, their expressions ranging from disbelief (Jake) to devastation (Kieran) and outright anger

(Ian). It might have been funny under different circumstances.

"No." Kieran began shaking his head as if he could dislodge the words and nullify them at the same time.

"It's what I want," she added, petting his arm as if she could soothe him, her voice softer. She wanted --- no, *needed* --- Kieran to understand. "Please try to understand, Kier. I just want to feel normal for a little while."

Lexi felt awful for hurting him, but it was the truth. She couldn't blame him for being upset. He'd always looked out for her, been her protector. This was like a betrayal in his eyes. She could only hope he would come to understand and forgive her someday.

Lexi smoothed away imaginary wrinkles from her top to hide her shaking hands. With willpower and courage she didn't know she had, she began walking toward the door, her head held high. With a glance toward Ian, she said, "You promised me a ride."

Then she walked through the doors and waited on the sidewalk, keeping her eyes directed away from the inside of the pub, hoping desperately that Ian would simply follow her out and no one would get hurt.

* * *

"If you hurt her I'll kill you," Kieran seethed. "I don't care how good you think you are, I'll slit your fucking throat in your own fucking bed." Then he turned and stalked away, leaving the others in stunned silence.

"Well, that went well," Jake breathed. "He took it better than I expected."

Ian shot him a scathing look before following Lexi outside.

He was almost as furious as Kieran. How could Lexi have said what she did? Was it possible that she actually believed that's all she was to him? Didn't she understand that she had become everything to him? Didn't she feel the same way?

He stormed outside with every intention of setting her straight, but pulled up short a few feet behind her. Her back was to him, but he could tell she was crying by the slight rise and fall of her shoulders. All of his rage was swept away instantly. The hurt he would deal with later.

Pulling her into his arms, he cradled her against him, drawing them back into a hidden alcove along the side of the building. "Ssshhh, Lex, it's all right," he soothed, rubbing her back.

"I hurt him."

"He's all right, baby. He's a big boy. He'll come around, you'll see. He's just trying to protect you."

Lexi wasn't a sobber or a wailer. Her tears were subtler than that, quiet hitches that drew little or no attention. He held her until she calmed down.

"What you said, Lex, it just isn't true." He lifted her chin and forced her to look at him. She had to know she was so much more than that to him. In the span of a few days she had become *everything*.

She attempted a smile, wiping impatiently at her eyes, neither confirming nor disputing him. "So. Do I get that ride or not?"

The sadness in her eyes faded into the background, replaced by that implacable mask he'd seen the day of her father's funeral. She was pulling away, distancing herself, and he hated it. But he also sensed that it was her defense mechanism, and it was not the time to push her.

"Yeah," he said, shelving the topic for later. "A deal's a deal."

An hour later, all bad thoughts faded into the background as he opened up the throttle. Lexi was snuggled securely against his back, her arms holding tightly around his waist. He'd taken it slow through town, letting her become acclimated to the feel of the bike, learning how to move with him. It required a fair measure of trust on her part, following his movements and instructions exactly until he was assured she wouldn't panic.

He shouldn't have worried. She was a natural, moving with him as if she were a part of him. Before long he felt confident enough to head out onto the twisting, winding mountain roads.

Having Lexi with him felt so right. Before long he felt the tension leave her body, replaced by childlike excitement. He could feel it in the way she held him, and in the little exclamations she let out every now and then. Ian pulled off the road near the top of the mountain. Her hair was windblown, her face flushed with joy, and her eyes glowed almost as brightly as they had in her hotel room after he'd spent hours making love to her.

"That's the most wonderful thing I've ever felt!" she exclaimed as Ian lifted her off the bike. He raised his eyebrow doubtfully. "Well," she amended, blushing a furious pink, "the second best, anyway."

Ian laughed out loud and kissed her. "Come on," he coaxed. "Bet you've never seen this before."

He led her along a barely visible path to a rocky shelf that overlooked the entire valley. "Oh, Ian," she said in breathless awe. "It's so beautiful."

"Yes," he said softly, sliding his arms beneath hers and pulling her back to his chest. "You are."

I am desperately, hopelessly in love with you, Lexi. Marry me and be mine forever. The words were right there in his head and on the tip of his tongue, all too ready to be spoken. He even took a breath in preparation to say them.

"You don't have to do that," she said quietly.

"Do what?"

"Say things like that. I already said I'd stay

through the end of the week."

Ian turned her around to face him, disbelief evident. "You think I'm kidding?"

She shrugged. Ian was dumbstruck. Lexi wasn't just attractive, she was gorgeous. Her clear amber eyes, the multi-hued hair that curved into her body. And that body! She was a Greek goddess in the flesh. But more than that, more than the physical features that had every man turning his head, was an inner beauty that was infinitely more attractive, yet she was completely unaware of it. She was at once vulnerable yet strong. Innocent yet passionate. Quiet yet intense. But how could he make her see that?

He couldn't. Not in words, anyway. So Ian resorted to the next best thing. He would show her.

Ian lowered his head and claimed her mouth with absolute possession. He poured everything he felt for her into that kiss, willing her to understand. Within seconds she melted against him, becoming pliant in his arms. That was his Lexi. He forced himself to pull away, his breathing nearly as ragged as hers.

"You. Are. *Beautiful*."

She gazed up at him with heavy-lidded eyes. He loved that he could do that to her with just a kiss. "Make love to me, Ian."

Ian didn't know what surprised him more --- the fact that she suggested it or the fact that he hadn't. The truth was that he had been perfectly content sharing the view with her in his arms, happy to simply be with her and share her excitement. Seeing things through her eyes was like experiencing them for the first time himself, whether it be sex, riding the Harley, or looking out over the breathtaking valley. Something told him that would never change, either. No matter how many times she gave herself to him, it would never be enough. They could come back to this ledge a hundred times and each time would be better than the last.

Now that she'd made the suggestion, however, the hunger was there, panting like a dog in front of a prime rib. He groaned, holding her body closely against his, his erection letting them both know that it was on board with that plan.

"Here?" he asked incredulously. "Now?"

"Yes," she breathed, her hands slipping down to his belt. "Right here. Right now."

He managed to coax her away from the overhang, pulling her to a more private location among the trees.

"Sweet baby," he murmured, helping as she tried desperately to remove his shirt. So hungry, so needful for that which only he could give her. Ian felt as though he had been given a tremendous gift. He laid his clothes over a fallen tree, easing himself back onto it. Once he was sure it would hold, he pulled Lexi onto his lap so that she straddled him. Her head flew back in rapture, her nails digging into his shoulders as he lowered her onto him, his hands guiding her hips with strength and unerring precision.

They made love with a slow, easy rhythm until the pressure became too great for her to resist and she gave herself over to him completely. Ian knew the moment she did, had been waiting for it.

"You're mine, Lexi," he whispered as he thrust upwards.

She buried her face against his neck, biting into his shoulder to keep from crying out. Ian swore under his breath and quickened his pace until her entire body closed around him. Relinquishing his own control, he took one, two, three mighty strokes and erupted deep within her.

"Thank you," she whispered into his neck, her words thick with an emotion he fully understood. Unable to speak, he held her that much tighter, as if by doing so he could hold on to the moment forever.

chapter nineteen

If this was a dream, then Lexi didn't want to wake up. She stretched out on the blanket, feeling the full moon on her naked back as if it were the midday sun. The night air was still relatively balmy in the high eighties, but the cool breeze coming in off of the lake was a welcome caress. Ian lay beside her, propped up on his side, lazily tracing the peaks and valleys of her curves with the pads of his fingers as if memorizing each and every inch.

How he had the energy, she couldn't fathom. After rowing out to a secluded spot on the far end of the lake, they'd shed their clothes and skinny-dipped in the cold, spring-fed waters. It must have super-charged Ian, because afterwards he was a driven man. He was a tireless lover, making love to her on the shore for several hours, bringing her to climax an astounding four times.

Her eyes drifted shut as she soaked up his warmth and the touch of his hand, sated and boneless, too tired even to sample the dinner they'd packed.

She was slowing down, she could feel it. The whirlwind pace of the last few days was catching up to her, the reduction in her meds exacerbating the fatigue and muscle weakness. Thankfully, Ian seemed to accept her lassitude as that of a well-sated mate, which was certainly true. Still, she would have to be careful, and try to do a better job of pacing herself until she could get back to Benton and her medicine cabinet full of miracles.

* * *

Ian smoothed the imaginary wrinkles from his crisp white dress shirt, feeling every bit as anxious as he had when he went to his first school dance. He did a quick self-inspection: black slacks, pressed and creased, check. Black shoes, matching and polished to a mirror-like shine, check. Tailored suit jacket and coordinated blue-striped tie, check.

He rapped his knuckles against the door, clutching the bouquet of miniature flowers (white rosebuds and sunset-colored lilies). Taking a deep breath, he reminded himself that he was a twenty-seven year old SEAL, and he had done far more difficult things than this.

Lexi was his *croie*. Taking her out to an exclusive restaurant and proposing was the next natural step. He would wait until after dessert, then

---

As they had once before, Ian's systems went into total lockdown when Lexi opened the door. Struck dumb, he could only stare.

"What?" she asked, taking a step back to let him in. "I look ridiculous, don't I? I told Taryn this was too much. I'm going to change."

"Don't." Ian forced the word out, his voice rough and husky, his eyes pleading. "*Please*. Just… just let me look at you, Lex."

His heart pounded against the inner walls of his chest as his eyes roamed the length of her body and back up again, certain that he was dreaming. Lexi was dressed in a form-fitting white sheath that had the draped looked of a toga, trimmed in gold with slight accents of blue. The dress showcased her lightly bronzed skin, now glowing with sun-kissed radiance. Slim bands of gold chains adorned her neck, her upper right arm, and her left ankle. Her unpierced ears held gold ear cuffs draped with sapphires. She wore her hair up, allowing streaked strands to fall loosely around her back and shoulders.

"Ian? What's wrong?" Lexi asked, her brows knitting together in concern.

"Just… give me a moment."

In his near thirty years, he'd never been quite so thoroughly stricken. Lexi had done what career soldiers could not; she had rendered him completely and utterly helpless. He struggled to breathe through the constriction in his chest.

"Ian? Are you okay?" Lexi took a step toward him, cupping his face gently in her hands. Ian suddenly knew what it was like to be touched by a goddess. She looked up into his face, those golden amber eyes filled with concern and love. *For him.*

He managed to put his hand over hers, only slightly aware that he was shaking. He closed his eyes and turned to kiss her fingers, saying a silent prayer of thanks. "I am now," he said softly.

Lexi's worried expression eased, replaced by a genuine, if not slightly disbelieving, smile, and in that moment Ian knew he would do anything to make her smile again. It would become a lifelong pursuit to make sure she smiled at him, just like this, every day for the rest of their lives.

"How did you ever manage to get us in here?" Lexi asked nearly two hours later. She was clearly impressed as they sat at a premier table in the back corner, the one usually reserved for special guests. From their seats, they had an unimpeded view of a magnificent waterfall flowing among pristine gardens.

Ian had never been to this particular restaurant before, but he knew of its reputation. *D'Armini's* was one of the most-sought after places to go, *the* top-rated restaurant in the Northeastern US, boasting the talents of one of the world's greatest master chefs, Francesco D'Armini. People came from all over the world to dine under his mastery.

Getting in, let alone on a Friday night, was next to impossible unless you were a high-ranking political figure or of comparable rock star status.

Or you knew someone who was and they owed you bigtime.

Ian smiled and shrugged as if it was no big deal. He'd had to call in a few favors, but seeing that look on Lexi's face would have been worth a thousand times more.

The dinner was exquisite. When Lexi sent her compliments to the chef, he came out personally, his eyes growing as wide as saucers when his eyes found Lexi. He was an older man --- Ian put his age somewhere around mid to late fifties --- with the shape of a man who took good care of himself but still loved his creations.

"Alexis!" the man cried in a thick Italian accent. "Can it be?"

She blushed as some of the other diners turned to look at the patron who had garnered the attention of the chef. "Most beautiful protégé I ever had," he said fondly with a kiss to each cheek and a warm embrace. "And my most favorite student, eh?"

Lexi blushed deeper, making the big man rumble with laughter. The waiters looked on in stunned silence, unused to seeing the chef quite so jovial.

"Ah, still shy I see," he said. "Such a rare treasure these days, to find a woman so enchantingly oblivious to the spell she casts on those around her."

"Chef D'Armini, how wonderful to see you again," Lexi said, rising to her toes to plant a kiss on his cheek. "As handsome and charming as ever, you rascal," she added, making him laugh even more. The world-renowned chef grinned like a schoolboy at the compliment. A few diners pulled out their Droids, no doubt sensing that anyone garnering such attention from Francesco D'Armini had to be Twitter-worthy at the very least.

"Come, *bella*," said Francesco, indicating that Ian should join them as well. "We will speak in a more private venue, eh?"

He ushered them into his private office. It was unexpectedly simple, but done with exquisite taste. Dark, rich fabrics and smooth, polished wood suggested understated elegance with a high price tag.

"You are very naughty, Alexis," he scolded with affection. "If I had known you were coming I would have prepared something special for you."

"Everything was fabulous," Lexi praised, making him beam even more. "And I didn't know we were coming here." She glanced at Ian, who stood against the wall like a bodyguard.

Chef D'Armini followed her gaze, and looked appraisingly at Ian. "This boy, he is treating you good, yes?"

Ian straightened a little. It had been a long time since anyone had called him a "boy", but he took it in stride.

"Yes, sir. He is." She flashed Ian a shy smile that melted his heart. There was a soft, ethereal quality to her voice that he only heard when she spoke to him.

"Ah, I see." The chef leaned in close, his face softening. "He is the one, is he not?" He spoke quietly, but Ian's keen ears heard every word. A lovely, familiar blush rose in Lexi's cheeks as she averted her gaze.

The chef turned to Ian. "You are a fortunate young man," he said, his voice full and somber. Ian detected something else in there, too. A warning, perhaps? It seemed as though Lexi brought out the protective male instinct in everyone.

"Yes, I am," Ian replied simply. He held the chef's gaze so that they understood each other. After a long minute, the chef nodded, satisfied.

"*Bene*. You will invite me to the wedding, no?"

* * *

Lexi was mortified. Turning at least a dozen increasingly dark shades of red, she looked down at the expensive carpeting, unwilling to see the look of 'not happening' on Ian's face.

"I'm sorry about that," Lexi said quietly as they made the hour and a half drive back toward Pine Ridge. Ian's mood had been subdued ever since they'd left the chef's private office. He'd barely spoken ten words to her over the coffee and dessert; his mind seemed a million miles away.

She wished it didn't bother her as much as it did. She knew her time with Ian was limited, knew that in less than forty-eight hours she would be on her way back to Benton. But there was some part of her that wanted to believe in fairy tale endings. She shut those thoughts down as soon as they began to surface, unwilling to let anything mar the time she did have.

"Don't be." The expression on his face was unreadable, his blue eyes crystal clear, like living glass.

The silence in the sleek black Jag (his brother Michael's) was making her paranoid. "The dinner was fabulous, Ian. Thank you."

"You're welcome." He offered a slight smile that made her want to scream in frustration. What was going through his mind?

"Look, Ian, don't pay any attention to what Chef D'Armini said. He's a hopeless romantic, always trying to play matchmaker. It doesn't mean anything."

"Doesn't it?"

"N-no," she answered, silently cursing the stutter she thought she had mastered years ago. Her face was flushed, the butterflies in her stomach multiplied a hundred times over. A familiar weakness started creeping into her extremities, brought on by the slight rise in her heartbeat and the decided lack of meds keeping her on an even keel. For the remainder of the ride she kept silent, concentrating on regulating her breathing before she made an even bigger fool out of herself.

The moment they got back to her hotel room she excused herself and practically ran into the bathroom. She breathed a sigh of relief when the welcome cooling sensation of the injection circulated through her body. Within a few moments she started to feel better, but it wasn't enough. She looked longingly at the last remaining vial, but wouldn't allow herself the extra fix. She had to save it to get through her last twenty-four hours. The ride home was going to be a bitch, but it would be worth it to have this extra time with Ian.

A stranger's face stared back at her in the mirror. Who was she kidding, anyway? She looked down at the dress, the jewelry, the shoes. Nothing but Cinderella dressing for the ball, except she'd stretched her one night of magic into an entire week. Soon her clock would strike twelve, and it would all go away. But it had been worth it. How many people got to live their dreams, even for a little while?

Lexi took a few deep breaths and pulled herself together. Her prince was waiting, and they didn't have much time.

"Come here."

Ian's voice was low, commanding, and Lexi felt a compulsion to do exactly as he said, but she fought it. She shook her head hesitantly, unconsciously taking a step back.

Ian's eyes burned a bright, glowing blue with an intensity that she felt all the way down to her toes. His unknotted tie hung loosely around his neck, the top few buttons of his dress shirt already undone. She stifled a whimper as he slid the belt from his slacks smoothly, then ran the leather through his hands suggestively.

Oh, God. She knew what was coming. She had practically begged him for it.

"Come here."

"No," she squeaked, barely louder than a whisper. Ian walked slowly toward her, a massive wall of pure male, his eyes never wavering, his gait predatory. Lexi stepped backward until the wall prevented any further retreat. He stopped mere inches from her, pressing his hands to the wall, his much larger body becoming a cage around hers without physically touching her.

But this was Ian. His very presence surrounded her, enveloped her, stroked her more masterfully than anyone else's hands ever could. What the hell had she been thinking, believing that she could ever handle this and emerge unscathed? Each moment in his arms, each night spent sharing a bed with him only reinforced the fact that she was in way over her head.

"Have a change of heart, did you?" he breathed, the delicious scent of his hot breath causing her to lick her lips.

"Yes."

"Liar," he scolded gently. "Don't be afraid of me, Lexi." He brushed a lock of hair away from her face. "I could never hurt you."

Lexi swallowed down the lump in her throat. Didn't he know that he had already destroyed her?

With infinite slowness, Ian lowered his head those scant few inches, hovering just above her lips. "Tell me no, Lexi, and I'll find some way to stop, I swear it."

But she couldn't tell him no. Not now, not ever. As terrified as she was, she would never deny him anything. When several long moments ticked by in silence, Ian groaned and touched his lips to hers. And she was forever lost. Her hands snaked up around his neck, and Ian lifted her to him, carrying her to the bed.

He took his time undressing her. With each piece of silken fabric he removed, he covered her bared skin with his hands and mouth, until only her jewelry remained. "My goddess," he breathed, his voice rough and strained with desire. "Will you give yourself to me willingly?"

"Yes," she whispered.

Pure white flames of hunger danced in his eyes. "Ah, baby. You have no idea what you do to me. All night long I've been dreaming of what I would do to you when I got you back here. How many times I would make you scream my name in pleasure."

He rolled her over onto her stomach. She felt the bed rise as he lifted himself from it. Eyes tightly closed in a mixture of fear and anticipation, she heard the soft opening and closing of the nightstand drawer. No, he wouldn't...

A tiny whimper escaped, despite her efforts.

"It's okay, baby." Within seconds his fingers slid through her slick folds, massaging in torturous little circles until she began pushing herself against his hand. Then he slid one finger into her, stroking masterfully at her sensitive nerves as she shook from the pleasure of it. One finger became two, scissoring within her relentlessly. When she was close, he pulled away. She knew he was preparing her for what was to come.

What she had asked for. A condition of her extended stay.

Lexi tensed as she felt the cool, smooth tip of her vibrator against her. Ian moved it slowly, teasing, turning it to its lowest setting. Just enough to stimulate, that's all. There was something insanely erotic about having him do this, of sharing such a personal act with him.

Just when she'd begun to relax, he moved it back and forth, hitting her most sensitive bundle of nerves. At the same time, she felt his hand on her backside. A smooth, arousing caress that added to her pleasure.

She gasped, her core clenching around empty

space. The simple sensations were too much. And not nearly enough. "Ian," she choked out, "I don't think I can do this."

"Yes," he crooned against her ear. "Yes, you can. You're going to give me this gift, Lexi, because you want it just as badly as I do, my naughty girl." Ian pressed himself against her, spearing her far too slowly for what she needed. His touch was too tender as he stroked and moved the small vibrator over her aching flesh.

Little by little Lexi found herself surrendering to his sorcerous touch, coaxing out the darker nature that lurked deep within her, the one she kept locked and hidden away with all of her deepest, darkest secrets.

Torture. Pleasure. Ache. Want. Need. Ian stoked the fire burning inside her with his mastery of her body, bringing her to her peak over and over again but never letting her plunge over the edge. The sound of desperate begging reached her ears, and Lexi, nearly out of her mind now, realized on some level that it was her.

"Ah, you're killing me, baby," Ian groaned. "So fucking hot, and all mine. You want this, don't you? Tell me you want this, Lexi. Tell me and I'll give it to you."

"Please, Ian," she pleaded, well beyond any rational thought or objection. He'd reduced her to a sobbing pile of need, of hunger. She needed him to fix this. He was the only one who could. There would only be Ian, ever. And she --- her body, her mind, her heart --- belonged to him. "I need you."

"That's my girl," he murmured approvingly. His fingers were suddenly gone as he rolled her onto her side, her back against his chest, and lifted her upper leg. "Here baby, you hold this..." He moved her hand to the vibrator, wrapping her fingers around it. "Use it. Make yourself feel good, Lexi."

Lexi barely had time to comprehend his words when she felt him lengthen his strokes. In this new position, he felt harder. Longer. Thicker. And with each thrust, he hit her exactly where she needed him most.

"That's it," he encouraged. "Let go. Give me everything, Lexi. I want it all."

Lexi's entire body tightened as the overwhelming climax consumed her, each sensation magnified by another. The pulse of her toy. The feel of having Ian inside of her, wrapping around her body, his teeth nipping at the tender curve of her neck.

Stars burst behind her eyes, relief exploding through her body with incredible force. She thought she might have screamed, but couldn't be sure. As if from far, far away she heard Ian curse, right before she felt pulsing jets of heat deep within while Ian's hands held on to her, anchoring her.

Then she gave herself up to the blackness.

chapter twenty

Ian willed his heart to slow down, to ease the fierce pounding against his chest for fear of waking her. Lexi lay limp in his arms. He had pushed her too hard, and she'd let him. He had tried to be gentle, but Lexi was like a drug coursing through him. With each fix, he wanted more. And tonight she had given him everything.

He lifted her carefully, wrapping her in a blanket and carrying her to the bathroom. She barely moved as he drew a warm bath, murmuring only slightly as he lowered her into the water and cleaned her reverently.

He frowned when he saw the blossoming purple marks along her hips. He hadn't realized he'd gripped her quite so hard, but then it was difficult to recall anything besides the blinding hunger that had driven him past the point of rational thought.

God, what he had just done to her! What she had given him. What she had somehow known he needed. Lexi had sensed his darker side, and yet she still loved him.

Ian dried her as carefully as he could, tucking her into bed before heading to the shower himself. It was a quick one; even a few minutes away from her were too much. He needed to hold her. He would, through touch, find some way to convey that in a few short days she had become the most important thing in his world.

He crawled between the sheets, thinking about the ring that still sat in the pocket of his suit jacket. He had planned on proposing at the restaurant, of taking her out into the gardens and going down on bended knee, the whole nine yards. But it just didn't work out that way. The mood had changed after their little tête-à-tête with the chef, and this wasn't something he would force.

Lexi was meant for him, he knew this. Besides, he thought with a grin as Lexi burrowed against him, she deserved a more unique proposal than that. Maybe he'd ask her atop the Ferris wheel at the county fair tomorrow…

* * *

It was still dark when Lexi woke. Ian's body was wrapped around her protectively, his deep, even breathing a soothing rhythm. How many times had she dreamed of waking like this in his arms? She could stay like this forever, she thought, her eyes drifting shut again.

A sharp, cramping pain sliced through her lower abdomen, jolting her back into alertness. She breathed through it the best she could. As it subsided, she tried to extricate herself.

"You okay?" Ian asked softly, his strong arm like a steel band around her.

Even though it was too dark for him to see, Lexi forced a smile, hoping it found its way into her voice. "I just need to use the bathroom."

Ian's grip loosened. "If you're not back in five minutes I'm coming in after you," he warned, his voice still thick and heavy with sleep.

Lexi kissed his forehead and smoothed his hair. He was asleep again before she slipped out of the bed.

Once inside the bathroom, she closed the door silently and sagged against the frame. Her entire body felt like it had been in a train wreck. Every muscle burned in protest, every joint felt like a toothache. A third cramp hit and she doubled over, sliding down to the floor until she could catch her breath again.

With a sense of dread, she forced herself to look down, knowing what she would see. Her legs were black and blue from her knees upward; patches of deep purple ringed her hips. Tears filled her eyes, a profound feeling of loss blossoming within her. Time was running out too quickly.

She had no choice. With a silent curse she reached for the last vial. She hated this. Hated what she was forced to do, just to pretend to live a normal life. This week had been a welcome respite from what her life had become – a structured series of tasks that carried her from one day to the next. But this week, this week she had actually *lived*.

When the pains stopped coming every few minutes, Lexi switched off the light and eased into the main room just long enough to grab her cell, moving slowly and carefully so as to not wake Ian. Once back in the bathroom, she tapped out a text, wishing she didn't have to. Then she pressed 'send' and settled against the cool wall to wait out the remainder of the night alone.

* * *

A knock at the door woke Ian. He heard Lexi's sweet, quiet voice, and seconds later the room was filled with the delicious smell of coffee and bacon.

"Good morning, sleepyhead," she teased, wheeling a cart over to the bed. "I wasn't sure what you'd like, so I ordered a little bit of everything."

Ian's stomach rumbled hungrily at the huge assortment of breakfast items displayed before him as Lexi uncovered plate after plate. Pancakes. French toast. Eggs. Bacon, Sausage, Ham. Several different kinds of pastries. And, God love her, two full-size carafes of coffee, one of which she was pouring into a pair of mugs. She handed one to him.

Ian looked her over carefully from tip to toes.

He'd slept soundly for the last few hours, but he was pretty sure Lexi hadn't returned to the bed. Now she was already dressed in faded capris that hugged her figure like a glove and a long-sleeved, light fabric peasant top. By all accounts she looked fine, but he sensed that something was off.

"You okay?" he asked, an edge of concern in his voice.

Lexi gave him a patient smile. "Yes. Stop worrying, Ian. I'm fine."

"Come here." She did, without hesitation, sitting beside him on the bed, though she did so rather gingerly.

"You're a rotten liar," he said.

Lexi had the good grace to look ashamed. "Okay. So maybe I'm a bit tender. But you don't hear me complaining, do you?"

"That's all?"

"Well, I think I'll have to skip the pony rides at the fair, but other than that…"

Amusement glinted in her eye, and Ian breathed a sigh of relief. "You know, I could help you with that soreness."

Lexi scooted off the bed, beyond his immediate reach. "Oh no you don't, mister," she scolded with a grin. "You promised me a county fair."

Ian smiled back, even if he was disappointed. Not too much, though. He could give her a couple of hours to rest. "That I did. And I always keep my promises."

* * *

The fair was as wonderful as Lexi remembered, even if it didn't seem quite as big as it once did. There were still dozens of food booths, games, shows, bands, animals, and rides. Truly something for everyone.

The entire Callaghan clan was there. For community-wide events such as this, the pub closed its doors so the men could take an active part in the festivities. Lexi got to meet some more of their extended family as well, the Connelly cousins. Johnny (whom she'd met), his brother Michael (not to be confused with Ian's brother Michael), his sister Lina, and their spouses. They'd taken over a pavilion at the far end of the grounds for their annual reunion.

Ian got dragged into a few spirited games with his brothers and cousins, while Lexi watched with the rest of the "wives". Taryn, she knew. Celina, Stacey, and Keely --- wives of Kyle, Johnny, and Michael (Connelly), respectively, were a riot to be around, and Lexi found herself enjoying the afternoon more than she ever thought she would. Odd as it seemed, she felt comfortable around these women, and they, in turn, seemed to genuinely accept her. It made her quickly approaching departure even more difficult.

"Uh-oh," muttered Taryn. "Here comes

trouble." As one, the women turned where Taryn was looking and saw Kayla approaching.

"She is trouble," Lina agreed.

They watched in silence as Kayla approached the pavilion, keeping to the far side, out of the line of sight of the men.

"Lexi," Kayla said, pointedly ignoring the others. "Can I talk to you for a sec?"

Lexi hesitated. Despite the smile, whatever Kayla wanted wouldn't be good. Still, there was no need to put these ladies through one of Kayla's outbursts.

"Sure," she said, rising from the picnic table. She looked out at the field where the pick-up football game was in full swing. Ian was currently at the bottom of a pile, with more jumping on.

"You don't have to do this," Taryn said quietly, her eyes shooting daggers at Kayla.

"Yeah," Keely agreed, speaking so only Lexi could hear her. "She can't take all of us."

Lexi bit back a smile. They would never know just how much their words meant to her. But this was her fight, not theirs. Especially not when three of them were clearly expecting.

"It's okay. I've got this."

Lexi met Kayla at the far end of the pavilion and they walked off together toward the woods.

"I don't like this," Lina said, rubbing her large belly.

"Me neither," agreed Stacey. "Maybe someone

should tell Ian."

"I don't think Lexi would appreciate that," said Keely. "I know I wouldn't. Let her handle this. We'll keep an eye on them and if things look like they're getting out of hand we'll call in the cavalry."

* * *

Kayla moved farther into the shadows of the trees, away from the others. Lexi followed along several paces behind, but was smart enough to remain in sight.

"What did you want to talk to me about, Kayla?"

Kayla stopped and crossed her arms over her chest, pinning Lexi with a hard glare. "You need to leave Pine Ridge. You don't belong here."

Lexi didn't argue. That was a given. She nodded. "Anything else?"

It took Kayla a moment to respond. Her eyes widened, her lips parted slightly. Clearly she'd been expecting more of a fight, but there was no point. "And you can't have Ian."

Again, Lexi didn't argue. She glanced down at her watch, silently calculating the time she had left before she had to leave for the airport. She didn't want to waste it by listening to one of Kayla's long-winded rants. The sooner they moved this along, the better. "Is that it?"

Kayla mistook Lexi's lack of response for mockery, becoming enraged from one heartbeat to the next. Without warning, her hands shot out and grabbed Lexi, shoving hard. Caught off-guard, Lexi went with the momentum of the shove, stopping abruptly when she felt the hard wood and rough bark on an oak press into her spine along with a sharp, sudden pain along the base of her skull.

"Ian. Is. Mine," Kayla hissed, her hands on Lexi's shoulders, pushing her back repeatedly into the tree with each word.

"He's not," Lexi managed, trying to push Kayla away, but she wasn't strong enough. Kayla was bigger and healthier and filled with rage; Lexi was struggling with barely enough energy to make it through the day.

"Yes. He. Is." Kayla spat back. "At least he will be when I tell him I'm pregnant."

Fireflies flitted across Lexi's vision with the next hit, but she was lucid enough to have heard the words. "You're... pregnant?"

"Yes," Kayla said with a cruel smile. "Ian was drunk, and I forgot to take my pills. Oops."

Kayla's smile faded when she saw the first drops of blood fall from Lexi's nose, then the side of her mouth. She got downright scared when it started to seep from the corners of Lexi's eyes, so that it looked like she was crying tears of blood. She quickly let go of Lexi as if she'd been burned, and Lexi was barely able to get her hands underneath her before she went down on her knees.

Lexi tried to wipe the blood from her eyes; her light-colored sleeve was now heavily streaked with red. "I won't stand in your way, Kayla," she said, pausing to spit out some blood.

"Jesus, Lexi, I didn't mean to …"

Lexi was shaking her head to clear it, her eyes unfocused as she tried to get her bearings. When she began to cough up blood, Kayla panicked, running back toward the pavilion for help. Lexi collapsed. Her cell vibrated with an incoming message.

"Oh, thank God," she whispered, her fingers tapping out a hurried response, praying she hit the right keys.

chapter twenty-one

Ian knew something was wrong the moment he looked up from the fields and saw Kayla running frantically from the woods, yelling for help. One look toward the pavilion showed that Lexi was not among the women now scattering. Keely was moving hurriedly toward the men, as fast as a woman pregnant with twins could; Taryn was taking off like a bat out of hell toward the tree line. Stacey was pulling out her cell phone.

Panic shot through him, and he knew with certainty that Lexi was in trouble. Shaking off his brothers, he rushed toward the pavilion as they all began to realize that something was very wrong.

"Where's Lexi?" Ian yelled, grabbing Keely. The look she gave him sent icy daggers into his heart. "The woods… Kayla…"

Ian felt his heart drop into his feet. Before she could finish, Ian was sprinting across the fields toward the woods. Several yards in, the coppery scent of blood hit him. "Lexi!" he yelled desperately. "Answer me!"

He found her another fifty feet or so in, lying face down in the scrub, Taryn by her side, trying to get some kind of response from her.

"Lexi, baby. Jesus Christ!" He turned her over, her face and shirt covered in blood. "MICHAEL!" he screamed, all pretense of control gone as he lifted her into his arms and carried her out of the woods.

He was met at the edge by a small crowd. Stacey's face drained of color when she saw Lexi in Ian's arms. Ian refused to let her go, forcing Michael to do a quick examination while Ian held her. When he pushed up her sleeve to check for injury, a collective gasp rippled among them. Michael lifted her shirt slightly and saw the same thing. Black, purple and blue blotches. Lexi looked like she had been thoroughly beaten.

Bright flashing lights and a wailing siren announced the arrival of an ambulance. Ian climbed in as Michael barked orders at the paramedics, while the others promised to follow along.

Ian paced the small waiting room with the look of a man possessed. His eyes were wild, his face as hard as if it had been carved in stone. Blood covered his torso and arms, big smears of it across his neck and jaw where he had tucked Lexi's head into him for the ride. None of it was his. He wished to God it was.

Michael had gone with Lexi into the examination room, and Ian was grateful for that.

Michael was a great doctor; he would fix this, whatever *this* was. He still had no clue what had happened.

Within minutes the rest of the family began arriving. Kieran was the first one through the door, looking almost as wild as Ian. His eyes found his older brother's. "How is she?"

"Mick's with her now."

"What the fuck happened?"

Ian gave him a pained look, one of shock mixed with fear. "I don't know. I don't *fucking* know.

"What's taking so long?" Ian asked, continuing his relentless pacing back and forth across the room. It had been an hour at least.

The door opened and a new face entered the crowded waiting room. "I'm looking for Alexis Kattapoulos. Where is she?"

Ian stopped his pacing at the sound of the unfamiliar voice. At the entrance stood a man with the looks of a movie star; golden blonde hair, cut short at the neck but rakishly long across the forehead and sides. Sculpted, well defined features. Clear brown eyes that were sharp and keen. He was dressed casually, but everything about him screamed wealth and power.

"Who are you?" Kieran asked. Not surprisingly, he was the first to approach the stranger. But Ian already knew who it was.

At that moment Michael came in to the waiting

room, his face grim. The room became instantly silent.

"Ian," Michael said. His voice was carefully controlled, but his eyes gave him away. Michael was shaken, and that was not a good sign from a man who had seen the horrors he had. "Anything you want to tell me?"

Ian's blood froze. "How is she?"

A tick worked along Michael's jaw. "She's bad. Real bad. She'd bleeding from the inside out, drowning in her own blood." His eyes grew ten degrees colder. "Her body's covered in bruises, like she's been severely beaten. We can't stop it. We can't stop the bleeding."

"You fucking son of a bitch!" Kieran roared and launched himself at Ian, knocking him down to the ground and landing blow after blow. It took several of the men to pull him off, pushing him back to the far end of the room.

Aidan stepped forward and addressed Michael. "You are Lexi's doctor?"

Michael nodded.

"She has a disease that makes her bleed easily. Like hemophelia, but worse. It's genetic. Very rare, passed from mother to daughter. She controls it with injections at regular intervals, but still she must be very careful."

"What meds?"

"These." Aidan handed Michael a small cooler-type bag. Michael looked inside, his eyes widening as he read the vials. He and Aidan shared a knowing glance, before Michael took off toward the exam room.

"Excuse me," Jack Callaghan said, pushing off from the far wall. "I don't believe we've met. Jack Callaghan."

Aidan turned and accepted the hand the older man offered. "Of course. Lexi talks of you all the time. Aidan Harrison."

"You are Lexi's boss."

Aidan smiled slightly, as if the thought amused him. "No one is Lexi's boss, Mr. Callaghan."

"Why are you here?" Ian asked gruffly, wiping at his bloodied nose.

Aidan studied him carefully before answering. When he did, he leveled his gaze. "Because Lexi asked me to come for her."

"You lie."

Aidan shrugged his shoulders elegantly, as if he could care less whether or not anyone believed him. "When she was not at her hotel, I used the GPS on her phone to locate her here."

"How did you happen to have Lexi's medicine?" Jake asked.

Aidan spoke slowly and carefully. "Lexi and I are very close."

"Meaning?" There was something far too intimate, too knowing in Aidan's manner. Ian didn't like it at all.

"If she did not share the details of her illness

with you, I don't see where I should." He ignored Ian's lethal stare and glanced around at the packed waiting room.

Michael came back through the doors. Before he could say a word, Aidan began walking toward him, already rolling up his sleeve. "Take mine," he said. "We are compatible."

At Michael's skeptical look, he added gravely, "I've done this more times than you can imagine, Doctor." Michael nodded, indicating that Aidan should proceed back toward the exam room.

"What's going on, Mick?" Ian asked.

"Lexi needs a transfusion. The meds are helping, but her blood is so thin it's not enough."

"Then take mine!" Ian said fiercely, but Michael shook his head. "Sorry, Ian, but your blood type's not an exact match, and she's not strong enough for anything else right now. It would kill her." He looked away from Ian's pained eyes, scanning the room until he found the one he sought. "Taryn? I could use a second donor. You up for it?"

Taryn was on her feet in seconds. "Like you even have to ask."

Lexi was in a medically induced coma until her body had a chance to recover from the damage and assimilate the meds. Jake and Shane escorted an exhausted, bloody Ian back to the pub for a quick shower, but only after Michael swore that there was nothing anyone could do and refused to allow Ian anywhere near her for a few hours.

He showered. He shaved. He put on clean clothes. And it was all done automatically, without thinking. Because the only thing Ian could think about was the realization that he almost lost Lexi, and the possibility that he still might.

What the hell had happened? She'd been fine the morning of the fair. Hadn't she? He thought back, recalling the purplish bruises he'd seen forming as he bathed her. But afterward... she'd been wearing jeans that covered her legs to right above her ankles, long, loose sleeves that extended to her wrists and tied right below her collar bone. *Sonofabitch.*

He still had some time before they went back to the hospital. He sought out Taryn, found her resting in her and Jake's room, looking almost as worried as he felt. It didn't take much to convince her to tell him what had happened that day in the kitchen.

Using that information and what he had managed to pick up in the ER, Ian sat down at the computer. Moments later, he stared in shock as screen after screen filled with data. Much of it was in medical terms and beyond his area of expertise, but he knew enough to get the gist of it.

He sat back, stunned, glad there was no one else around because what he found scared the shit out of him. Lexi had a rare blood disease, a form of hemophilia that kept her blood from clotting properly. It was hereditary, inherited from her mother. She'd been undergoing treatments for years, each one more risky than the last by the look of it. Daily injections allowed her to live a fairly normal life, but even the smallest cut could be life-threatening.

It was all beginning to make sense, not the least of which was Kieran's overprotective behavior. No wonder Kieran had been so freaked out over the raspberry bushes. He was one of the few who knew that one good scratch in the wrong place could make her bleed out. Kieran had also apparently figured out what happened in the kitchen that day, and confronted her with it. For the first time, Ian began to understand the pain and worry his brother must have been feeling all along.

He had been so rough with her. He felt sick to his stomach, remembering the way her body had been battered. Kayla had admitted to shoving and pushing her, but it hadn't been Kayla that had done all that damage. It had been *him*. Barely managing to make it to the bathroom, Ian fell to his knees and threw up. He'd almost killed the woman he loved.

Lexi remained unconscious for the next two days. They all took turns sitting with her, though Ian and Aidan put in the most time, each reluctant to leave her alone in the company of the other.

"Why, Lex?" Ian asked for the hundredth time as he sat beside her. "Why didn't you tell me?"

Aidan snorted derisively as he stood by the window, staring out over the park below. It was such an uncharacteristic action from the smooth, composed man that Ian turned to look at him. "What?"

"You are an idiot."

"Excuse me?" Ian stood, power radiating from every limb.

"Do you know how many times I've been in hospital rooms like this? How many times I've stared out the window, waiting for her to wake up?" Aidan turned from the window, looking at Ian as if he was a child. "This disease is life-threatening, Mr. Callaghan. Lexi knows exactly what she must do, knows that even the slightest deviation could have devastating effects. Yet here she is, her body battered beyond limits, and not enough medicine to see her through the week. Why do you suppose that is?"

Ian didn't have an answer to that as the gravity of Aidan's words fell over him like a heavy shroud. Aidan. The one with whom Lexi had entrusted her secrets. The one whose timely arrival had probably saved her life.

"You are in love with her." It wasn't a question.

Aidan smiled slightly. "Yes. But not in the way you think. She is family to me. And she is in love with another man; I have always known this." He paused briefly. "I always wondered what kind of fool would let a woman like that go. Now I know, don't I?"

"I never knew." But he had, hadn't he? If he

was honest with himself, he had to admit that some part of him knew. Some part of him recognized her feelings for him, and capitalized on them without reservation.

Aidan shook his head. "That makes you even more of an idiot then, doesn't it? Even now you *still* don't get it. Lexi risked her life. And for what? *To spend a few more days with you.*"

* * *

Lexi heard their hushed low voices through the haze. She'd been drifting in and out of consciousness over the past day or so, her blood chemistry finally returning to some semblance of normalcy. Her body still felt as if it had been the bulls-eye for a freight train, but at least she was breathing on her own, so technically, she'd been worse, a lot worse.

She hadn't been able to work up the courage to face any of them yet. Only Michael knew. He'd asked lots of questions. Lexi explained what had happened in the woods, but that she'd already been in pretty bad shape by then. That yes, Ian had caused some of her injuries in a way, but it wasn't his fault. Michael had to understand that without her meds, even a jostle in a crowd was the bruising equivalent of a blind-sided tackle.

She left out many of the details, but Michael was smart. He'd already pieced most of it together, and his exams were thorough. His expression had remained calm, his blue eyes caring, his touch gentle, but she could sense his discomfort every time he looked at her injuries. She didn't have to go into graphic detail for him to figure out exactly what had happened.

She would have expected to feel more ashamed than she did. As it was, her biggest concern was defending Ian, stressing the fact that he hadn't known, that he was always careful with her. It was hard to determine if Michael really believed her, but she did her best.

"Aidan." Aidan's familiar eyes met hers. She gave his hand a weak squeeze as she forced the words through her parched throat. "I knew you'd come."

"As if I would be anywhere else," he said tenderly, leaning over to kiss her forehead.

"Are you alone?" she rasped.

"For the moment. You really scared me this time, Lex," he told her as he poured a glass of water. He gently placed one hand behind her back to support her and held the cup to her lips.

"I'm sorry, Aidan. You always get stuck taking care of me, don't you? Sucks for you."

Anger flashed quickly across his features before he smoothed them back into concern. "Don't ever say that again," he said softly, smoothing the hair away from her face in an easy, familiar gesture. "We take care of each other."

Lexi saw the telltale bandages along his arm, traced them with her fingers. "You gave me another transfusion."

"Yes. But it wasn't enough this time. A woman named Taryn donated as well." His lips curled in a smile. "Bold, that one, but I like her."

"Yeah, she's awesome," Lexi agreed with a weak smile. She would miss Taryn. The woman came closer than anyone else to being a real friend, something Lexi's never really had. "And you're a good man, Aidan. What would I do without you?"

"I don't know, Lex. I leave you alone for a week and look what happens." He attempted a smile, but Lexi didn't share it.

Aidan might have been teasing, but he was more right than he knew. She didn't do well on her own, obviously. Her innate tendency to let her heart rule over her head got her in trouble more often than she cared to admit. If anything, this was a stark reminder that she could not lead a normal life, not ever.

"I want to go home, Aidan."

Aidan glanced over toward the door, as if expecting to see Ian's shadow there, listening. If not him, then one of the others. "I don't think they'll let you go that easily, sweetheart."

"I can't stay, Aidan. I just can't." Tears began to well up in her eyes. Who had she been kidding, anyway? Before, only Kieran knew about her secret, and look how he'd treated her. Now everyone knew. She couldn't bear the way they would look at her from here on out. Or the way they would baby her, protect her like some fragile piece of china. It made her want to scream.

That was one of the many wonderful things about Aidan. He never tried to stop her from doing anything, but he was always there to pick up the pieces when she did something monumentally stupid. Like coming back to Pine Ridge. That had to be the granddaddy of them all.

Aidan was skeptical. "You're sure about that? It's what you want?"

"Yes," she sniffed. "I'm sure."

"What about Ian? He hasn't left your side for days, Lex. He's the one, isn't he? The one who's held your heart for all these years?"

Lexi was quiet for several long seconds. Was it that obvious? Yes, she supposed it was. She'd been like a lovesick puppy around Ian, always had been. The only one who hadn't seen it was Ian, though she suspected even he was finally catching on.

"No," she said finally.

"Alexis," Aidan scolded gently.

She looked at her hands, folded neatly across her stomach. "I - I thought he was, but I was wrong." The words tasted like bile in her mouth; her stomach ached at the wrongness of them. God would punish her for such a bald-faced lie. But surely He would understand.

"There is nothing here for me, Aidan. Please.

Take me home."

"I'll talk to the doctor, okay?" he placated. "We'll see what he says."

Lexi shook her head. That wasn't good enough, and it would waste too much time. Aidan was right; the Callaghans wouldn't let her go so easily. She pushed herself into a sitting position, pausing to wait for the room to stop spinning. Aidan was there, like always, steadying her.

"No. Get the plane ready, Aidan. Call Dr. Fahs and tell him we're on our way. He knows the drill. I'm signing myself out."

"Lex, I'm not convinced this is the right thing to do."

"Fine," she said, mustering as much power as she could behind the words. Physically, she was beat, but the fire burned inside her, giving her strength. "I'll do it myself."

Gritting her teeth, she managed to swing her legs over the side of the bed.

"What do you think you're doing?" Michael asked as he entered the room.

"I'm leaving," Lexi said firmly.

"I don't think so," Michael answered, swinging her legs back onto the bed as if she was a small child. "Why would you even consider that a possibility?"

"Michael," Lexi interrupted softly. "Michael, look at me." Lexi waited until Michael's eyes were focused on hers. "You examined me. You know why I need to go. Don't you?"

Michael stared into her eyes for a long time before answering. Lexi endured his probing gaze, willing him to understand. Thankfully, he did. "All right," he said finally. "But I do so against my better judgment."

"Thank you, Michael."

Michael looked at Aidan. "Can you put me in touch with her regular doc?"

With a grim nod, Aidan removed a small mobile device from his pocket.

"Going somewhere?" Ian entered the hospital room sometime later. Clearly Michael had given him a heads-up. Lexi would have expected no less. She needed to say her goodbye, no matter how painful it would be.

"Yeah," Lexi said, attempting a weak smile and failing miserably. "Home."

She was already dressed. The loose, lightweight cotton blouse had long sleeves; the matching skirt went down to her ankles. The outfit concealed the bruises that still marked her, though they were fading quickly as her body started to take care of itself again.

Ian shoved his hands down into his jeans. "Mick's okay with this?"

"He doesn't have a choice. It's my decision."

"This is what you want?"

No. Why did everyone keep asking her that? "Yes." Again, Lexi half-expected a lightning bolt to strike her right there in her hospital bed for telling such a huge lie.

"And where do I fit into all this, Lex?"

You are the epitome of everything I want and can't have. The words burned a hole in her chest, right over her heart, but it was the truth. For a while she'd had a chance to live her dream, but that's all it could ever be. There was no way she could keep up the pace she had this last week; it would kill her. Almost had.

No, as much as she might want to, she could never be the kind of woman Ian needed. He was a free spirit, and she came with far too much baggage. Besides, he was going to have enough responsibility on his hands soon enough. She wondered if Kayla had even told him about the baby yet.

Oh well, it didn't really matter. Nothing much mattered anymore, except getting the hell out of there before she made a complete idiot out of herself. She could not tell him the truth: that leaving him was breaking her heart. That she couldn't imagine one day without him, let alone the rest of her life.

"I'm sorry, Ian. It just wasn't meant to be." Where the words came from and the strength it took to say them, she didn't know.

"And this last week was...?"

Ian's jaw clenched, his blue eyes blazed. Lexi knew that beneath the cotton button-down his body was tensed and as hard as a slab of marble, yet against her skin it would feel warm and smooth. She had to look at something else before she lost her courage to do the right thing. Her eyes locked onto the I.V. pole, the now-disconnected tubes hanging without purpose. It was exactly the reminder she needed of why this was necessary.

"Fulfillment of a young, foolish girl's fantasy." They were the same words she'd said to him once before. It was much harder to say them now, because now she knew for certain that the reality was a thousand times better than the fantasy, no matter what the cost. Given the choice, she would do it all again, without question.

"That's all?"

"Yes."

"I see." Ian walked further into the room until he stood mere inches away from where she sat on the bed. He was close enough for her to feel the heat radiating from him, and oh, how she wanted to feel all that heat against her when she felt so very cold inside. To be held in those arms until the terrible ache in her heart began to ease.

"Look at me, Lexi, and tell me that again." His voice was low and deep, a lover's caress to her senses.

Lexi couldn't do it. She couldn't look into those magnificent blue eyes again or she would lose the courage to do what needed to be done.

"Look into my eyes and tell me you don't love me, Lexi," he persisted. "Tell me, and I'll leave right now."

Lying was one thing. She could justify the untruths by telling herself it was for the greater good. For a child that needed a father. For a man who deserved a woman who could promise him something other than a lifetime of hospital visits. But to look into his eyes and lie? She didn't need to worry about God striking her down; her heart would never survive it.

"Ready, Lex?" Aidan appeared in the doorway with a wheelchair, granting her a reprieve. Aidan took one look at the two of them and added. "Perhaps I should come back in a few minutes."

Ian said 'yes' at exactly the same time Lexi said 'no'. Aidan paused hesitantly.

"It's all right, Aidan. We're done here."

"Are we?" Ian asked quietly.

"Yes." This time Lexi had no problem looking into his eyes, because it was the truth.

chapter twenty-two

Seven Months Later

Ian cursed when he saw the big black Expedition snaking its way along the driveway. He briefly considered shutting off the solitary light and leaving by way of the back door, but it would be pointless. Jake already knew he was here, and he was too goddamn old and too goddamn tired to be playing hide-and-seek.

"You couldn't tell me you were back?" Jake said by way of greeting as he barged into the room. "I hate it when Shane knows something I don't," he griped, plopping himself down on the only piece of furniture in the living room: a soft, comfortable sofa large enough for his big frame. "The smug little bastard. He's going to be even more full of himself now."

Ian sighed. Jake sitting down meant Jake was staying for a while. Great. Still, it could have been worse. It could have been one of the others, there to tell him to get over himself already. It was one of the reasons he'd moved out of the pub and taken up residence here, in Lexi's grandmother's place.

When he wasn't off on suicide missions, that was.

Ian tossed him a cold beer from the fridge. "Never should have showed him how to use the trackers," he commented. Each one of the Callaghan men had tiny chips beneath the family crests tattooed on their upper arms. It was Ian's idea. He'd thought it would be good to be able to locate any of them at any given time, given what they did for a living, though he was currently reconsidering the wisdom of that.

"Bad one, huh."

"Yep." Of course, they would know all about it by now. Ian had been instrumental in taking out a small terrorist cell in South America, though he had blatantly ignored orders to wait for back-up. His father would probably kick his ass and give him another lecture. Nothing he hadn't heard a hundred times over from the well-meaning souls that seemed to think he gave a shit.

They sat in silence for a while, pulling on the long-necks. Two brothers, so in tune that conversation was often unnecessary. Yeah, Ian thought as the minutes dragged on. He should have called Jake, at least to let him know he was still in one piece.

"So how's Taryn?" Ian drained his bottle and grabbed two more.

"Good. We're expecting."

Ian shot a surprised look at Jake, for a moment forgetting he didn't care about anything anymore. He, like the rest of his brothers, knew that Taryn had lost their first child at the hands of a monster a little more than a year earlier. It had broken something in Jake, but made him stronger, too. "Yeah?"

"Yeah," Jake said, grinning. "Found out a few weeks ago. Due in March."

Ian chuckled. Of the seven brothers, all were either conceived in March or born in March. It was an inside joke among them, and the reason they all had "Patrick" as a middle name. "A real Callaghan, then."

"Yeah."

"Congrats, man."

"Thanks."

They settled into that comfortable silence before Jake spoke again. "Heard anything from Lex?"

Though he'd been waiting for it, Ian tensed; his hand gripped the bottle so hard it was in danger of breaking. Ian downed the rest of his beer in one long pull before answering. "Nope."

"Lexi called the pub. Taryn answered, told her about the baby and all."

Ian said nothing. What the hell was he supposed to say? Every phone call, every letter, every email he made or sent went unanswered.

"Funny thing was, Lex asked if Kayla had the baby yet."

Ian's head snapped up, his eyes like blue flames.

"Yeah, thought that would get you," Jake said soberly. "Taryn was pretty stunned too. Before she could ask Lex what the hell she was talking about, Lex apologized for asking, said it was none of her business, and hung up."

"Why would she think Kayla was pregnant?" Ian demanded.

Jake pinned him with a hard stare. "Yeah. Excellent question, that."

It was as if someone had thrown open the windows in his mind, letting in cool, clean air and sweeping away the fog. Kayla had spoken to Lexi right before she collapsed. In the hospital, Lexi had refused to meet his eyes. "Sweet Christ. Lexi thinks I got Kayla pregnant."

Jake nodded approvingly. "That's what Taryn thought too, so she tracked Kayla down and asked her." Ian almost smiled at the thought. Taryn was as fierce and protective as any of the men. If she thought for one second any of them had been wronged she was on it like a mama tiger.

"She *asked*, did she?"

Nearly all of Jake's teeth showed in the resulting grin. "Yep. And guess what?"

Ian didn't have to guess. He knew. All of the pieces started falling into place. "I have to talk to

Lexi."

Jake's smile faded. "Lexi's gone, man."

"Gone?" Ian's heart seized up and refused to beat for several interminable seconds. "What do you mean she's *gone*?"

"Fuck," Jake cursed, immediately apologetic. "Not like that. Gone, as in moved out of her apartment. Leased it out to some single mom or something, someone she knew from the restaurant whose husband's MIA. She quit her job. Seems to have just disappeared. Taryn's been trying to reach her. Her number's been disconnected, email comes back as undeliverable."

Ian started breathing again. Fuck the English language and all the words that could be so devastatingly misinterpreted. "Aidan knows where she is." Ian would bet his life on it.

"Most likely," Jake agreed. "She's hidden well, and you don't get that kind of cloaking without some major cash and influence. He's not sharing though." Jake paused, and Ian sensed there was more.

"What are you not telling me?"

"Taryn Googled her. Society pages caught wind of something going on there. They're speculating that Aidan asked her to marry him, but she turned him down, then did her vanishing act."

Aidan asked Lexi to marry him? *Son of a bitch.* "There's got to be a trail."

"Shane and Kieran have been taking turns

hacking your machines, but no luck so far."

Ian's eyes glowed with life again. "*I'll* find her."

* * *

"Bed rest sucks."

Aidan chuckled as she pouted at him, her arms crossed over her chest, her amber eyes defiant. At least they still held the signature spark, and as long as it was there, there was hope.

"So you keep telling me," he said, sliding off his shoes and easing up on the edge of the bed so they were sitting side by side, propped up against a myriad of pillows. It was something he looked forward to every day, this quiet time with Lexi. Sometimes they talked. Sometimes they watched TV. Sometimes they did nothing at all, just enjoyed one another's company.

"Personally, I kind of like it. I always know exactly where you are."

Lexi stuck her tongue out at him, making him laugh even harder. She did it for his benefit, he knew. So he wouldn't dwell on the dark circles beneath her eyes, or the paleness of her complexion.

"So…" she said, brightening as she peered over him to the shopping bag he'd casually dropped alongside the bed. "What did you bring me?"

"Who says I brought you anything?" It was a ritual, this light bantering back and forth.

She smiled. "Because you *always* bring me something. You spoil me rotten, Aidan."

"Hmm. Maybe I should stop then." It was an idle threat, they both knew it.

"Yeah, you probably should." Aidan waited, counting off the seconds in his head until she added, "But not tonight." He grinned again, reaching for the bag.

The exquisite aroma hit her the moment he opened the airtight seal of the container. "Fresh baked cinnamon rolls?" she asked, her eyes glowing. "From Antoine?"

Aidan nodded as she held the rolls to her face and inhaled, her face rapturous. He'd known women who hadn't been as pleased with multi-carat diamonds as Lexi was with the simplest things.

"Go on. There's more in there." Lexi squealed excitedly as she picked out the remaining items. He'd learned long ago that expensive trinkets meant little to her. But a hand-picked flower, an Abbott and Costello DVD with a bag of buttery popcorn, and fresh baked rolls from Antoine --- those things made her eyes light up like a Vegas nightscape. He would do anything to see his best friend smile again.

"Aidan, you are truly a prince among men." As always, a familiar warmth spread through him at her praise. The kiss to his cheek didn't hurt, either.

Lexi wasted no time in taking a big bite of the decadently gooey cinnamon roll. "Are you sure I should be eating this?" she asked, even as she chewed.

"Absolutely. Why, the endorphins released by just one of Antoine's rolls have been clinically proven to reverse the aging process."

Lexi raised a skeptical eyebrow. "It's true," he insisted, taking one for himself. "Look it up if you don't believe me. Cures scurvy, too."

Lexi laughed, holding her hand over her mouth lest any part of the delicious roll be sacrificed. "I guess that explains why I don't have scurvy *or* wrinkles."

"Now you know."

Two hours later, as the final images from *The Time of Their Lives* faded, Lexi yawned and began gathering the remnants of their little pig fest, reaching across Aidan to grab the bag to put it all in.

"Hey, what's that?" She pointed to the plainly-wrapped brown package that sat upon the bedside table.

"It was delivered to the restaurant." Aidan handed it over to her; it was about two inches thick and approximately the same dimensions as a stack of standard size copy paper. Lexi's name was scrawled across the front in flowing calligraphy, the name of Aidan's restaurant appearing in the c/o below.

Lexi turned it over curiously in her hands, her grumbling temporarily forgotten. Aidan had already inspected it. He knew that there was no return address, no post mark to identify from where it had come. Lexi shook it tentatively. "It feels like a book or something."

"Whatever it is, someone wants to make sure you get it. One of these was hand delivered to each of the restaurants."

"Hand-delivered?"

"Apparently." He didn't tell her that the hostesses at all three restaurants described the delivery man as exceptionally tall, dark, and handsome with striking blue eyes. "Open it."

With a grin that reminded him of a child on Christmas morning, Lexi tore at the paper. "Oh…. Oh, my…"

Aidan shifted to see what she had revealed. It was a bound manuscript, with an artist's rendering on the front, depicting a woman looking remarkably like Lexi. Multi-colored layers of hair curling seductively around her gleaming white gown. Realistic amber eyes. In the background, hidden in the shadows, a pair of familiar blue eyes watched over the image. *By Salienne Dulcette* was hand-scripted down in the lower right hand corner.

"Th-There's a note," Lexi said, her voice shaking nearly as much as her hands as she pulled the stationary from the clip and read it aloud:

Dear Lexi,

Enclosed is my latest manuscript,

tentatively titled "Celtic Goddess". Sorry, I know I stole the name from your restaurant, but you were my inspiration (please ask Aidan not to call the lawyers just yet for copyright infringement ☺). I want you to be the first to read it and tell me what you think. Kieran drafted the cover art. Didn't he do a fabulous job?

I'm also enclosing a picture of our little guy. I'm sorry I didn't get a chance to say goodbye before you left. I really hope we'll meet again someday. Ian needs you, Lexi.

Hope you enjoy the book.

Love,
Stacey Connelly

A small photo was paper-clipped to the back of the note. "Holy shit," Lexi breathed in amazement."

Aidan leaned over to get a better look. The picture included a pretty, dark-haired woman with silvery eyes next to a large blonde man holding a tiny, swathed newborn. Both looked exhausted but extremely happy. "Do you know them?"

"Yeah… Johnny is the guy who came out to my grandmother's house about possible renovation, and Stacey is his wife. Holy shit, Aidan. *Stacey Connelly is Salienne Dulcette.*"

"Who?"

"She's a famous author. I have all of her books. I can't believe I met Salienne Dulcette."

"You know, she probably says the same thing about you. You're kind of famous yourself."

Lexi ran her fingers over the cover. "It's not the same. Wow, Aidan. Look at this. I knew Kieran was talented, but this is amazing."

"It is uncanny," Aidan murmured, looking at the cover as well. "He's captured you perfectly. Are you going to read it?"

Lexi bit her lip and shifted a little. She seemed to be holding her breath, then let it all out at once. "Um, no, not right now."

"Why not?"

"Because my water just broke."

"Son of a bitch." Aidan was on his feet in a flash, hitting the speed dial on his iPhone. A few harried comments later he sprinted across the room for the bag she'd had packed and ready to go months ago.

"Aidan," Lexi said less than an hour later, her voice groggy from the I.V. Dressed in scrubs, he held her hand while they prepped her for the operating room. "If anything happens…"

"Nothing is going to happen, Lex. We've got everything covered. Piece of cake." Aidan smiled in reassurance and tried to stay calm, but inside he was scared to death. They'd practiced this drill over and over, but nothing could have prepared him for the real thing.

"But if it does..." she insisted between gritted teeth, bracing against the pain that even with meds, was enough to crush the bones in his hand, "... promise me."

Aidan avoided her eyes. He knew exactly what she wanted, and God help him, he couldn't do it. Lexi had a special contract drawn up the day she found out she was pregnant. One of the stipulations was that all measures be taken to save the baby, even if it meant sacrificing her own life. Another was that should she end up on life support, it was to be discontinued after thirty days if there was no sign of improvement. In the case of either event, Aidan would be free to contact Ian as he deemed necessary and appropriate.

But outside of those circumstances, he was not to say a word to *anyone*. It was a source of major contention between them. Aidan thought Ian should know he was going to be a father. Lexi agreed to tell him, but only after the baby was born. Aidan understood that she had her reasons, but that didn't mean he agreed with them.

"It's time," the doc said as they stopped in front of the OR. The room was packed with specialists; they were prepared for any emergency. "Mr. Harrison, if you would, please." One of the masked men gestured to Aidan. Over the past few months they'd been stockpiling his blood. He would be prepped to give more should it become necessary.

"Promise me, Aidan," she pleaded.

"I promise."

She smiled drowsily. "Thank you, Aidan. Piece of cake."

"Piece of cake," he agreed. "I'll be waiting for you, Lex."

chapter twenty-three

Jake's Irish Pub was usually crowded on a Friday night. But when St. Patrick's Day fell on a Friday, the place was over-the-top insane. Every member of the Callaghan clan tended, taking care of their loyal customers and all of the honorary Irish who came out to have a good time. It took a while, therefore, for Ian to notice the familiar face of Aidan Harrison in the crowd.

The two men locked gazes. Ian searched the other man's face for a clue to explain his presence, but his expression was unreadable. Aidan pulled a legal-sized manila envelope from the inside of his coat and slid it across the bar as he leaned in to speak. Despite the roar of the crowd, Ian heard his cryptic words as clearly as if the other man had spoken across an empty room.

"It'll take about an hour for my private plane to refuel."

Before Ian could respond, Aidan was gone, swallowed up by the crowd.

Ian picked up the envelope and took a step back from the bar. With his heart pounding, he reached in and extracted a photo of a beautiful baby boy. Pink-faced and chubby, with a shock of jet black hair and piercing blue eyes. His eyes locked on the little boy's, and he *knew*.

He had to lean against the back wall when his legs went weak. Reaching in again, he pulled the only other item from the packet: a record of birth for Patrick Brian Kattapoulos, born January twenty-seventh, weighing in at seven pounds, three ounces, and measuring twenty-one inches long. The mother was listed as Alexis Kattapoulos. The father: Ian Patrick Callaghan.

Ian felt his eyes fill with tears; he had to lean over and braced his hands on his knees as he fought for breath. *He had a son.*

"Ian, man, what's up?" Jake asked a few seconds later as the crowd around Ian became eerily quiet, their curious attention focused on him. Ian could only shake his head, holding out the papers for Jake to see.

"Jesus Christ," Jake said, scanning the contents. A moment later, Ian felt himself being grabbed by the arms on either side and hauled toward the back kitchen.

"Aidan's got a plane waiting," he managed to choke out after a minute or two.

"Then what the hell are we waiting for?" Jake barked. "Let's GO! Shane! Cover for me, man, I'm taking Ian to the airport."

* * *

Lexi yawned and stretched, feeling pleasantly drowsy. Her breasts, heavy with milk, ached like crazy. Looking at the clock, she started to panic. It was nearly six a.m. and she'd put the baby down around midnight. He was nursing about every two hours. How had she slept through two feedings? Oh, God, what if something was wrong?

As quickly as she dared, she slid her feet over the side of the bed and began to pad quietly across the lush carpet toward the crib at the far side of her room, holding her breath. In the brief three seconds or so it took to get there, her post-partum hormones managed to convince her that her baby was in mortal peril --- or at the very least starving --- and that she had to be The Worst Mother Ever.

Relief flooded her as she looked down and saw that the crib was empty. Then fear gripped her again an instant later. *Where was her baby?* Oh, God, someone stole her baby in the middle of the night while she was in bed sound asleep, selfishly dreaming of how the baby was conceived....

Worst. Mother. *Ever*.

Lexi gripped the rails and forced herself to breathe. In. Out. In. Out. Aidan must have come back late last night. Yeah, that was it. He'd checked on them, like he always did, and fed the baby from the milk she'd pumped and stored in the fridge. He was probably in the living room right now, rocking the baby and watching infomercials. So help her, if he ordered one more gadget from QVC…

The thought of nursing made her overly-full breasts ache. Wet circles formed across the front of her nightgown. She pulled on a light robe and headed for the kitchen, hoping Patrick was still hungry.

The smell of freshly brewed coffee, bacon, eggs, and toast met her the moment she opened the bedroom door. Her fears immediately melted away. Aidan *was* here. The man was nothing less than a saint. He was going to make some lucky woman very happy, she thought, her emotions now definitely on the up side of the roller coaster. Maybe he would finally ask out that private duty nurse that came by every afternoon. The nurse was very pretty, soft-spoken and gentle, and she definitely had eyes for Aidan. He probably hadn't even noticed. Lexi made a mental note to talk to him about asking her out very soon. Tonight would be good, since she'd gotten so much sleep.

Lexi froze as she neared the kitchen and heard the quiet humming in a deep, bass tone. She knew that voice; it called to the very depths of her soul. She knew that song, too. It was an ancient Irish lullaby, the one her grandmother used to sing to her.

Taking small, hesitant steps, Lexi made it to the archway. Her hand flew to her mouth as she blinked, once, twice, three times. She pinched herself lightly, sure that she must still be dreaming.

The broad, muscular back. The jet black hair, so shiny it looked blue, longer than she remembered, extending beneath those strong shoulders. The narrow waist, the gorgeous backside hugged by faded blue jeans, the heavy, corded legs.

Ian.

As if he sensed her presence, he turned around. There, safely ensconced in the crook of one elbow was her son, looking perfectly content, sampling his tiny fist. Two pairs of identical blue eyes looked at her with keen interest.

"Perfect timing," Ian said softly, never taking his eyes from her, shifting the baby up toward his shoulder gently as if he had plenty of practice. *Of course he has*, she thought suddenly, a bitter taste in her mouth. *This isn't his first.*

"How did you get in here?" she asked. *How did you know?*

"Later," Ian said huskily, his eyes dipping to her chest. "My son is hungry." Ian looked pretty hungry, too.

A million questions floated around in her head, but the sharpening ache in her breasts overrode them. She forced her numb legs toward the padded rocking chair and sat down, untying the top of her gown. Ian brought their son to her, reverently placing him in her arms as he knelt before them. His face filled with awe as he saw his son snuggle into her, his tiny mouth searching until he latched on, his pudgy little fists on either side of her breast, possessively holding on.

As the baby's powerful tugging began to ease some of the ache, Lexi studied the man before her. God, how she'd missed him. He was even more breathtaking than the pictures in her mind, the ones she'd locked away and brought out to get her through the next minute, the next hour, the next day.

"Christ," he whispered, stroking his son's head lightly with trembling fingers. "That is the most beautiful thing I've ever seen." He swallowed hard and raised his eyes to meet hers. In them, she saw raw, powerful emotions swirling restlessly, held carefully in check, but her reckoning would come soon, she knew.

As soon as the boy's eyes drifted shut and his little body relaxed, Ian took him from her, holding him to his chest and rubbing his back. Lexi frowned, feeling a bit cheated. She loved holding her baby up against her, caressing his soft skin, inhaling his perfect baby smell. One look at Ian, though, and she felt ashamed. No matter what had transpired between them, Patrick was his son, too.

"Now it's your turn," Ian said, walking toward the kitchen. The child remained asleep in his arms; he made no move to put him down. Lexi knew just how he felt.

She heard the microwave door open and less than a minute later, Ian brought her a covered plate. He went back for silverware. Again for coffee. Once more for juice, doing everything one-handed, never once relinquishing his hold on his son.

It was hypnotic, watching him move. He had a silent, masculine grace that radiated strength and control like some lethal predator, yet he held their son with infinite care. Like someone who had been in the dark for ages and was then suddenly permitted to gaze upon a spectacular sunrise, she could not turn away.

There was no denying that Patrick was Ian's son. The boy was barely two months old but it would be clear to anyone not legally blind that the resemblance went beyond the black hair and blue eyes. Already her son had the same stubborn set to his jaw, the fierce temper, and the ability to melt her heart with only a look. Seeing them together stirred something inside of her, something at once beautiful and sad. Yes, Patrick was Ian's son, but he was hers, too, and there was no way hell she would ever let him go. The only way that child would be taken from her was over her cold, dead body.

Ian stopped moving and stared back at her. As if sensing her thoughts, his big hand came up protectively against the back of Patrick's head.

"Ian..."

He flashed those blue eyes at her, a look that breached no argument. "Eat," he commanded, his voice quiet but with unquestionable authority. "Then we'll talk."

Her eyes flashed right back at him, but the loud growling from her stomach lessened the impact. Her traitorous body was betraying her left and right this morning, wasn't it?

The meal was hot and delicious, but despite her hunger, she had trouble swallowing. Ian was here, in her apartment. He waited patiently, holding Patrick, and watched her with an intensity that did absolutely nothing for her appetite. Only when she laid down her fork and refused to take another bite did he stir.

Without a word, he removed the dishes one by one. Then, with a kiss to the baby's forehead that melted her heart, he laid their son down in the bassinet and began to pace, running his hand through his hair. *Here it comes*, Lexi thought, bracing herself.

But instead of saying anything, Ian suddenly appeared before her, pulling her to her feet. The next thing she knew she was wrapped tightly in his arms, his body crushing gloriously against her, his mouth devouring hers.

The raw emotion in his kiss was staggering. In it, Lexi felt paralyzing fear, relief, elation, hunger, anger, and desperation. She was swept away in a fast, swirling current, clinging to him as if her life depended on it.

Eons later, he finally broke away, gasping for breath. The cage of his arms didn't weaken in the slightest, though, as he rested his forehead against hers. "I thought I lost you," he said, his voice tortured. "Never, *ever* do that to me again. I swear to God, Lexi, I won't survive it."

* * *

Her heart beating against his chest encouraged his own, and he focused on that until he felt strong enough to release her. Unwilling to relinquish all contact, he entwined his fingers with hers and guided them both to the couch.

"Why, Lexi?" he asked finally, following up his one-word question with several others, one after the other. Once he got going, he found it hard to stop. "Why did you leave? Why didn't you answer any of my emails, phone calls, texts? Why didn't you tell me you were pregnant? *Why did you risk your life?*"

"Because I love you," she whispered quietly.

For the life of him, he didn't understand. He heard the words, but they made no sense to him whatsoever. He opened his mouth to respond, but couldn't seem to figure out a way to express the complete state of confusion in which he found himself.

She sighed, focusing on where their hands met, moving her thumb slowly over his skin. "You have to understand something, Ian. I've been in love with you since the first time I saw you," she confessed. "Wildly, madly, passionately in love with you, before I even knew what love was."

Yeah, his brothers had told him as much. The

ones that were still talking to him, anyway.

"Kieran brought you home with him after school," he said.

Lexi nodded. "It was in ninth grade. My first year of public high school. I met Kieran my first day." She smiled at the memory. "I was totally lost, standing where two hallways intersected, trying to figure out which way to go. He turned the corner and plowed right into me, leveling me like the bulldozer he is. My lip split and, as you can imagine, it was a total bloodbath. Thank God we were both running late and no one else was in the hallway at the time."

"He was freaked out, but he handled it better than most. He picked me up and carried me to the nurse, refusing to leave even though they threatened him with detention for not going back to his classes. That's when he found out my secret. He swore he wouldn't tell anyone, and instantly appointed himself my protector."

Yeah, thought Ian. That sounded like Kieran. Even when they were little, their mother used to call him her little white knight. The rest of them teased him mercilessly about it. Still did.

"Anyway, we started hanging out after that. Well, it was more like I tried to hide and he kept finding me, but he started growing on me after a while. One day, football practice was cancelled, and he wanted to walk me home after school, but I was in no hurry to go back to my house. I knew Kayla would be there with her friends."

She shrugged, seeming to grow smaller as she subconsciously shrunk back from the memory. "I swear they spent hours coming up with new ways to torment me. I didn't care; I'd learned to ignore them. But I would have been mortified if they'd humiliated me in front of Kieran. He was pretty much my only friend. I couldn't chance that. Kayla was beautiful, outgoing, and popular. Boys were always asking her out, but me, well…"

Yes, Kayla had been popular. She'd been in Ian's class. He had been just as enamored as the rest of them when she first moved to Pine Ridge, but that was the stupidity of adolescent boys, wasn't it? Kayla never had any qualms about flaunting her assets in front of them. Still, Kayla was one of those girls boys liked to take out, not take home. She made it easy. *Too* easy. There was a huge difference between that kind of "popularity" and the genuine kind, though he doubted Lexi understood that back then.

"When he realized I wasn't going to let him walk me home he suggested I go home with him instead, feigning some excuse so I wouldn't feel bad. That was the first day I met you."

"You were in the kitchen," Ian recalled quietly. "Making cookies."

"Yeah," she laughed softly. "I wanted to do something nice for Kieran since he'd been so kind to me. Given the size of him, I figured anything involving food was a safe bet, and baking was one thing I could do well. Little did I realize I would end up feeding a small army."

Ian smiled at the memory. The aroma had drawn him and his brothers to the kitchen like moths to a flame. They'd been without a mother for several years by that time, and needless to say, Jack Callaghan was not much of a baker. Things that other kids took for granted, like having a mom around that made fresh-baked cookies after school, were highly coveted in their household.

"I remember thinking that Kayla would have done anything to be in my place that day," she recalled fondly. "There I was, alone, surrounded by an entire room full of Irish demi-gods." Ian raised an eyebrow and Lexi blushed. "That's what all the girls called you guys."

"Then you came in," she said, looking at their joined hands again. "You were bummed because all the cookies that had come out of the oven so far were gone, and the others were razzing you about it. 'Don't worry,' I said, pulling out another tray. 'You can have these.' You leaned against the counter, looked me right in the eye, and said ---"

"*You are a goddess.*" It came back to him in a rush and suddenly he was back in that kitchen, looking down into her beautiful face, tilted up toward his, more exotic-looking than any girl he'd ever seen. Those wide, innocent eyes, blazing amber. The dark pink that quickly suffused her light bronze skin. The way her dark, full lips parted slightly, giving him an instant hard-on. Embarrassed by his reaction to her, he'd grabbed a few cookies right off the tray, ignored the burning in his palm, and beat feet out of there before any of his brothers (or more importantly, *she*) took notice.

"I swear my heart stopped in that moment," Lexi continued quietly. "It was like being hit by lightning, except instead of being fried to a blackened crisp, I felt like a part of me suddenly woke up. It was just like in all those fairy tales. You know, love at first sight and all that? Except this was *real*, and it was happening to *me*. I wondered if you felt it too, but…"

Yeah, he knew. He'd taken off like the devil himself was on his ass, but hell, he had been nearly eighteen at the time, and she was Kieran's age. He had no business having a reaction like that to her. And even if she had been older, he probably would have done the same thing. Because he *had* felt something, and it scared the shit out of him. So much so that he forced himself to bury it so deep he didn't have to face it.

"I tried to tell myself that I imagined it," she said. "That it was all in my mind, a product of my overactive imagination. Too many books, too much time alone. But each time I saw you, I felt it a little stronger than the last, until it got to the point where I could barely function if you were around. Your brothers started to notice, Kieran especially, and I felt like a total idiot, but there was nothing I could do. Eventually, I think, you started sensing it too, or maybe one of them said something to you about it, because after a while, you seemed to go out of your way to avoid me."

It was true. He had. But not for the reasons she thought.

"And then, well, Kayla found out where I was spending my spare time. To say she was livid was an understatement. And somehow --- I swear I don't know how --- she found out about my feelings for you. That was the night you got roped into picking me and Kieran up from the basketball game. And you know the rest of that story." She let the silence hang heavy between them for a long time.

"Why did you leave Pine Ridge?" he asked quietly.

"Ah, Kieran didn't tell you," she said. "Always my protector. I guess it doesn't matter anymore." She took a deep breath. "The night of the basketball game – well, I saw you and Kayla and, and I don't know, I just lost it. Something just… snapped. I waited for her at home, and when she finally came in, I said I was going to tell Dad what she was doing every night when she snuck out of the house to go meet boys. Things got loud and we ended up waking our parents."

"We heard them coming a mile away. All of a sudden, Kayla got this really funny look on her face. Before I realized what was happening, she hit me hard and fast – twice in the face, once in the stomach. I was caught completely off-guard. She'd never done anything like that before. Most of her abuse was verbal, though sometimes a push here or a shove there, but nothing like that. I think I was more surprised than physically hurt, but as you can guess, it looked horrible. By the time my parents opened the door I was doubled over, bleeding profusely from the nose and mouth."

"Son of a bitch," Ian murmured. He'd known Kayla was cruel, but he'd never imagined this.

"Then, it was as if someone flipped a switch, and Kayla went from raging psycho to concerned sister. All of a sudden Kayla was on the floor with me, pressing a balled-up shirt to my face, crying and stroking my hair. It was a great show; she always was a consummate actress with a flair for the dramatic. With her hand holding the shirt in my face I couldn't say anything. Kayla told them ..." Lexi paused, steadying herself with a deep breath. "... she told them that I'd been ... attacked. That we had been fighting because she insisted I tell but that I wanted to keep it quiet, to protect the one that did it. My father went absolutely ballistic. My stepmother went into hysterics." Lexi shook her head.

"Who did Kayla say molested you?" Ian asked, sensing he already knew the answer.

"Kieran," Lexi answered, her voice thick with tears, confirming his worst fears. "She wanted to hurt me, and she figured out the two best ways to do that. Oh, I've always known that she was behind that scene in the parking lot," she told him. "And the thing with Kieran? I think that was just a bonus."

"Lexi," he breathed, pulling her closer. "I'm so sorry."

"I told my Dad and Patricia it wasn't true, but if they accepted that then they'd also have to accept the fact that Kayla had been the one to attack me, and I don't think either one of them was ready to face that. Patricia, I could almost understand, but not Dad. He knew your family, knew your dad forever. Thought of you boys as his own. I think he knew in his heart that Kieran would never do such a thing, but he had to do some serious damage control. Patricia insisted on calling the police right away, but Dad managed to talk her out of it. He did, however, forbid me from seeing Kieran ever again. Or any of you, for that matter." She sniffed. "It was for your protection as much as mine."

"If Kayla was bad before, she was unbearable after that. I did what any young teenage girl would do. I ran away. More than once, actually. Except each time, my dad would call your dad on the sly, and Kieran or Shane would find me. They would always find me."

"I guess my dad couldn't take it anymore. One day, it was just me and my dad at home. That should have tipped me off; Patricia always felt threatened when my dad and I spent any time together, so she made sure it didn't happen often. We both knew things couldn't keep going the way they were."

"My dad was in a tough place. Divorce wasn't an option, and I told him if they stayed, then I'd just keep running away. When he told me about my great-aunts in Georgia, I was so hurt and angry. I said I wanted to go."

"Next thing I knew, your dad came over and talked to my dad. Then Uncle Jack was driving me to the airport, telling me everything was going to be better from then on." She paused, her eyes far away, the memory of that day as clear as if it had just happened. "I'll never forget the look on my dad's face when I got into that car with Uncle Jack. I couldn't believe he was actually letting me go."

"He was trying to protect you."

"Yeah," she sniffed. "I figured that out. Eventually." Lexi took a deep breath, and that helped her go on. "I think he was scared, too. He didn't want to lose me the same way he lost my mother. He made sure I had the best doctors and that I was well taken care of. He came to visit me too, sometimes. I don't think they ever knew, which was probably for the best."

"Except for missing my dad, I had a good life. My aunts were nice. Aidan's dad took me under his wing, sent me to the culinary academy and gave me work when no one else would give me the time of day. Aidan was one of the few who knew my secret. His dad had arranged for him to be wherever I was, and he quickly assumed Kieran's role as my guardian."

She laughed, but it was a sad laugh. "I think he resented it at first, almost as much as I did. But then we became really close. I don't know what I would have done without him."

Ian was grateful for everything that Aidan had done, he really was. But it still chafed to have her talk so fondly of another man. "He loves you."

"And I love him. But not like you think." Ian might have had his doubts before, but Aidan had been brutally honest on their two hour flight from Pennsylvania to Georgia. Between telling him what a monumental ass he was, Aidan also saw fit to set Ian straight on a lot of other things as well. But then Lexi didn't know that. Aidan hadn't told her what he was up to. He'd told Ian as much.

"We take care of each other. I would do anything for him, but he knows as well as I do that there was only ever one man for me."

Something swelled inside Ian's chest. "If you really felt that way, then why did you leave me, Lexi? Why did you shut me out? Not tell me about our son?"

"That week in Pine Ridge was the best seven days of my life," she said honestly. "I should have been honest with you. I should have told you about my medical condition right up front and that I didn't have enough meds to last me more than a few days. But you asked me to stay till the fair, and I could never deny you, Ian. Not ever."

"You *left*." It was still hard for him to fathom. Each time he thought about that day he felt a knife slicing right through his heart.

She nodded. "I had to, Ian. You... you're so strong and fierce, so vibrant, so alive. I could never expect you to understand. The last thing you needed was to be saddled with someone for whom a paper cut could be a life-threatening situation. And Kayla had probably already told you about the baby. Even if you didn't plan on marrying her, I knew you'd do right by your own child. You're too good of a man to ever walk away from something like that."

Anger lit Ian's eyes from within, making them glow. "*Saddled* with you? Jesus Christ, Lexi. Is that what you think? Don't you know I'd do *anything* to be with you? Under *any* circumstances?"

It was Lexi's turn to look surprised. "I thought once Kieran told you, you'd see things differently."

"Kieran didn't tell me shit. Hasn't talked to me since you left, as a matter of fact. Blames me for everything." He held up his hand when she opened her mouth again. "I wish I had known, Lexi. I would have done things differently, been gentler with you, made sure you had your meds so you wouldn't have to leave me, ever. *Nothing* could change the way I feel about you, Lex. *Nothing*."

"But Kayla ---"

"Kayla was never pregnant," Ian said, his voice bitter. "She *lied*. Made that up because she was jealous that you were able to do something in one week that she couldn't do in a lifetime."

"And what's that?" Lexi asked quietly.

"Make me fall totally, completely, and irrevocably in love with you."

"I did?"

"Yes, Lex. You did. But it doesn't excuse the fact that you kept your pregnancy from me. Were you even going to tell me I had a son? Christ, when I think about you going through everything alone…"

"I wasn't alone," she argued, averting her gaze.

Yes, he knew about Aidan. And it burned his ass that another man was taking care of his *croie* when it should have been him. Yes, he was grateful for everything that Aidan had done, but goddammit, he never should have had to.

"You didn't return my calls. My emails. I staked out every restaurant Aidan owns, hoping to catch a glimpse of you. I sat outside your apartment for days, just for the chance to talk to you, Lex. I couldn't find you. I never felt so helpless in my entire life. Explain to me why, please, because God knows, I just can't understand why you would keep something like this from me."

"At first," she said, her voice shaky, "I didn't know. Looking back, all the signs were there, but I just assumed it was because of what happened." Not to mention a shattered, destroyed, pulverized heart. "And one of the side effects of the meds I was on was an inability to conceive, not that that was ever really a concern for me before."

"But you weren't taking your meds properly, were you?"

"No," she agreed. "It never occurred to me that by lessening the dosage and stringing them out I was doing anything other than trying to spend as much time with you as possible."

"It's a miracle the meds didn't hurt the baby when you started taking them again."

"I was terrified that they did," she said quietly, and Ian heard the residual terror in her voice. "And that's part of the reason I didn't want to tell you. Once I realized I was pregnant, I stopped taking everything. But by that point, there was a very high probability that one or both of us wouldn't survive the pregnancy, or the delivery. I couldn't do that to you."

She paused, and he held his breath, suddenly afraid of what she would say next. "They wanted me to terminate the pregnancy, Ian," she said, and the last resolve in him shattered. "I couldn't do that. This was our baby. Ours. I knew it would be strong, I knew he wouldn't be anything less than perfect, because it was a miracle he was even conceived in the first place. He was meant to be, Ian. And I was going to tell you, once I knew everything was going to be okay."

"He *is* perfect," Ian agreed, nothing less than absolute reverence in his voice. From the moment he'd first held his son in his arms he had known that. But he had still counted toes and fingers, gazed in awe at the intelligence in his infant eyes, swelled with pride at the strong grip on his finger. His son hadn't cried once, seeming to know Ian was his father. He knew he was probably crazy, but he and the boy *bonded*.

"Aidan stuck by me, told them all to go to hell. Said we'd find different doctors, and we did. They put me on different meds. They weren't as effective but were safer for the baby."

"And what about you, Lex? How are you?"

"Better now," she said evasively.

"You look tired." She was a hell of a lot more than tired. Again, Aidan had pulled no punches, giving Ian a brutally honest review of her health on the flight down. Lexi was wearing herself down, struggling stubbornly to do everything, and her fragile body was weakening at an alarming rate. Aidan told Ian point-blank that he had to do something, because he seemed to be the only one Lexi ever listened to.

She laughed lightly. "Show me a new mother who isn't."

"True, but most women don't have the same challenges you do."

Her eyes glowed, and Ian saw the familiar defiance. "He is my son."

Ian's shoulders shifted back just slightly, his back straightened. Subtle changes, but the overall effect was an unquestionable air of command, of authority. "He is my son, too. And I'm going to take care of both of you."

Without another word, he stood up and scooped Lexi into his arms, carrying her back toward the master bathroom.

Chapter Twenty-Four

"Would you prefer a shower or bath?" he asked, lifting the milk-soaked gown over her head. His eyes lingered over her full breasts, her ample hips.

Lexi placed her hand over her belly self-consciously, all too aware that the pregnancy had added curves to the ones she'd already had.

Ian clasped both hands around her wrists and pulled them away. "Never hide yourself from me," he said huskily. "Jesus, Lex. You just had my child. How can you think I would see you as anything less than the goddess you are?"

"But I'm so… soft," she mumbled as she looked down at the pooch where she had once been flat. She'd never been a hard-body, but the swimming and careful diet had kept her trim and relatively firm. Months of bed rest and the pregnancy had really taken a toll. Her eyes trailed up Ian's tight, hard physique, so lean and drool-worthy, and she felt the now-familiar welling of tears behind her eyes. God, she hated the hormones.

They were turning her into a paranoid cry baby.

Big, strong hands caressed her gently. "I like you soft," his voice rich and thick like honey. "And believe me, sweetheart, I'm hard enough for the both of us." Taking her hand, he pressed it against some rigid proof of that statement.

Just that quickly, tears were replaced by a quick flash of heat zinging through her body. *Ian wanted her.* She stroked him through his jeans, following the shaft all the way to the tip of his waistband. He allowed her to do that a few times, then gently caught her hand and brought it to his lips.

"Uh-uh-uh," he chastised. "Not for a while, baby."

"For me, yes," she agreed, her voice dropping. "But not for you." Lexi went for his belt.

"Later maybe," he growled. "Let's take care of you first."

"Shower with me then," she said, pointing to the wet spots on his shirt. "Looks like you're a casualty of my overzealous let-down reflex, too." Before he could refuse, she added, "You can scrub my back."

Ian's hesitation was not lost on her. After everything that had happened, she couldn't blame him. He was worried, she got that. But that didn't mean she was going to let him off that easily. The worst of the danger had passed. She had survived, and their son was perfect. Clearly she was stronger than anyone (including herself) had given her credit for.

She was being given a second chance, and she was determined not to blow it this time. "It's all right, Ian," she said softly. "I really want this."

Lexi silently cheered when Ian began removing his clothes. The step-in shower was easily large enough for two people, and included a seat for Lexi. No less than six gleaming shower heads were positioned along three sides. Ian stepped behind her, his hands gently pushing her down onto the seat that had been placed in the middle, and he began to wash her hair.

She tilted her head back, enjoying the slow, lazy circles he made with his fingers. It felt so good, it almost made up for the fact that she couldn't ogle him from this position. "Oh, God, that feels good," she moaned. "Don't stop."

Ian chuckled softly behind her. He took his time, massaging her scalp, then her neck, then shoulders and back.

His hands felt wonderful; she had forgotten how magical Ian's touch could be. Judging by the few side glances she'd managed, he was every bit as affected as she was, too. There wasn't much she could do to alleviate the ache in her core, but there was no reason he had to suffer.

When he turned away to replace the body wash on the shelf built into the corner, Lexi made her move. The second he turned back around, Lexi's hands were clutching his hips, drawing him between her lips.

"Ah, fuck!" he ground out, his hands flying to her head. Lexi smiled around his thickness, grateful that the shower seat placed her at the perfect level for this. She devoured him greedily, starved for the man she had thought she'd lost forever.

Nine months, two weeks, and four days. That's how long it had been since she had last seen him. That's how long she had been dreaming of being with him again. She couldn't have stopped herself even if she'd wanted to (she hadn't).

"Baby," he growled in warning, but Lexi had already sensed his rising climax. Like a woman driven, she sucked him deeper, harder, one hand cupping his tight sac, one finger lightly stroking his seam. It was his undoing.

Lexi took everything he gave her, suckling him for more until every last drop was spent. Then she looked up at him and smiled.

Satisfied that she had gotten her way, Lexi gave him no hassles whatsoever about going back to bed for a little while, but fate had other plans. A loud wail sounded from the other room, their son anxious to remind them of his presence. Ian brought him back to her a few minutes later, smelling all clean and baby-like.

"You changed his diaper?" she said, impressed.

"Of course I did," Ian said, acting affronted.

"I knew there was a reason I fell in love with you."

Ian grinned. "Say that again."

"I love you."

"I love you, too. Now feed our son."

Lexi laughed. "I'm not sure who's more excited about this, Patrick or you."

"Me," Ian said, with a look of anticipation as he settled himself in front of her, mesmerized by her fingers as she parted her top. "*Definitely* me."

* * *

Ian watched as Lexi nursed their son. If there was ever a more perfect image, he couldn't imagine it. Even now, weary as she was, she was the most beautiful woman he had ever seen.

Christ, he loved her so much. She had been through so much, and she'd had to do it without him. Never again. Never again would she have to face anything alone, because he was going to damn well make sure of it. Nothing would ever hurt her or his son.

Including him.

He didn't know how he was going to find the strength to resist his baser urges, though. The pregnancy had given her more curves than a mountain road. Denying himself the pleasure of that would be the ultimate test of his resolve. That, and the unspoken challenge in her eyes.

Never take your eyes off the enemy. That was a mantra drilled into every soldier's head from day one, one that Ian was reminded of earlier in the shower. He had turned away for a second, one second, and she'd managed to annihilate every one of his defenses until the only thing he could do was hold on. He hadn't had the heart nor the will to push her away, not when she looked up at him with those big amber eyes and managed to convey, without words, just how much she loved and wanted him.

He was awed by it. But as glorious as it had been, he couldn't let it happen again.

* * *

Lexi's heart swelled as she took in the scene before her. Ian was sprawled out on the recliner, eyes closed, chest rising in a steady, easy rhythm. Patrick lay across his chest in almost the exact same position, the child's back to his father's front, Ian's large hand protectively holding him in place. Both heads were tilted slightly but at exactly the same angle, two sets of legs identically extended.

It was how she had come to find them each morning as of late, things settling into a familiar pattern. After the second feeding of the night, Patrick was usually not interested in going back to sleep right away. Ian would take him into the other room, allowing her to rest for a while longer. It was a nice thought, and very considerate, really. But she would have much preferred Ian's body next to hers on the bed over a few more Z's, especially considering that once he left, she found it impossible to rest anyway.

Her need for him, her dependence upon him continued to grow. Every day with him only ingrained him that much more in her heart and soul, and she worried about what the future would bring.

They hadn't discussed it, and that was part of the problem. A lot depended on the results of her next checkup, for that would be when they would decide the next course of action. So far they'd just been taking things one day at a time, avoiding the subject.

Despite Ian's presence over the last couple of weeks, his life was back in Pine Ridge. That was clear, even though he didn't come right out and say it. His family was there. His friends. His jobs, both the legitimate and covert, were based in the sleepy little Northeast town as well. Until recently, she would have said hers was here in Benton, with her job, her doctors, and Aidan. But Ian's presence changed everything, and she was coming to realize that where she really wanted to be was wherever Ian was.

Except as time went on, he was putting more distance between them, finding more ways to avoid being close to her, especially at night. She frowned at the pillow and blanket on the couch. For the last two weeks, Ian had been slipping out of her bed the moment he believed she'd fallen asleep. At first he'd stayed with her at night, curling his warm body around hers. He'd kept his sweats on to reduce temptation, but she'd understood, believing it to be a temporary thing until her post-birth recovery was complete.

Unfortunately, it wasn't turning out that way.

Granted, she *had* made it difficult for him, especially in the beginning. Reaching for him in the middle of the night, slipping her hand beneath his waistband, loving the heavy feel of him in her hand. If she was lucky, he'd let her stroke him, sometimes even guiding her. Once she'd gotten really lucky, and had managed to get her mouth on him, but it was only once. And each time, just like that first time in the shower, he'd withdrawn almost immediately afterward, finding some excuse to avoid any further intimate contact. Now, he had progressed to double-knotting the drawstring of his pants, ensuring that he woke up before she managed to get too far.

So she'd taken the hint, keeping her hands above the waist in an attempt to make him feel more comfortable. But if anything, it seemed to make things worse. If she snuggled up to his back or placed her hand on his arm, his body tensed and she would back off, feeling each rejection more keenly than the last. Then he started disappearing before she had any chance at all, using her exhaustion against her.

It was strange, really. She felt more alone now than she had before he had arrived. So far she'd been able to hold her tongue, but having him so close and yet so far away was taking its toll. Her appetite was nearly non-existent, and the only sleep she managed were short catnaps here and there.

At least he and Patrick had taken to each other. To say that they adored one another was an understatement. Ian's eyes glowed with pride when he looked at his son. At the sound of Ian's voice, Patrick would instantly calm. And, Lexi swore, they actually communicated with each other, simply by staring into the other's identical blue eyes. It was a little freaky sometimes.

As if sensing her distress, Ian's eyes opened and locked right on her. God, she thought, those eyes should be declared lethal weapons. They bore right through her with the precision of a laser, cutting through every defense she'd constructed.

Concern etched his features when he spotted the glistening in her eyes. Without another word, she turned and went back to the bedroom, the soft click of the door informing him quite plainly that it was not an invitation.

* * *

God, he hated this. Every cell in his body screamed to be with her. To hold her. To kiss her. To show her that she and his child were his world. Being within a hundred feet of her gave him the hard-on from hell, and she felt the need to do something about it. He totally got that. Loved that she loved to please him. But it was too one-sided, and he wanted, no, he *needed* to pleasure her, too. And he couldn't.

It ate away at him. No matter how many times she tried to explain that she was okay with having to wait, he'd still end up feeling frustrated and helpless afterward. No matter how many times she tried to tell him that it gave her great satisfaction to care for him, that it was another way of loving him, he just couldn't accept it.

He'd seen the hurt in her eyes, wished to God he hadn't been the one to put it there. But just being close to her was driving him insane. Feeling her breasts pressing against him. Her soft, sweet breath across his skin. Those soft sighs she made in her sleep. It was more than he could bear.

He swore he would never, *ever* lose control around her again, but goddamn it, she made that difficult. Images of what she'd looked like in that hospital bed, bruised and battered, appeared in his head, made his belly sick with disgust. *He* had done that to her. And God help him, some sick part of him wanted to do it again.

Not to hurt her, no; he never wanted to hurt her. But he did crave to be with her again in that fiery, unbridled way, where everything else ceased to exist. To be inside her, feel her hot, tight sheath loving him; to feel her legs wrapped around his hips as he drove into her over and over again, marking her, filling her until she couldn't remember her own name.

But to do so was to risk her life. And he would never, ever do that again.

These were the demons he faced, and Lexi simply didn't understand that every time she took him in her mouth, every time she stroked him into ecstasy, his hunger, his need for her grew. Now it was so strong, it scared the shit out of him. He knew Lexi was waiting for her next doctor's appointment, waiting to get the green light for sex, but secretly he was dreading it. He was terrified that he'd hurt her again.

Yes, it was hard to see the hurt and confusion on her face each time he pulled away. It cut him up inside like a thousand little knives. But it was better than looking down at her battered body, worried that each breath she took might be her last.

chapter twenty-five

Ian heard the shower go on and off. Heard the soft sounds of drawers opened and closed. The gentle hum of the breast pump. He frowned. Patrick would be up soon and ravenous as always. That kid was a Callaghan through and through, eating enough for a couple of kids. Why would she be pumping milk if she was going to feed him soon?

The light chime of the door bell sounded, deepening his frown.

"Aidan," Ian greeted, stepping aside to let the other man in. "Wasn't expecting you, man."

A puzzled look crossed over Aidan's face, but he covered it quickly. "How's the prince today?"

It was a joke they shared, the nickname given to Patrick at the hospital by the doting nurses since he'd been treated royally from the moment his existence became known.

"He's good," Ian said, shifting him slightly. The boy, now awake, reached toward Aidan. Aidan gave him his finger and a huge grin.

"You know, it's scary how he looks at you like

that," Aidan said as Patrick focused on him. "Like he's already got it all figured out."

"Yeah, that's what Lex says, too. Not to be rude, buy why are you here?"

Lexi made her appearance at the moment, looking fresh and lovely in a pretty aqua sweater, black skirt, and sandals. Her hair was brushed to shining, forming soft waves that curled in toward her body. She wore just a hint of makeup, but it was enough to take his breath away.

"Hey, Aidan," she greeted when she spotted him at the door. "What are you doing here? I called for Fritz."

The other man nodded. "I know. Fritz is off today, his wife's home in bed with the flu, so I'll be your ride."

"Oh, that's too bad," Lexi said with genuine concern in her voice. "I'll make her some soup later."

"I'm sure she'd like that."

Feeling like the odd man out, Ian shifted slightly. "Going somewhere?"

"Yes, actually," Lexi answered without looking at him. "There's plenty of milk in the fridge. I left a big bottle out on the counter. It's still warm." She took Patrick from Ian's arms and rubbed her nose into his neck, making him giggle. "Be good for daddy, sweetie. Mommy will be home soon."

"Where are you going?" Ian asked, hating the needy undertone of his voice.

"I have a few appointments. Should be back by dinner."

Ian glanced at the clock. It was barely nine a.m. "What appointments? There's nothing on your calendar." He knew, because he had looked. Worried that Lexi might try to do too much too soon, he had taken it upon himself to ensure that didn't happen. Thankfully, he had found an ally in Aidan, who handled the business side of things.

Without answering, she handed Patrick back to Ian and looked at Aidan. "I'm ready. Let's go."

"Lex ---" started Ian, but she was already out the door. He turned to Aidan. "What the hell was that all about?"

"Not sure. But shot in the dark? Lexi's pissed."

Ian nodded, barely managing to bite off the "no shit, Sherlock" comment before it made it past his lips. "What appointments does she have today?"

Aidan shrugged apologetically. "That, I honestly don't know. But when I heard Lex had called for Fritz, I figured something was up. Don't worry, Ian. I'll keep her out of too much trouble."

And *that* grated against Ian's nerves like steel wool on his skin. Aidan shouldn't have to be doing anything of the sort. That was *his* job.

"Maybe you should keep an eye on Patrick," Ian suggested. Aidan was probably the only person outside of his own family that he would trust with his son. The man had proven himself more than enough over the past seven months. "Let me take

Lexi wherever she needs to go."

"Do I *look* stupid to you?" Aidan said, shaking his head. "You still don't get it, do you?" Opening the door, he took one step into the hallway. "But honestly, Callaghan, I hope you figure it out soon, because I don't think either one of you is going to make it through another one, and you've got the kid to think about now."

Stunned, Ian stood in silence as he watched Aidan insert his private key and step into the elevator. Lexi was already long gone, no doubt waiting below in the sleek limo. As he closed the door, Patrick grabbed tightly onto his hair and pulled until Ian gently disentangled his fingers.

"Yeah, I get it little man. You're hungry. And Daddy's an idiot. Come on. At least I know how to fix one of those things. You might have to help me with the rest, though."

With a smack of his pudgy hand against Ian's jaw and gurgle of agreement, they headed for the kitchen.

* * *

"All right, Alexis. You may get dressed now." Dr. Elena McKenzie put her hand lightly on Lexi's shoulder, the slight crackling of the paper gown as loud as an Alaskan avalanche in the quiet space.

Lexi sat up, holding the gown in place, which seemed kind of silly, really. The doctor had just performed a thorough exam; there was nothing she hadn't already seen. It made about as much sense as folding her underwear and hiding it between the other articles of clothing when she undressed, yet she always felt a strange, prudish compulsion to do so.

She dressed quietly behind the silk paneled screen, hand-painted with a landscape scene while recessed lighting radiated a light, warm glow. All around her, the walls were a brushed hue of... well, it was hard to describe, really. Something between orange and pink, Lexi guessed, a solid attempt to recreate the hue of a perfect sunset, she supposed. Soft classical music played in the background. Water flowed gently over plates of colored glass in one of those zen-based sculptures, no doubt designed to instill a sense of calm and tranquility, just like every other feature of the room. No sterile white walls and hard-on-your-butt exam tables here; it was first class all the way. Considering that each office visit sucked a nice four digits out of Lexi's bank account, it should be.

"Well?" Lexi tried not to fidget, but it was difficult. The doctor had her head bent down over some device that looked like what an iPad wanted to be when it grew up. As the specialist other specialists deferred to, Lexi had come to expect nothing but the best from Dr. McKenzie in everything.

Dr. McKenzie looked up. It was a slight glance;

her head didn't move, only her eyes. Lexi suddenly felt like a child about to be scolded. After an eternity, the rest of the doctor's head followed. The flat digital screen was placed on the carved mahogany desktop.

"I'm sorry," Lexi said, the words coming out in a rush. "I just... well, I..."

If the doctor had a surprised look, Lexi knew she was witnessing it right then, though beyond the slight rise of an eyebrow, there was little to distinguish it from any other. This woman was the epitome of professionalism, her implacable face rarely giving anything away. Lexi reddened under her gaze, feeling more like an impatient child than ever.

"This is not like you, Alexis," the woman said, her voice as smooth as the glass in her tranquility fountain, an unusual accent slightly coloring the enunciation, "to be so impatient. Something has changed in your situation, has it not?"

Hell, yes. "My ... ", she started, then faltered. How exactly should she refer to Ian? What reference would be appropriate here? Boyfriend sounded so juvenile in this distinguished space, and he really didn't fit that mold anyway. Husband was an even further stretch. Every word she came up with seemed just as inadequate. Friend? *Um, no.* Acquaintance? *Uh-uh.* Love of my life? Soul mate? Accurate, but probably not appropriate.

"Patrick's father is in town," she blurted out

finally. Yeah, that would work. The small sentence got a full quarter-inch tilt from the eyebrow. Big-time stuff.

"Ah, I am beginning to comprehend. He knew not of the little prince until recently." Lexi nodded, feeling a brief, momentary vibe of disapproval from the doctor before the atmosphere leveled out again. "And now? How does he perceive the situation?"

Such an odd pattern of speech, Lexi thought, wondering for the hundredth time exactly from where the enigmatic Elena McKenzie had come. Her manner of speaking, the slightest hint of an unidentifiable accent, gave Lexi the impression that the doctor was originally from somewhere in Eastern Europe, but she'd been unable to pin it down to one specific region.

At least she could answer the doctor's question fairly easily. "He is the world's proudest father," she said with a smile. "He and Patrick, they're inseparable. Ian feeds him, bathes him, talks to him. And Patrick just adores his father." The words tumbled out in a rush, but they were all true. Ian was an incredible father.

Dr. McKenzie's head bobbed just slightly, a single nod of comprehension. "And what about you, Alexis? How does the prince's father perceive you?"

Well, that was the million dollar question, wasn't it? One that wasn't quite as easy to answer. "I think he's... afraid." It felt like a betrayal of sorts to suggest that her hard, strong SEAL was scared, but even as the words left her mouth she felt the truth of them.

Green eyes studied her with more than just clinical interest. Lexi could practically sense the doctor's brain processing the situation behind them, connecting the dots at inhuman speed. Lexi was used to that. But what weirded her out was the subtle emergence of a woman from behind the impeccable clinical façade. The sharp edges softened, just a little.

"He should be," Dr. McKenzie said softly, her words a carefully metered cadence. "As any male of worth should be. His dalliance nearly killed you."

A surge of irrational anger rose up within Lexi quickly, rolling over her like a wave. "It was no dalliance!" she said defensively, surprised at her own vehemence. The mere thought that what she and Ian had shared was anything less than the realization of a life's dream for her was completely unacceptable. "Ian is the most honorable, loving, good man I've ever known. *I'm* the one that left him, Doctor."

"And yet one must wonder, if he is as good a man as you profess, why you would do such a thing."

They were way beyond the typical doctor-patient conversation, but Lexi didn't care. She needed to talk to someone, and she was skinny on the BFF's at that moment.

"Because I love him more than anything," Lexi admitted. "Because I did not want him to live in fear of what might happen every time he touched me." *Like he is doing right now.* "He is a strong, virile man, Dr. McKenzie. Tying him to someone like me would be like trying to domesticate a wild tiger. It would be cruel."

But would she ever have the strength not to let him go? She would never keep Patrick from him, so how could she handle seeing him on a regular basis?

"You are not so fragile, Alexis. I am confident that with proper care and preparation, no door is closed to you."

"More meds," Lexi said, shaking her head, knowing what the recommendations would be: more toxic chemicals with side effects as bad as or worse than the disease itself. She'd refused everything because she wanted to breast feed her son. Dr. McKenzie knew this.

"We've discussed this. I will give my son every advantage I can. No drugs."

"It puts you at great risk."

Lexi sat up straighter and lifted her chin. "So be it."

The doctor tented her fingers, an oddly masculine move for a woman who never wore slacks and was always coiffed to perfection. "Have you considered a compromise, Alexis?"

"A compromise?"

"Nurse your young one for six months. Begin mixing easily digestible cereals into your breast milk at four months. From what you tell me, the boy is strong and soon your milk will not be enough to sustain him adequately. Store and freeze as much as you can to extend the benefits of mother's milk beyond that. You do pump regularly, do you not?"

Lexi nodded.

"Excellent. I am quite optimistic of a new treatment plan, one that is based upon purely natural, non-chemical substances."

Lexi looked at her skeptically, hardly daring to hope. A natural solution? No more pumping her body full of industrial-grade poison?

"Yes, Alexis. It was your own unique heritage that spawned the idea, a joining of two different but ancient and powerful cultures that may yet hold the answers we seek. It was the doctor who tended to you in Pine Ridge who developed the idea. However, I do not think it is wise to change anything at the present time for fear of disrupting the boy's routine. From what you tell me, he is flourishing."

Again, Lexi nodded in confirmation. "He is. His pediatrician says he is beyond where he should be."

"That is good," the doctor said approvingly. "A further indication of good genes, and the strength of his parents. And the timeframe, it is reasonable, is it not?"

Lexi inclined her head. "Yes, it is. But in all honesty, I don't know if I can wait that long." *Because he's slipping away from me a little more every day, and I feel like I'm dying inside.* Not to mention that Ian's presence called to her on such a base, primal level. Her feelings for him went way beyond anything she could logically understand. She craved him. Ian Callaghan was as necessary to her survival as food and water and air. These last few weeks, as difficult as they had been, had been like the arrival of spring up north, when everyone opened their windows, letting the clean fresh air breathe new life into stale, closed spaces.

"I see no reason why you cannot resume a physical relationship, although I would strongly recommend that it be of a gentle nature until we can begin a viable treatment plan."

Gentle? Lexi had lots of ideas running through her head, and gentle wasn't on the program. The doctor paused, as if deciding whether or not to continue. "There are a lot of options for pleasuring one another that would not place you in danger. Will your man be accepting of this?"

My man. Boy, Lexi liked the sound of that. She realized with a jolt that he really was hers, wasn't he? Her possessive instinct was nearly as strong as her mother's instinct. But asking Ian to be gentle? That would be like ordering an entire chocolate silk pie and only allowing herself one bite.

It would be worth it, though. One bite of Ian

was better than a whole truckload of goodies with anyone else. And, if she handled this right, she should be able to convince him that she would not shatter into a thousand pieces.

The thought had the corners of her mouth curving. There were a lot of things she'd read about, actually, that sounded wonderful. Things she had dreamed of Ian doing to her, things she would never have the courage to ask for. But now, well now she was just desperate enough to do it.

"I think he might," she said cautiously, but inside her core muscles were doing the wave.

chapter twenty-six

By the time Lexi got back to her suite that night, she was nearly a basket case. It was the first time she'd been away from Patrick for more than a few hours, for one thing. She wasn't worried about his safety; there was no place safer for him than with his father.

What if he'd reached for her and she wasn't there? What if he needed the comfort of his mother's arms while she was off selfishly taking care of herself instead of her baby? Or, sweet Mary, what if, in his infant mind, he believed she had abandoned him?

Despite the racking guilt, the afternoon had been therapeutic and long overdue. After leaving Dr. McKenzie's office, she sent Aidan away and visited the spa and salon. Now she was waxed, exfoliated, plucked, and moisturized. Her hair was trimmed and styled; her nails buffed, shaped, and polished. She certainly felt more womanly than she had in quite a while, and she was going to need all the help she could get if she was to pull off her plan.

The foyer was illuminated only by the soft recessed lights, and she had to give her eyes a moment to adjust from the brighter lights of the outer entrance. The penthouse was divided into two suites, both accessible by the key-driven elevator and secured private stairway. Aidan's was to the left; Lexi's, to the right.

Lexi slid her digital key into the lock, not quite sure what she would find on the other side. It was just around dinner time, and she was hoping to persuade Ian to order in tonight while she fed, bathed, and got Patrick settled in his bed. Then, with any luck, she would feed, bathe, and *un*settle Ian in *her* bed afterward.

The spacious apartment was quiet. Too quiet. Like the foyer, the lights were dimmed. The sound of her footsteps was practically nonexistent, absorbed by the plush carpet and double-padded underlay as she worked her way through the living area. The soft, muted sounds of the flat screen in her room settled her nerves. Ian was probably in there with Patrick sprawled out on his chest, two men bonding over ESPN Sports Center.

Kicking off her shoes, she stopped first at the kitchen to unload the bottles of milk she'd pumped throughout the day. One thing about having such a ravenous child: her body was on full-scale dairy mode. She'd learned quickly that her body was going to answer the call every two hours whether she was home or not, and ignoring it was the quickest way to aching boobs and drenched shirts. Thankfully, there had been private areas at both of the places she'd visited, allowing her to stay on schedule and keep her dignity intact.

"I hope you haven't eaten yet." Ian's deep, velvety voice startled her.

"I thought you were in the bedroom with Patrick."

"I was. He's sound asleep. You smell wonderful." Ian dipped his head down toward her neck and inhaled deeply. Lexi fought the urge to bury her hands in his hair and hold him there. A second later, he stepped back, as if he had realized what he'd just done and regretted it. "Have a good day?"

"Um..." she said, trying to focus on the question. Ian's intimate sniff had railroaded her thought processes and left her freshly-waxed, sensitive womanly parts tingling intensely. "I'm sorry. What?"

That sexy half-smile of his --- the one that devastated her every time --- made her knees weak.

"Did you have a good day?" He took the miniature cooler from her and stacked the bottles neatly on the shelf.

"Yes." Lexi regained some of her poise, but not enough. The sight of Ian's delectable backside as he bent into the fridge was a major distraction. Thinking about sex all day had definitely put her on edge. Discreetly, she pressed her thighs together as she reached for a glass and held it under the drinking tap. "I saw Dr. McKenzie today."

"I thought that appointment wasn't for another two weeks," he said carefully. "Are you having problems?" Ian's voice was too level, too neutral. Undoubtedly, he already knew about the appointment. *Aidan*. Since when had he become Ian's little narc?

"No, everything's fine," she assured him, but he probably already knew more about the results of her exam than she did. She wondered if anything she and the doc had spoken about afterward was transcripted into her records anywhere. "In fact, everything's better than fine."

"Is it now?" Hunger warred with doubt in his eyes.

"Mmm-hmm," she answered, working hard to keep up her courage, but it wasn't easy. Ian moved back, putting several feet between them, his body language guarded and closed. She put her arms around herself, feeling a sudden chill. "I thought maybe we could order dinner in tonight. I could tell you what she said. If you're interested."

"I'm interested," he said, but his tone was not what she wanted to hear. *I'm interested*, it said, *but it's not going to change anything*. A dull ache started in her Lexi's chest.

"Okay then. If you don't mind ordering, I'll just go start getting Patrick's bath ready."

"He's already had his bath."

"Oh. Well, I guess I could feed him, then. It's still a little early, but I'm sure he won't mind."

"He just finished a bottle about fifteen minutes ago. He's good for a couple of hours."

"Oh." Lexi was torn between feeling grateful for all that Ian had done and feeling disappointed that they had managed so well without her.

"He really missed you, though," Ian said a little too quickly, no doubt spotting the moisture quickly accumulating in her eyes. "He was a very unhappy camper there for a while, and completely skipped his afternoon nap."

She nodded, biting her lip. That probably shouldn't have made her feel as good as it did. Still, if Patrick was all taken care of, then there was really no reason to delay. If she could just get Ian interested.

Lexi stepped up behind him as he pulled the take-out menus from the magnetized clip that hung on the side of the fridge. She slipped her arms around him, laying her cheek against his back. He felt so good. So strong, so warm, so ---

Ian's entire body tensed beneath her. "What would you like? Chinese, Indian, Italian?"

The shutdown was cold and complete, as if someone had just flipped a switch. Suddenly, Lexi wasn't feeling quite so brave anymore. She couldn't do it. Without Ian's willing cooperation, this was not going to work.

"Never mind," Lexi said, dropping her arms

and pulling away. She wouldn't be able to eat anything anyway with the way her stomach was doing flips. The intense swing of emotions from pulsing lust and hunger and need to humiliation and regret and despair was brutal, and once again she cursed her hormones and her totally messed-up body chemistry.

She started shutting down, her natural defenses assuming control. It was strange, really, how the numbness mixed in with the pain, a necessary dilution to keep her functioning. Visions of how Ian had once looked at her shattered in her own mind, like pictures someone had thrown against the wall. Oh, when she thought of the things he had done to her, the places he had taken her... But that felt like an entirely different lifetime, and in a way, it was. That was when Ian still thought of her as a healthy, vibrant, passionate woman.

She wondered what he saw her as now, then decided it would probably hurt too much to know. The bottom line: Ian wasn't interested. He kept his distance. Cringed when she got near him. How could she tell him what the doctor said now? How could she ask him to do any of those things she'd dreamed about when he couldn't even stand her touch?

"Lex, what's wrong?" Ian asked carefully.

"You know what?" she said, backing away slowly, her arms wrapped defensively in front of her. "I'm really not hungry. I'm very tired, it's been a long day. I'm just going to check on Patrick and then go to bed."

"Lex."

"Goodnight, Ian. Thanks for taking care of Patrick today. I'll take it from here."

Lexi forced herself to keep a steady pace as she walked back toward her room, refusing to look at the pillow and blanket neatly tucked and folded along the sofa. Then she closed the door and locked it. She wouldn't be needing Ian's help any more tonight.

* * *

Ian felt a shiver run through him. That wasn't Lexi's voice. It held no warmth, no affection whatsoever. None of the love it normally did, and he didn't like it. Not at all.

Fuck. Ian wished he was on active duty at that moment, because he really wanted to kill something. He was losing his mind trying to say and do the right thing, to not put any pressure on her, to not take advantage of her. His body was going to explode if he didn't get inside her soon. And *still* he was screwing this up royally. How the hell was he supposed to deal with this?

He simply wasn't good at this kind of thing. Taking out the enemy? He was on it. Cracking a system? Nobody better. Taking care of his woman? Big, fat suck-fest on a stick.

It took a while, but Ian finally came to a conclusion and began a deliberate march across the suite. To hell with what he was *supposed* to do. He was going to do what he *had* to do. He reached out, twisted the knob, and found the bedroom door locked.

Well, that was a clear message there, wasn't it? It was the first time she'd done that, and it only strengthened his belief that he was doing the right thing. Things were getting way out of control, the very thing he was hoping to avoid. Within seconds, the lock was disabled and he was inside, poised to duck as he half-expected a solid object to come flying his way.

Nothing did. She wasn't even in the room. The flat screen still droned on ESPN at a low murmur. Patrick lay sleeping soundly in his crib, though Ian could see that Lexi must have picked him up. The slightest tint of bronze was on his head where she had pressed her lips to him.

God, she had looked so beautiful standing there in the kitchen. Her hair was shiny and full, her skin radiant. And, oh, did she smell good. So good that he'd forgotten himself and gotten too close. His chest ached, his arms burned with the need to hold her.

He barely heard it over the soft, muted sound of running water, as if… He listened closer, all doubt fleeing. It was the sound of someone crying. Into a towel by the muffled nature of it.

"Lex, open the door," he commanded, his voice holding the edge of the panic he felt. The door was locked; he raised his fist and pounded against it. "Jesus, Lex. Open the goddamn door."

He was just about to break the thing down when he heard the soft click and she opened it a few inches. Huge eyes, rimmed in red, her dark liner smudged, looked up at him and his heart broke. Those once-glowing amber eyes were cold. Dead.

After a brief hesitation, the door opened a little wider. "Lex, I ---"

"One of us needs to leave."

A bomb went off in his head somewhere, and he was only vaguely aware of the shrapnel raining down within his mind, shredding what little was left of his sanity. Surely he'd heard wrong. "What?"

"You heard me. This is not working, and I can't do this anymore. It's not fair to either one of us."

"What the hell are you talking about?"

Lexi opened the door and stepped into his body, pressing her breasts against his hard chest, weaving her hands up around the back of his neck, tangling her fingers in his hair. For a moment, for one glorious moment, his hands went around her waist and onto her butt, his hips grinding against hers. Then his eyes snapped open, his hands gripped her shoulders and pushed her back about six inches.

Lexi let her hands drop, and Ian realized that he had done exactly what she had expected him to.

"*That's* what I'm talking about." She stepped

back, twisting away from his hands. "We'll have to work out something."

"Damn straight." Working something out together sounded good to him, because he wasn't doing so well on his own.

"I'll take nights, you take days."

"What?"

"With Patrick. Assuming you want to. You do want to spend time with your son, don't you?"

"What kind of a question is that? Of course I do."

"Good. You can have him during the day, which will work out quite well, actually, because I need to start working again."

"You're not going back to work."

"Fuck. You. I'm not asking. I'll work mornings and afternoons, then we'll switch. You're planning on heading back to Pine Ridge, right?"

Ian couldn't answer; he could only stare at her, stunned. Where the hell was all this coming from?

She didn't wait for him to respond. "Look, I know your life is there. I get that. And I would never keep you from Patrick, so this is the only way I can see making it work," she continued. "You have your place at the pub, you work nights. I'll get a job at Francesco's and live in my grandmother's house. Assuming Uncle Jack didn't sell it, that is."

"He didn't." Ian's lips thinned. No, his father hadn't sold it. He'd given it to Ian, and Ian lived there now. So it was all good. "You'll live with me, where I can take care of you. *Both* of you."

"At the risk of repeating myself: fuck you."

Ian growled. The sound originated from somewhere around his navel and built as it rose up through his chest. His muscles strained with tension, his jaw clenched, and he went utterly, unnaturally still.

"Once we're married --- "

Lexi's eyes widened. "Married? Wake up, Ian. I am not marrying you."

Another bomb went off, this time in his chest. "Of course you are. Patrick --- "

"--- is our son," she completed for him. "He deserves the love and attention of both of his parents, and he'll have that."

"You're right about that. And you *will* marry me." Ian thought about the ring that he still carried in his pocket, just as he had every day since he bought it. Damn it, he hadn't wanted it to come out this way, but there really was no choice here. There never had been any doubt in his mind, not since she first fell asleep on his arm on that God-forsaken bus.

"No, Ian, I won't."

"You need me." *Please, God, let that be true*, he prayed. He needed it to be true, because he couldn't live without her.

Lexi softened her tone, as Ian had softened his. "Patrick needs his father."

"And what about you, Lex? What do you

need?"

Her arms wrapped around her mid-section as if she was trying to hold herself together. She bit her lip while he held his breath, wanting to hear her answer and dreading it at the same time. When she spoke, her voice was barely more than a whisper. "I need a man who will love me the same way that I love him: with every last piece of my heart, my mind, and my soul."

Relief flooded his chest. "Lex, I do love you like that. I swear to God."

She held up her hand to stop him from saying anything further, the look in her eyes so pained he felt it acutely in his chest. "No, Ian, you don't. Because there is nothing in this world or any other that could ever keep me out of your arms or your bed as long as you wanted me there."

Ian felt like an eighteen-wheeler had just hit him head on. "You think I don't want you? Jesus Christ, Lexi, it's killing me not to wrap myself around you and bury myself deep inside you till you don't know anything but me."

"Then why don't you?" she asked, her voice rising. "Do you have any idea how hard it is to have you shrink away at my slightest touch? To lie awake all night, thinking of nothing but being in your arms, and hearing you pacing in the next room because you can't stand to be near me? To know that every time you look at me, all you can see is the ugliness inside of me?" Tears fell freely over her cheeks. "Is that how you love me, Ian?"

"I can't hurt you again!" he yelled. "I won't!"

"You didn't hurt me, Ian. That was *my* fault. And I wanted it, all of it. I still do. The only way you can hurt me is by turning away from me now. Please, Ian. I need you to hold me. I need to feel your heart beating against mine."

More than anything, Ian wanted to take her into his arms and show her exactly how much she meant to him, but his legs wouldn't move. As much as his heart cried out for her, his brain still flashed visions of her lying in that hospital bed, looking like she'd been tortured. What if he lost control again? He couldn't take the chance.

Very quietly, Lexi nodded, a silent affirmation that her worst fears had been realized. Her hands dropped to her sides. With slow, heavy movements, she walked around him to the crib where Patrick was now crying. Lifting him up to her, she padded toward the door and out into the softly lit hallway. She paused, but did not turn around.

"I'm sorry, Ian," she whispered softly. "But I want a husband, not a housemate." Then she was gone.

chapter twenty-seven

"Francesco D'Armini?" Aidan said in disbelief as the private limo crossed the Maryland-Pennsylvania border. "Why don't you just plunge the knife into my back and twist a little harder?"

"We've been over this, Aidan. Patrick needs to be near his father," she said wearily.

"So he can't move to Benton?"

"I don't want him in Benton. He has a life here. A home, a job, a family. If he came to Benton he'd expect to move in with me, and that is so not happening."

"You don't think he's going to want to live with you here?" Aidan asked, shaking his head. "I thought you were smarter than that, Lex."

"There's no reason for him to," she sniffed. "And he's already agreed to move back to the pub." Lexi had made it a condition of her and Patrick's permanent relocation to Pine Ridge. Ian would get to spend every day with his son, and she wouldn't have to deal with his rejection.

Aidan snorted. "You haven't actually signed

anything with Francesco yet, have you?"

"No. I was planning to talk to him once we got settled."

"Do me a favor, will you? Don't call Francesco just yet."

"Why not?"

"I've got an idea. Something I've been thinking about a lot lately."

"What idea?"

He sighed heavily. "Lex, we have always been there for each other, haven't we?"

"Yes, of course."

"Then please, just do this for me."

"All right, Aidan. I'll wait. But I do wish you'd tell me what's going on in that devious mind of yours."

Aidan smiled and patted her hand. "Soon, Lex. Soon."

Three Months Later, Fourth of July, County Fair, Pine Ridge, PA

"Wow, he's pretty fast for a six-month old," Lina commented as Patrick made his way across the huge quilt on his hands and knees, trying to get to his slightly older, larger cousins. Lina's and Stacey's sons were about the same age. Keely's twin boys were just a bit younger, but nearly as large, and seemed to have adopted Patrick as one of their own.

"Yeah, he is," laughed Lexi. "He started crawling at five months, and he hasn't stopped since. I'm just glad he's got more of his father in him than me," she added as Lina's son reached out to grab Patrick and he tumbled, laughing hysterically.

"I don't know," said Stacey, offering Lexi some iced tea. "I think his mom is pretty strong, too."

"I'm getting there," Lexi said. "But I have to thank you guys for that." Moving back to Pine Ridge had its share of challenges, but the close camaraderie and friendship of these ladies had been a godsend.

"You're starting your new treatments soon, right?" Keely asked.

Lexi nodded. "Monday."

"Want me to watch the little guy?" Taryn asked, cradling her newborn daughter.

"Thanks, but he'll be with Ian."

As one, four sets of female eyes turned on her. "Ian's not going with you?" Keely asked quietly.

"No, why would he?" Lexi said defensively. The last thing Ian needed was daily, blatant reminders of her condition. He already treated her as if she was made of spun glass.

The other women exchanged glances. "You shouldn't have to do this alone, Lex."

"I'm going with her," Stacey spoke up. "She

won't be alone."

Lexi gave her a grateful look. Stacey understood her better than anybody, having gone through her own personal medical crisis. Her husband, however, had dealt with things better than Ian apparently.

"Maybe you could ask Johnny to talk to him, Stace," Lina suggested. "After all, you went through something similar."

"Me and Michael, too," said Keely, nodding her head. "But then we talked it out and everything was okay."

Taryn snorted. "Yeah, you guys *talked* long and loud. Repeatedly, from what you told me at the Christmas party." With only a slight tinge of color to her cheeks, Keely grinned from ear to ear. She loved her big, physical husband, and made no secret of the fact.

"Thanks, but no thanks," Lexi said, suddenly feeling awkward among these happily married women. From the other side of the grove, she saw Ian and his brothers moving toward them. It took some effort to get to her feet. When she scooped up Patrick, she tried unsuccessfully to hide her grimace.

"Here," Lina said, grabbing Patrick until Lexi could right herself. "You're not leaving, are you? It's almost dark. The fireworks will be starting soon. Boy, he's a big one, isn't he?"

"Don't go, Lex," Stacey said. "Watch the

'works with us. Best show ever."

"She's not kidding," Lina laughed. "But that's what happens when you get a computer genius and a few demolition experts together."

Lexi shot another look toward the men who were closing the distance quickly. From where she stood, she could see Ian hardening himself, the way he always did when he got close to her. They rarely spoke at all anymore unless it was to share information about Patrick, though the very air between them practically crackled with electricity. It made it uncomfortable for everyone.

"Maybe next time," she said, forcing a smile as she took back her child. There was no way she was going to ruin this for everyone. "Thanks, girls. This was fun."

They watched in silence as Lexi made her way across the fields, her steps deliberate and methodical, as if each one was a tremendous effort.

"Hey, the fireworks will be starting soon!" Jake announced, as the men returned from the initial setup. His gaze followed Taryn's. "Is that Lex?"

"Yeah." There was an awful lot in that one word. They watched as she disappeared behind the booths.

"Well?" Taryn asked, turning to her brother-in-law and poking him in the chest.

"Well what?" Ian looked down at her, his expression hard, as if he could scare her into holding her tongue. It didn't work.

"Aren't you going to go after her?"

"No," he said flatly. "Why would I?"

"How can you be so cold?" asked Taryn. A few seconds later, under the combined, disapproving stares of his family, Ian turned and walked off in the other direction.

"Talk to him, Jake," Taryn pleaded.

"Don't you think I've tried?"

"We all have, Tar," Johnny said quietly. "He won't listen. He thinks he's protecting her, and nothing any of us say or do is going to change his mind."

* * *

Three Months Later, October

Ian looked at the ancient wall clock in the pub kitchen. It had advanced three whole minutes since the last time he checked, which, he decided, was physically impossible since at least two hours must have passed. Patrick chattered happily in his high chair, telling a long-winded tale in mumbles and grunts to Taryn and Jake's daughter Riley, who was mesmerized. Riley had deep, violet eyes, just like her mom, and they were focused solely on her playmate. The two had become inseparable, each happy when in the other's presence. It made for some pretty easy days.

Lexi was late picking Patrick up. Again. Okay,

so technically she wasn't late. She was supposed to pick him up by six p.m., and it was five forty-five. But she used to come over by five o'clock to chat and have coffee with Taryn, and this was the third night in a row she hadn't.

Ian missed her terribly. He looked forward to that hour at the end of the day, when Lexi was ending her work day and before he started his shift at the bar. Other than a quick greeting and an exchange of Patrick-related information, they didn't speak much to each other directly. Their relationship, if you could call it that, had been reduced to little else.

But for that one hour he would find some reason to hang around, just so he could look at her, to know that she was safe and well. He could listen to her voice as she spoke with everyone else and hear about her day, what was going on in her life. That precious hour was the only thing that made his life bearable, got him through from one day to the next. He loved their son, treasured the time he spent with him, but without Lexi by his side, he felt as if part of him --- the biggest, best part --- was missing. It was the price he paid, every day, to keep her safe. From him.

During the day, at least, he had Patrick. They did all kinds of things together. Evenings he worked the bar, so that provided some distraction. Nights were the worst. He would lie there, staring at the ceiling, remembering what it felt like to have her body snuggled against him, warming him. To hear her little sighs as she dreamed. To bury his head in her hair and smell the fresh, musky scent of her, knowing that with little more than a soft touch she would open for him, cradling his body with her own.

At night, he allowed himself to let go, to dream and remember. But it was all he could allow. The reality was that with a word from him, she would give him everything, without hesitation, without regard to herself. Ian knew this. It was exactly why he had to be the one to protect her and keep her safe, because she would never put herself or her needs above his.

At least she seemed to be going on with her life, which was both a blessing and a curse. Ian wanted her to be happy, but he wished he could be the one making her that way.

She had a lot going on. She was on that new, experimental treatment plan. She didn't talk about it much when he was around, but he knew it was brutal. For several hours each week she was hooked up to a machine that basically filtered her blood and reintroduced it back into her body with plant-based additives that were supposed to be well-tolerated. Michael described it as a type of 'organic chemo' that was supposed to stimulate her natural body chemistry to start creating the clotting factors on its own.

Ian wanted to go with her to the treatments, but

she had vehemently opposed that idea. The first couple of times he found himself at the hospital anyway, sitting outside the treatment room and waiting, blending into the shadows when she was wheeled in or out. But then she'd spotted him and pitched such a fit that he reluctantly agreed to stay away.

Renovations were an ongoing thing at the house, too, and that was certainly keeping her busy.

If that wasn't enough, Aidan had secured property on the mountain (Ian still wasn't sure how he'd managed that) and was in the process of building what promised to be his finest restaurant yet. From what Ian had gleaned, it was to be built in the style of an ancient Greek temple, built right into the mountainside itself, affording diners a spectacular view of the valley below. With aggressive plans to open for New Year's, it was being touted as the number one most sought-after reservation on the East Coast, with a waiting list already a mile long.

Yes, Lexi's life was full. And his... not so much. He'd withdrawn. His family didn't try to talk much to him anymore, knowing they wouldn't get a response. He loved Patrick, loved spending the days with him. But the time he loved most of all? The time that made him feel the most alive? The one hour when he, Lexi, and Patrick were all together, in the same room, at the same time. Like a real family.

Only she was late. *Again.* His hour, the one chance he had to be with her, had now been reduced to ten minutes.

Taryn shot him another glance as she placed a handful of Cheerios in front of Patrick. He grabbed them with his chubby hand and held them out to Riley. "You're pacing again."

"Is there something I should know about?" Ian stopped pacing and looked directly at her.

Taryn looked away, avoiding the question. "Why do you ask?"

"Lexi's late again."

"She's not late. She's just not as early as she usually is. Look, I've got things covered here. Why don't you just go on in and help Jake?"

Ian's eyes narrowed. Not only was she avoiding his gaze, she was trying to get rid of him. "What are you not telling me, Taryn?"

She didn't answer, busying herself with cleaning up. "Why is she late?" he asked again.

"Why do you care?" She threw back at him. "God, Ian. You act like you're married or something." It was a direct hit, a knife in an open, festering wound.

"If it was up to me, we would be," he said through gritted teeth, trying to keep his voice level in front of the kids.

Taryn's violet eyes pinned him. "Why? So you could treat her like a leper in the comfort of your own home?"

"You don't know what you're talking about." Everyone believed he was cold, cruel, for keeping Lexi at arm's length. But none of them understood that what he did, he did out of a love so deep, so true that he would sacrifice everything to keep her safe. Living like this was hell, but it was nothing compared to what life would be like if she wasn't in it at all.

"Maybe not. But let me tell you what I do know. I know that Lexi loves you more than anything else in the world. That she would give anything if you would treat her like the loving, caring woman she is instead of a contagious disease. And that she still cries herself to sleep every night, holding on to a pillow that's wrapped in a shirt you left behind in Benton, because you can't man up and be there for her when she needs you the most."

Ian blinked. She still slept with his shirt? He remembered the first time he saw her wearing his T-shirt, how good that had made him feel. It still did, only now it was accompanied by a familiar ache, the one that made him cranky. Because *he* wanted to be the one she held on to, the one she turned to in the middle of the night, not his shirt.

But to suggest that he wasn't man enough to be there for her? Christ, he felt like he was dying inside. Staying away from Lexi was the hardest thing he had ever done.

Ian gave her a look that could have frozen

Niagara Falls, but she just waved him off. "Don't even try, Ian. Jake's death scowl is much scarier than yours. And let me tell you this: you think you're protecting her, but you're killing her more than that damn disease ever could."

"Hey," said Shane, blowing into the kitchen and grabbing some of the Cheerios from Patrick's tray. "What's up, big man?" He put his hand up for a high-five and Patrick obliged. Then he tickled beneath Riley's chin, making her giggle. Shane didn't acknowledge his brother. Ian was used to it. At first they had pleaded with them. Then they pointedly avoided him. Now they just ignored him.

"Have you heard anything yet?" Shane asked Taryn.

"Not yet." Taryn's eyes shot over to Ian and back in a silent but blatant warning. Shane took the hint and rerouted himself toward the fridge. Ian narrowed his eyes suspiciously, but said nothing.

Sean thundered in, giving his twin a shoulder bump. "Well?"

Ian materialized out of the shadows. Normally he was more than happy to stay out of their group discussions, especially where Lexi was concerned, because those discussions inevitably turned into something akin to an intervention. Today, however, he was already on edge, and their non-attention was pissing him off.

Something was going on, and it had something to do with Lexi. Ian felt that despite his own self-imposed distance, anything to do with Lexi was his business. Before he could say anything, Taryn's cell rang, the sweet sounds of AC/DC's *Highway to Hell* filling the kitchen.

"Yeah?" she answered into the phone, the hopefulness in her voice unmistakable. At that moment Riley decided to let out a wail, so Taryn stuck one finger in her ear and turned away. Even from where he stood Ian could easily see the slump of her shoulders.

"I see... And there's no... Yeah, okay... No, no problem, I can do that... Yeah, thanks Stace.... 'K... Bye."

She disconnected the call and took a deep breath before turning around. She looked at each of them briefly (Ian excluded) and shook her head.

Judging by their reactions, it was not good news. Shane and Sean shared a look, then made their exit, but not before shooting daggers at Ian.

"She's not coming," Ian said.

"No," Taryn agreed. "Patrick's going to hang out with us tonight, aren't you, big guy?" Taryn said with false cheeriness, picking up a washcloth and wiping the Cheerio remains from between his fingers. He grinned and giggled.

Lexi lived for her son. There was no way she would just leave him there without a damn good reason. The cold weight in Ian's stomach intensified. "Why not?" The mountain sized chip on his shoulder seemed a lot smaller suddenly.

Taryn paused. "You really don't know, do you?"

"*Taryn*," he warned.

"Ah, damn. Lexi's probably never going to speak to me again for this, but…"

chapter twenty-eight

"There's nothing I can do, Ian." Michael's expression was as calm as ever, but Ian could sense the turbulence, see the frustration in his brother's eyes.

Ian sat across from him in a state of mild shock. It wasn't the first time he'd heard those words come from his brother's mouth, but those other times had been few and far between, and they had never applied to someone in their family. And Lexi was family, which was the only reason Michael was even discussing this with him in the first place.

The test results from Lexi's first three months of the treatment showed very little improvement in her blood chemistry, and her overall health had taken a decided downturn, so much so that Michael had admitted her to a private room for the night for monitoring and rest.

"I thought the treatments were working." Ian's voice was hoarse.

There was sympathy in Michael's eyes. Sympathy and something else. Disappointment?

"That's what she wanted everyone to think." Yet based on what Taryn had told him earlier, no one else besides him seemed to be fooled.

"Talk to me, Mick."

Michael's eyes glittered, the only indication of the powerful emotions he kept hidden away. With each interminable second that ticked by, the vacuum in Ian's chest expanded. For Michael to hesitate that long, it had to be bad.

"She's exhausted," Michael finally said. "She's not sleeping, not eating, not taking care of herself. She puts everything she has into Patrick, the house, and the new restaurant. She's weakening to the point that the treatments are doing more harm than good. And the mind-fuck you're doing on her is not helping."

It wasn't possible. It simply wasn't possible. Ian saw her every day. Yes, she looked tired, but she had so much going on. And strained, yes, but he'd just assumed that was because of his presence. Ian imagined he looked much the same way. Being around each other, trying to hold it together, was hard.

He clenched his jaw and wrapped his hand around the arm of the chair so tightly it cracked. Michael leveled his blue-eyed stare at him. Two men, brothers, with equally intense Irish eyes, who had done and seen more together than most brothers do in a lifetime, faced off.

It was Ian who breathed first. "Tell me what to

do, Mick."

Michael shifted in his chair. "It's all or nothing, Ian. This is not something you can walk away from, because I'm telling you right now: if you turn away from her again, it will kill her. And then, hell, I might just have to kill you myself."

Flames flared in Ian's eyes. He would expect those words from Kieran, or Jake, or any of his other brothers. But Michael? Michael was the healer, the one who never took sides. It was a testament to just how much of an asshole he'd been.

"I can't lose her." Ian's head lowered. He rested his forearms on his powerful legs, his hands rubbing at his eyes. All of the rigid, hard lines of his body sagged. "Fuck, Mick," he said, his voice weary. "I just can't do this anymore. I swear to God…" His voice failed him for a moment, until he took a deep breath and gathered himself. "If I can't hold her in my arms again…"

Ian felt a big, warm hand on his shoulder. It was nearly his undoing. He'd allowed no one, with the exception of his son, to get close enough to touch him these last six months, afraid the human contact might finally break down the last of his defenses.

"All right, then," Michael said softly. He gave Ian a few moments before he started outlining a plan.

* * *

It was hard to open her eyes. It felt as though fifty-pound sandbags had been laid over her lids. Her head pounded with the force of a thousand out-of-sync sledgehammers. Her mouth was so dry she didn't even attempt to swallow, knowing it would hurt. She was so tired of hurting.

"Morning, Lex." The words, though spoken in Michael's deep, soothing voice, were like a bullhorn wired directly into her aural nerves. She winced, making her head throb all that much more.

"Son of a bitch," she whispered hoarsely. "You drugged me."

"I'm sorry about that, Lex," Michael said, his voice reduced to a whisper. "Your body needed some time to rest." The regret in his words was genuine.

"Go to hell." Lexi's eyes were shut tight against the pain.

Unfazed, he wrapped his fingers around her wrist to check her pulse, then nodded in approval. "Much better."

Unable to help herself, she groaned.

"Hangover's a bitch, huh?" he asked, though his words were gentle, receiving a barely perceptible nod in response. "I can help with that." A few clicks and swishes later, she felt a wonderful, cooling sensation flowing through her body as the pain started to ease almost instantly.

"Better?"

"Mmmmm," she answered, her face relaxing. "That's nice."

Michael chuckled. "So I've been told."

"Keep it coming and maybe I won't have to kick your ass."

Michael smiled. "Tease. Feel up for a visitor?" he asked. "Someone's very anxious to see you."

Michael nodded toward the door and Ian entered, holding Patrick. The little boy's eyes lit up at the sight of his mama, his chubby arms extended as he reached for her.

Lexi avoided looking directly at Ian, concentrating on her son's face instead. Michael raised the bed slowly so that she could hold him in her lap. Patrick nuzzled his lips against her face and mumbled, his words still unintelligible but his meaning clear. Lexi's eyes filled with tears. "I missed you too, buddy."

His eyes were so like his father's. They had the power to fill her heart with so much love her chest felt like it might just explode.

"She can leave as soon as she's ready," Michael said to Ian.

Lexi's gaze snapped up. Michael smiled and winked at her. "Later, beautiful." And then the sneaky son of a bitch was gone.

"What is he talking about?" Lexi said, narrowing her eyes at Ian over her baby's head.

"You're coming home with me," Ian informed her, placing the overnight bag on the chair.

"The hell I am."

Ian ignored her, pulling out a pair of jeans, and a cotton T. He made a show of holding up the silken thong and matching bra for a moment, admiring them, before adding them to the pile. When his eyes met hers again they held a promise she hadn't seen there in a long, long time.

He laid the clothes beside her, pulling Patrick back into his arms. "Come on, buddy," he said. "Let's let mommy get dressed. Unless she needs help, that is." His eyes flashed at her again, raking across her body and Lexi felt a quick, sudden spasm across her middle. He held her gaze for a long moment, as if daring her to defy him.

Taryn chose that moment to breeze into the room. "Easy there, big guy," she said, pushing Ian toward the door. "I got this one."

Ian looked back at her one more time, and she thought she saw a flash of disappointment in them. Surely it was just a residual effect of the happy juice Michael had been pumping into her.

"Ready, Lex?" Taryn asked.

A familiar band tightened around her chest, the instinctual warning that told her she'd been set up. "*Et tu?*" she said icily.

Taryn laughed, looking happier than Lexi had seen her in ages. "You bet your ass," she said with a grin that extended from ear to ear. "You're coming back to the pub, which means you and I are going to have some real quality girl time, Lex. And, might I say, it's about time. Too much testosterone, not enough estrogen in that place, you get me?"

When Lexi made no move to get out of bed, Taryn whipped the sheet from Lexi's legs, ignoring her death stare. "I don't want to go to the pub," Lexi said, hating the childlike pout she heard in her own voice.

"Tough shit."

"Excuse me?"

"You heard me." Lexi had always secretly admired Taryn for her hard-ass attitude. Now that she was on the receiving end of it, not so much.

Lexi tried to pull away from Taryn as the other woman coaxed her out of bed, but Taryn's grip was like iron. Was Taryn that strong, or had Lexi allowed herself to become that weak?

"You're a real bitch, you know that?"

Rather than be insulted, Taryn laughed again. "I've been trying to tell everyone that for years. Don't know why everyone acts so surprised. Now come on. Everybody's waiting on you."

Lexi tried to hold her head high as she was led in through the private, back entrance of Jake's Irish Pub, Ian's strong hand stubbornly held at the small of her back. If she hadn't let herself get so weak she would have kicked him good and hard. As it was, he didn't even acknowledge the few times she'd tried to stomp on his toes, other than the slight flexing of his hand in warning.

"Try to move away from me," he'd whispered

against her ear earlier, "and I will sling you over my shoulder and paddle your ass." It was an empty threat, she knew, but it still sent a shiver up and down the length of her spine.

Every available space in the oversized kitchen was filled with Callaghans. She felt almost as awkward as she had the first time she'd been here more than a decade ago. She had the sudden, intense urge to make them all a batch of cookies. But instead of Tollhouse morsels, she'd slip in some chocolate Ex-lax...

The welcome was understated, but sincere. Each of them hugged her, and with each embrace, she felt the anger slipping away a little more, stripping her down to the part of her that scared her the most: her heart. It was the streaming sixty-second video feed from Kieran, stationed God-only-knew-where, though, that broke through the last of her shields.

"I'm coming home soon, Lex," he said into the camera, "and I'm hoping you'll be there when I do."

Lexi suddenly felt ashamed. Somewhere in her battles with Ian she'd forgotten how much Kieran's friendship and support meant to her. By shutting them out, she was doing to them exactly what Ian was doing to her. And she knew better than anyone how much that hurt.

"I'm so sorry, Kier," she whispered into the mobile device. "I'll try." From somewhere behind her, Taryn sniffed and excused herself while the others exited quietly.

chapter twenty-nine

Ian sensed Lexi's rising tension as she looked around, no doubt bemused by what she saw. Her clothes, make-up, and a few other personal items had been moved into Ian's suite of rooms on the third floor. Riley and Patrick would be sharing a nursery, he told her. At the moment, both children were on the floor, Patrick eagerly pulling toys from the brightly-colored storage box and offering them to Riley while Taryn watched over them protectively.

Lexi set her jaw and crossed her arms over her chest. "I didn't agree to any of this."

Ian shrugged and closed the door to his bedroom, giving them some privacy. Whether she agreed or not at this point didn't matter. He'd be damned if he'd watch her destroy herself. She could fight him as much as she wanted, but they both knew she'd lose.

"Explain to me again what you think you're doing?"

"It's all very simple," he said as he sat down on

the overstuffed chair in the corner of his room and patted his leg in an invitation to join him. Instead of joining him, however, she lifted her chin and took several steps in the opposite direction. That little show of defiance had him aching already. He shot her a look of warning, but she ignored it.

"You and Patrick will live here, with me, at least for the time being, while renovations continue on the house. Then we'll see. I'll take you wherever you need to go during the day. You can rest here at night while I'm working downstairs. Taryn will be here to help with the kids and whatever else you need."

She smiled. When she spoke, her voice was far too sweet to be genuine. "Really, Ian, you can't possibly be serious."

"Oh, but I am, baby," he said, his voice deliberately pitched low and seductive, though his heart was pounding. It wasn't going to be easy winning her over, he knew that. But he would.

He patted his lap again, beckoning her. "Come here and let me show you how serious I am."

"I don't think so." Her tone was cool, uninterested, but he knew it was a lie. Her eyes gave her away. His heart leapt with hope, along with his arousal.

"Don't make me come over there and get you, Lexi," he growled, deepening his voice. She shivered, but stood her ground.

"Don't make idle threats, Ian. I have nothing

you want, you've made that perfectly clear. But if you're feeling a little anxious, I'm sure there's some young thing downstairs that'll have you. You know, someone strong and healthy enough to handle a big, tough guy like you."

He absorbed the blow, seeing it for what it was. A self-defense mechanism. There was no defense for the all-out attack he had planned.

"I don't think so." He made no attempt to hide his body's natural reaction to her as he stood up slowly. Her eyes flicked the length of his body and back up again. "Only one woman can satisfy me, baby."

"Yeah?" she taunted, but he saw the familiar flare of heat in her eyes as she took a step backward. "And who might that be?"

Ian's eyes dipped lustily toward her chest as he stepped toward her, his movements smooth and graceful like the predator he was. "Come here and I'll show you."

"Go to hell, Ian."

"I've been there, baby. For more than a year. And I'm ready to come home."

"Aren't you afraid you'll hurt me?" she asked, continuing to back up until she felt the wall behind her. Ian continued his unhurried advance until he was only inches away. His palms pressed against the wall on either side of her head, caging her as he leaned forward until nothing separated them but the thinnest slice of air.

"Yes," he admitted, his voice a tortured whisper. "But I'll die before I hurt you again, Lexi. And I'm going to trust you to be honest with me this time. Can you do that for me?"

"I never lied to you," she protested.

"You let me ravage you, Lexi," he said, his lips skimming across her forehead, along her temple, her cheeks. "And it hurt you."

"You didn't hurt me, Ian," she gasped, lifting her chin to give him access to her neck. "You never hurt me."

"I saw the bruises, baby. I have nightmares about what I did to you." Ian kissed his way along her jaw, his touch scorching, yet infinitely light. Lexi bunched her hands into his hair, and he wanted to shout at the bliss of it.

"Not your fault…" Lexi arched into him. Ian groaned, low and deep, the rumble vibrating through both of them.

"God, I love how you taste, Lexi." His mouth dipped lower, his tongue licked along her collar bone as one hand reached up under her cotton T. She sucked in a breath, encouraging him. Her mouth could say anything she wanted, but her body told him the truth.

"Ian," she gasped, grabbing fistfuls of his hair. "Don't tease me, Ian. I can't bear it."

Ian growled low in his throat. A second later her T-shirt was being lifted over her head and he was kissing his way down to the swell of her breasts. His hands cupped her, his thumbs rasped almost lazily across the nipples, so hard beneath the silken bra she wore.

His hands moved lower as he took one breast into his mouth, suckling her through the material, biting back a curse when he felt her ribs clearly beneath the skin.

"*Ian...*" she warned breathlessly. He pulled away just enough to look into her eyes, now half-dazed with hunger. The need he saw there speared through him, nearly knocking him on his ass. For the first time in a long time, he allowed himself to see what was there, and it humbled him greatly.

"I don't deserve you," he murmured, wrapping his arms around her waist and lifting her. She was like nothing in his arms; too light, too thin. How could he not have seen what he was doing to her? He'd thought he could keep her safe by keeping his distance, but the reality of the situation finally hit home. Lexi needed him. She fucking needed him, and he would never let her down again.

He laid her carefully on the bed, slipping off her shoes. Next came her jeans, and it was all he could do not to cry out in anguish when he saw the bones protruding from her hips. She was still beautiful, always would be to him, but he missed the full, hot flesh of her curves.

"Twenty pounds," he whispered, placing hot, stinging little kisses across her sunken abdomen as he removed her thong. "I want you to gain at least twenty pounds. And for each one I'm going to do this…"

Lexi's back arched, as Ian pressed himself between her legs, kissing the inside of her thighs. His hot breath blew over her sex and she trembled. It fed his hunger, made his eyes glitter with need. "Christ," he whispered, awed by her reaction. He'd never been so needed, so wanted, by anyone. He must have been a complete idiot to believe she would be better off without him.

He placed tiny, light kisses along her sex as his hands pressed her legs open wider. A long, languorous lick of his tongue had him groaning again. There was nothing like his Lexi. He buried his face, nose to chin in her sweet, slick folds. He felt her heels against his shoulder blades, her legs slung over his shoulders as she surrendered herself to him. He would reward her greatly for that, for this chance to love her again. To feel her fingers in his hair again, scraping against his scalp. Ah, it was heaven.

The muscles in his back flexed as he took her with his mouth, rimming her entrance with his tongue before dipping into her. She cried out softly, tugging on his hair, pushing him into her with her legs. She was close, on the edge, and he wanted her falling off, right into him.

Ian began a steady, methodical pattern that had her writhing beneath him. A few short, quick suckles against her sensitive nub. Long, full strokes along her lips. Teasing circles around her entrance, then dips of his tongue deep to stroke the sensitive inner flesh until she held her breath. All the while, his hands stroked over her belly, her breasts, her hips. Then, just as she was about to come, he'd begin all over again.

"Ian, oh God, Ian," she begged, raking his scalp with her nails. They were too short. He wanted them longer. He wanted her talons gripping him hard enough to draw blood.

"What do you want, baby?" he asked in between licks.

"Please, Ian. I need to come. Make me come, Ian."

"Say you love me, Lex."

"I love you. I love you so much," she sobbed.

"I love you too, baby. Say you'll stay with me."

Lexi hesitated, her fingers stilled. Ian flicked his tongue over her a few more times, holding her hips in place.

"Say it, Lexi," he coaxed, blowing softly on her, making her shudder. His heart beat faster, stronger, needing to hear her say the words. "Say it and I'll let you come, baby. Promise me."

Lexi wriggled beneath him, but he wouldn't allow her to move an inch. "You'll stop..."

"No, I promise you, I'll never stop. As long as you stay, I'll never stop again. I swear it." Ian dipped his tongue into her again, swirling, filling his senses with his woman.

"I'll stay." She breathed the words so quietly he wasn't sure he actually heard them. He lifted his head enough to look up across the span of her body, caressing her with his chin. "What was that?"

"I'll stay," she said, stronger this time. "But only if you let me love you, too."

Ian grinned in triumph. "That's my good girl," he crooned, before submerging himself within her with renewed fervor. Lexi was several inches off the surface of the bed when he finally took her over the edge. He held onto her as she seized beneath him, crying out his name in tortured whispers.

When the tremors began to fade, Ian crawled up along her body and held her to him. Only then did he realize she was crying. A few moments of intense fear gripped him. Had he hurt her again? But then her arms wrapped around him and she pressed her body close to his, and he knew the truth. They were tears of joy, of relief. Because he had finally come home.

"Sshhh, baby, it's okay," he told her as she gripped him. He felt the tension returning to her body, felt the desperate hold she had on him. It didn't take a genius to figure out what she was thinking, and he hated the fact that he had put so much fear, so much uncertainty into her heart. He kissed the top of her head, making a silent promise to spend the rest of his life rectifying that.

"You're not leaving?" she asked, her voice shaky.

"No." His gut twisted as she burrowed into him a little more, knowing she was trying to decide whether or not to trust him. Her fingers had a death grip on his shirt.

"Lexi," he said, his voice low and resonant. He felt her body tense all over again as she held her breath, waiting. "Lexi, touch me, baby, before I die from the want of it."

Slowly, her fingers uncurled from his shirt, enough to slip beneath the hem. His stomach curled in as he felt her hands on his bare skin. His arm tightened around her as she ran along the ridges of solid muscle there, skimming teasingly along the waistband of his jeans. Her touch was more tentative than it had once been, as if afraid he would run away if she made one false move.

"Ah, baby, I love when you have your hands on me," he encouraged, hoping to feel the bold heat which with she once touched him; her fearless, hungry exploration of his body. With a heart beating so hard and fast he could feel it against his ribs, she moved her palm over his abs, along his ribs, across his pecs, re-learning the feel of him. He forced himself to be patient, to control the urge to flip her onto her back and take her till she was screaming his name again.

* * *

Lexi closed her eyes and moved her fingers

over his heated flesh, tracing the contours of the steel beneath the skin. Just the feel of him against her filled her with a peace she had not known for far too long. His strength and power seeped into her, making her feel alive again. The dark, masculine scent that was pure Ian filled her lungs, sending delicious tingles through her entire body.

Feeling emboldened, Lexi began moving her hands downward, keeping her movements slow, giving him the chance to stop her. He didn't. His hands moved restlessly over her back and arms; she could feel him flexing his fingers with the effort to hold back.

Lexi stroked him through his jeans, running the length of his shaft from the tip of his waistband all the way down between his legs. He gave a low growl, a purely masculine sound that had juices flowing from her once again in preparation for what she wanted.

"More, Lexi," he pleaded. "*More.*"

Her fingers were trembling so badly he reached down with his free hand and helped her, undoing the clasp himself. She was able to pull down the zipper, immediately cupping him through his boxer briefs. He sucked in a breath and cursed. Seconds later he was shucking the remainder of his clothing completely.

Lexi could not turn away from him. Her Ian was magnificent. Incredibly hard and thick, his cock strained toward her. She encircled as much as she could with her hand, stroking it lovingly, feeling him jerk beneath her. Ian was her man. The only man she had ever touched in this way, the only man she'd ever wanted to. And he always would be, no matter what, at least in her mind. There was only Ian.

Her first. Her only.

Lexi knew exactly what she wanted to do, but memories of consequences incurred the last time she followed her natural urges kept her from doing so. God, she loved him. Wanted to taste him so badly her mouth watered at the thought of it. Still, she was hesitant. What if he pushed her away again? No matter how much she wanted him, she couldn't risk losing this closeness he was offering her without being sure.

Lexi lifted her head up enough to look into his face. "Can I?" she asked.

"Yes," he answered, his voice strained even as his eyes begged her. "Please, Lexi. It's okay, I swear it."

She slid down his body, again slowly, giving him the chance to change his mind. He didn't. Instead, he lifted his head up enough to watch. Lexi's lips parted, hovering just above him. She looked questioningly into his eyes once more, praying he wouldn't refuse her.

"Yes, Lexi. Suck me, baby. I'm begging you. Please. I need you to love me with that sweet, sweet mouth of yours."

Her eyes half-closed slowly as she gave herself over to the hunger raging for control. Lexi held him in her hand, pressing soft, wet kisses along his shaft until he fought to breathe. Then she began to lick him, base to tip, swirling around his balls, then starting all over again. Ian's hands fisted in the bedding with her exquisite torture. When she finally took him in her mouth, his hips bucked, but he made no move to stop her.

His body tensed as he grew closer to his peak. Lexi felt it coming, too. She doubled her efforts, sucking harder, stroking faster, squeezing him with gentle, agonizing pressure.

"Baby," Ian whispered, pulling her on top of him and holding her like a precious treasure. "I need to be inside you," he whispered. "Straddle me, Lexi. Take me inside you."

She needed him, too. So badly. Before he changed his mind, she allowed him to guide her onto him slowly, holding her hips to keep her from moving too quickly. The hiss he let out as she came down around him was music to her ears.

"Yes, Lexi. Jesus. Ride me, baby."

Lexi placed her palms on his chest and began to move. She rocked her hips forward and backward, lifting up and then impaling herself again. It only took a few strokes for her to begin to lose herself.

Lexi tossed her head back. Ian was inside her. *Ian was inside her*. Nothing had ever felt better, more right. She was so tired of worrying about what was going to happen next. Right now, at this moment, she had her man inside her, and all was right with her world.

When she came, she came hard. Ian held her in place and pumped into her from below, one, two three thrusts before lifting her up and pulling out. She collapsed on his chest, feeling the hot jets of his release shooting across her behind, up onto her back. It was one of the most erotic things she'd ever felt, but it was disappointing, too.

"You pulled out," she said quietly, after their heartbeats had begun to return to normal.

"Yeah."

Her finger traced little circles against his chest as she lay tucked beneath his shoulder, her body half covering his.

"I didn't want to," he said.

"I know." And she did know. Just as she knew exactly why he had done it. Because another pregnancy right now would probably kill her.

Ian's hand moved slowly up and down her back. As if sensing her thoughts, he said, "I want more kids with you, Lex."

"You do?"

"Hell, yes. But if it's not right for us, then I'm okay with that, too. As long as I have you and Patrick, I don't need anything else."

Long moments of silence passed between them. Michael had told her that if the new treatments were successful, there was no reason she couldn't live a fairly normal life, including having more children, something she'd been terrified she would not be able to do.

It wouldn't be easy; she would have to be extra-careful, even more cautious than usual, but it would be worth it. And she definitely would like Patrick to have a little brother or sister someday. Maybe several. But in order to make that happen, she had to do a lot better than she had been.

"I love you, Ian."

"I love you, too, Lexi."

chapter thirty

"Lexi, baby, time to wake up." Ian's big body was curled around hers. She hadn't slept much. She'd drifted in and out of slumber, half-expecting Ian to be gone if she allowed herself to fall asleep too deeply. It was exceptionally difficult. Wrapped in his strong arms, suffused with his warmth, her body melted against him, feeling safe and secure.

Her mind, on the other hand, refused to relax. If he left again, she wanted to know right away instead of thinking everything was okay when it wasn't. But Ian hadn't left. He'd stayed right there beside her throughout the night. And when she reached out to him in the darkness, he didn't turn away. After getting up to check on Patrick, something she still did several times a night, he'd been waiting for her, pulling her into him as if she'd never left.

One eye peeked open, expecting to see sunlight. The bedroom, however, was still dark. The glowing numbers on the nightstand clock read four a.m.

"What's wrong?" she asked, her mother's

worry spiking across her consciousness. "Is Patrick okay?"

"He's fine," Ian assured her, pulling back the covers gently and planting a kiss on her shoulder. Even that was enough to have her stirring.

"Oh, no," he chuckled at her sensual moan. "Not this morning."

No sex? Then what was the point of getting up this early? Lexi grabbed the bedding and pulled it right back up to her chin, burrowing into her pillow with a growl. "I don't get up till seven," she informed him, her voice muffled by the down.

"Not today you don't," he said, yanking the covers down again. "Coffee, a light breakfast, then you're due at the fitness center by five."

"I don't belong to a fitness center," she grumbled. "But please, feel free to go on without me. Wake me up when you get back."

"Doesn't work that way, baby," he said, the smile evident in his voice. He slipped his arms beneath her body and lifted her like a doll. She curled into his chest, burrowing her face into his neck. The next thing she knew a blast of cool water was streaming down over her.

"Ian!" she shrieked, clinging to his body for warmth against the sudden shock of cold.

"Sshhh," he warned. "Everyone else is sleeping."

"Of course they're sleeping," she said through gritted teeth. "It's still the middle of the night."

The corners of Ian's mouth quirked as he slipped out of her grasp. "You've got ten minutes," he told her, holding her under the water. Then he was gone, leaving Lexi to wonder how difficult it would be to shove a bar of soap up that arrogant yet delectable ass of his.

She was still grumbling when she appeared in the kitchenette wearing the loose Capri sweats and T he'd set in the bathroom for her.

"You know," he said, his eyes amused as he looked her up and down, "I don't recall you being this grumpy in the morning."

"That's because waking up for early morning sex is infinitely preferable to being tossed in a cold shower."

His lips quirked. "You're not strong enough for early morning sex yet." His eyes began to glow. "Once a day, baby, till we get you healthy again. Follow the program, keep up with your treatments and we'll take it from there."

Once a day? Was he insane? And what the hell was this program he was talking about? She looked at the food he'd laid out on the counter: coffee, soy milk, a banana, and a whole grain muffin with peanut butter. She narrowed her eyes.

"So what are you telling me? If I'm a good girl and do as I'm told you'll reward me with sex?" she asked facetiously.

"Exactly." Ian's eyes glittered.

Lexi had to make a conscious effort to keep her

jaw from hitting the floor. "You must be joking."

"Not even close," he told her, sliding a paper in front of her. "This is your schedule for today."

Lexi glanced down, not believing what she saw. Every hour of her day was planned out, including meals, workouts, rest periods, with a few hours allotted for working. "You're insane," she said, pushing the paper away. "I'm not doing this."

"Yes, Lexi, you are." Ian didn't raise his voice, but his tone took on an authoritative quality that breached no argument. He pushed the paper back toward her. "And I'll tell you why you are going to do it."

Lexi watched, her eyes widening as Ian reached down into his sweats, his arousal obvious as he stroked himself. It was so incredibly erotic she had to tighten her thighs. "Because I need you, Lexi. And I think you need me, too. You're not the only one who misses early morning sex."

She swallowed hard, licking her lips. He had no idea just how much she needed him. Or did he? It was both a relief and a disappointment when he tucked himself away and leaned back against the counter.

"What are these numbers?" she asked, noticing the values etched next to the various items on the schedule.

"Weighted point values," he said, grinning. "Points earn you rewards."

"Rewards?"

He nodded. "Rewards. Positive reinforcement for good behavior. Be a good girl, Lex, and you will be rewarded, baby."

"And what exactly are these rewards?"

He shrugged. "Whatever you want. Rides on the Harley. Midnight picnics. Sexual favors." At the mention of the last, she inhaled sharply, making him laugh, though his eyes reflected the same hunger she was sure was in hers.

A soft knock at the door had her reining in her wild thoughts.

"Now who is that at this ungodly hour?" Lexi asked, but Ian didn't seem surprised in the least. She understood why a few moments later when Shane appeared, looking wide awake in light sweats and a muscle shirt under a black jacket. Without apology, he grabbed her coffee mug and downed the rest of the contents in a single swig.

"Let's go, Lex."

Lexi looked questioningly at Ian, expecting him to say something. He didn't. She started getting a bad feeling in her stomach. "Go where?"

"To the gym."

Ian grinned. "Meet your new personal trainer, baby."

"Oh no. Oh *hell* no."

"Oh hell yes," Shane said, his eyes sparkling.

"Ian, do something!" she said helplessly.

Ian ignored her pleas and regarded Shane. "Have her back by eight-thirty. Aidan's expecting her at nine o'clock."

"Ian!" she shrieked as Shane grabbed her hand and tugged her toward the door. Ian, however, made no move to come to her aid. He leaned against the counter, one leg crossed casually over the other at the ankle, feet bare, coffee in hand. "You're not coming?"

"Fuck no," he said cheerily. "Too goddamned early. I'm going back to bed."

* * *

The gym time (an hour of swimming, followed by an introductory yoga class) was followed up by meeting with Aidan over breakfast, then working for a few hours. Ian's schedule allotted four hours a day to start, which allowed Lexi to make progress on planning the menu, lining up suppliers, and so forth. It was much less than the ten hours a day she had been putting in, but Aidan was just as immovable as Ian when she tried to discuss it with him.

"So, you were in on this, too, I take it." Lexi sipped her herbal tea (apparently she was only permitted one cup of coffee per day) as Aidan pulled out yet another folder of natural food suppliers in the Mediterranean. It wasn't as much of a question as an accusation, but it was spoken without any sharpness.

"How long have we known each other, Lex?"

He left the file unopened and sat back in his chair. For the first time, Lexi noticed how tired he looked.

"A long time."

Aidan smiled. "Yeah, a long time. And I have never been as worried about you as I have been these last few months. All the times you were in the hospital, all the times you needed a transfusion, I didn't worry so much, because I always knew that you'd come through it okay. You had so much life in you, Lex. So much inner strength. I never doubted you, not once."

"But then... I don't know. You gave up. And I, like everyone else who cares about you, had to sit back and watch you destroy yourself a little more each day. So when Ian called me and told me about what he and Michael had cooked up, hell, yes I jumped on board. And I'll not apologize for it."

He smiled wryly. "I'll admit it's a shot to my ego, though. I kind of liked playing hero all by myself."

Lexi laughed softly. "You *are* my hero, Aidan. You think I was the strong one, but you were the one holding me up all these years. I never could have made it this far without you. I am so sorry I made you worry so much."

"Just promise me you'll work with us on this, okay?" he said, his eyes shining.

"I promise."

The meals and the workout kept Lexi focused, and by the end of the four hours, she was amazed at what she had been able to accomplish. Ian arrived to pick her up with Patrick in tow. He was taking her to the nearby town of Birch Falls for a lunch appointment with Johnny to discuss renovations on the house. Lexi was forbidden from doing any of the work herself, but Johnny assured her she would be pleased with the results.

The best part of all was having Ian by her side, smiling at her, talking with her, touching her and sneaking kisses whenever he could.

After meeting with Johnny, Lexi was required to "rest". Ian told her that could include anything not too physically demanding. Fortunately, he was flexible enough to allow for some "rewards" and "incentives for good behavior" while Patrick took his nap.

Dinner was prepared in the pub kitchen. By popular demand, Lexi was allowed to oversee and assist in the meal preparation. Jack Callaghan joked that it was the first time so many of his boys ate a meal together in years, and hoped that it would become a regular event.

Lexi was not allowed to clean up the kitchen afterwards. She didn't protest that one too much.

After dinner, Lexi retired upstairs with Patrick. Together they watched movies, played games, read books, often with Taryn and Riley. When the kids went down for the night, Lexi had time to herself. Sometimes she and Taryn would curl up with a movie and popcorn; sometimes they'd go their separate ways, each comfortable in the knowledge that the other was only a soft knock away.

The support she received was overwhelming, and Lexi felt blessed.

chapter thirty-one

Lexi nuzzled Patrick on his belly, making him laugh. It was a beautiful fall day; the region was in the midst of an Indian summer. The unseasonably warm temperature and clear skies were perfect for spending an hour or two by the nearby lake.

"So. You doing okay?" Ian asked, leaning back on his elbows, watching them play together.

Lexi turned to smile at him, and felt her heart skip a beat. Somehow, she knew it always would when he smiled at her like that.

"I have to admit, it's going pretty well." And it was. Each day was better than the last as she grew accustomed to the new routine. She felt better than she had in a long time, and this afternoon's check up with Michael had been encouraging.

"You say that like you're surprised. Does my woman doubt me?"

His woman. Is that what she was? Her mind answered with a resounding *Yes!* She always had been, and she was beginning to realize that she always would be. She laughed softly, shaking her head. "It's too early to tell, but... I think this could actually work."

Ian rose a little higher. "Yeah?"

"Yeah."

Patrick crawled up his daddy's leg and stood on his lap, gripping his shirt with two beefy hands. Looking at the two of them, Lexi couldn't have been happier. Right here, right now, was exactly where she wanted to be.

Could it have been only a week ago her life seemed so bleak? She had sat in Michael's office, knowing the results of her tests before he opened his mouth. And she hadn't really cared. The only thing keeping her going at all had been her son, and even that was barely enough some days. On those days, she saw how happy Patrick was with Ian and Taryn and all of his doting uncles and grandfather, and wondered if he wouldn't be better off without her. More than once, she felt guilty for taking him away from all that.

A tear slipped down her cheek.

"Hey," Ian said softly. "Are those tears?"

She nodded, too afraid to trust her voice.

"Are they good tears?"

She nodded again, and Ian pulled her against him. Patrick relinquished his hold on Ian with one hand, grabbing for Lexi so that he held both of them. In a move so tender, so sweet, Patrick studied Lexi's face and touched his hand to her tears and then looked straight into his father's eyes questioningly.

"It's okay, bud," Ian told him. "Mommy's happy 'cause she loves us so much."

Patrick grinned, showing all four of his teeth.

Three Months Later – January

"So?"

Ian sat hand in hand with Lexi, neither of them touching the back of their seats. Lexi's leg bobbed in anxious anticipation, but Ian was unnaturally still. Michael's face gave absolutely nothing away. He looked down once again at the papers in his hand.

"Jesus Christ, Mick. You must have read that thing ten times already. What does it say?"

Michael looked at his brother, his blue eyes as intense as Lexi had ever seen them. He put down Lexi's latest test results and pinched the bridge of his nose between his thumb and forefinger, sighing. Lexi felt her heart drop clear out of her chest, landing somewhere around her feet. Her bottom lip began to tremble.

She had done everything right. She had kept to her diet, exercised every day, took her treatments diligently and without complaint. She forced herself to rest, to pace herself --- something that was increasingly difficult as the new restaurant got closer to opening its doors.

Of course, everything was much easier once she opened her heart and accepted the love and support of her new family. Whenever it started getting too hard, they would keep her going. Whenever she was tempted to overextend herself, someone was always there to rein her in.

By far the biggest motivation was the wedding, slated for the end of February. Lexi wanted everything to be perfect when she and Ian started their life together "officially", not the least of which was the desire to fulfill Ian's wish for more children.

Worst of all was the feeling that she had let everyone down, especially Ian. He would be devastated, and no doubt find some way to blame himself. If he pulled away again, she simply wouldn't survive it.

Slowly she turned to face him. She would be strong for him; she would show him that she wasn't ready to give up. This was a minor setback, that's all.

But when her eyes met his, she did not see the disappointment she'd expected. Nor was there any trace of anger, frustration, or sadness. His clear blue eyes were dancing, one side of his mouth curving into that sexy half-smile that made her catch her breath. What the hell?

Apparently Ian had seen something that Lexi had not in Michael's dramatic pause, and she had the distinct impression she was missing something.

She cast a glance toward Michael, who, despite his best efforts, was curling his mouth into a smile as well.

Before she realized what was happening, Ian leaned over and captured her mouth with his. There was no gentleness in the gesture, just a flood of emotion as he cupped the back of her neck and deepened the kiss. Michael cleared his throat a few times before Ian released her.

Light-headed from Ian's sudden and unexpected possession, she looked dazedly at Michael. "Why do I feel like I am missing something? The results were bad, weren't they?"

"No," Michael said, smiling. "They are good. Very, very good. So good in fact that it's going to be a nightmare."

She blinked, more confused than ever. "And this is bad why?"

"Because," he said, with a long-suffering sigh. "You've just made medical history, Lex. You have just proven that this treatment can work. They'll be coming out of the woodwork trying to get to you." Lexi paled visibly at the thought.

"Did I tell you my brother was a biochemical genius or what?" Ian said proudly. "We have to keep them at bay, though, Mick. I don't want Lexi showcased as a lab rat or anything."

Michael nodded. "Agreed. I'll call Dr. McKenzie this afternoon and take care of things on this end. We'll work something out. The best thing would be to keep Lexi's name out of it entirely, but it might take some effort on your part. There will be lots of records to be adjusted."

"Not a problem," Ian assured him.

Trying to follow a conversation between these two was like being carried downriver on a swift current, only catching glimpses of what was speeding by, but she was starting to get the gist. "You mean," she said slowly, looking at Michael, "you aren't going to take any credit for this? Why?"

He smiled enigmatically, his face as calm and serene as ever. Michael had been the one to find the right combination of organic compounds. He'd been the one to take Dr. McKenzie's raw ideas and turn them into something viable, practical, and apparently, effective. Yet he was going to remain quietly in the shadows and let someone else take the credit?

"Seeing you healthy is all that matters to me, Lex. The fact that I won't have to watch my brother destroy himself is a bonus." He winked. "Though admittedly, I do have five others, and he is arguably the most irritating."

Lexi was speechless. "I don't know what to say."

Ian squeezed her hand. "Make his day and tell him he doesn't have to wear a tux at the wedding."

* * *

The celebration that ensued was a memorable one. Though not yet officially open to the public, with quite a few well-placed phone calls and a natural deviance Lexi had been fostering for years, she reserved a special room at the new restaurant and managed to prepare a surprise feast in appreciation of her new family.

They all, of course, worried that she had done too much. And as they arrived, one by one, they proceeded to gang up on her. Lexi didn't mind. By that point everything had been prepared and she could allow herself to sit and enjoy the evening with them.

The food was excellent. The atmosphere, divine. But as Lexi looked around, there was nothing quite as wonderful as the family and friends that now surrounded her.

"You have outdone yourself, Lex," said Aidan quietly afterward, sneaking up behind Lexi as she personally thanked each of the staff for helping her with her special surprise. Keeping the celebration from him had been one of the most difficult challenges, but she had managed. "However, if there are any more surprises, I think I might just have to fire you."

She laughed. "Only one more, and I think it's on its way out now."

Aidan raised an eyebrow, just as he heard roaring laughter and cheers coming from the private room. Together they peeked through the window, and Aidan couldn't help but laugh when he spotted the biggest plate of chocolate chip cookies he had ever seen being delivered to the table.

Thanks for reading Ian and Lexi's story

If you liked this book, then please consider posting a review online! It's really easy, only takes a few minutes, and makes a huge difference to independent authors who don't have the mega-budgets of the big-time publishers behind them.

Log on to your favorite online retailer (or Goodreads) and just tell others what you thought, even if it's just a line or two. That's it! A good review is one of the nicest things you can do for any author.

As always, I welcome feedback. Email me at abbiezandersromance@gmail.com. Or visit my awesome website at abbiezandersromance.com and subscribe to my newsletter to be the first to know about new releases, sales, sneak peeks, and updates.

Like my FB page (AbbieZandersRomance), and/or follow me on Twitter (@AbbieZanders).

Thanks again, and may all of your ever-afters be happy ones!

♥ *Abbie*

Also by Abbie Zanders

Contemporary Romance

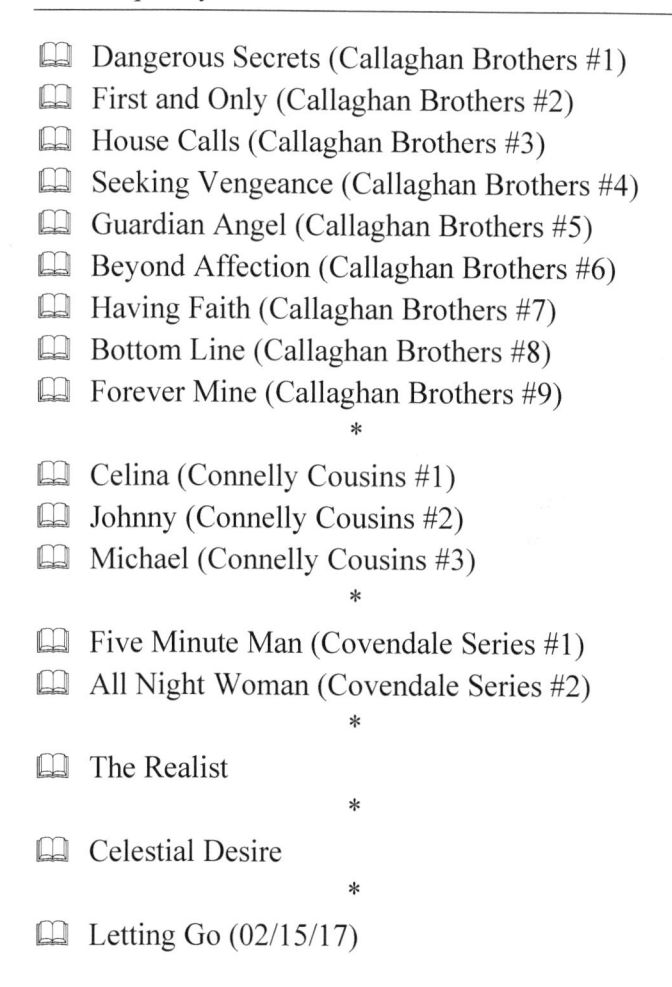

- 📖 Dangerous Secrets (Callaghan Brothers #1)
- 📖 First and Only (Callaghan Brothers #2)
- 📖 House Calls (Callaghan Brothers #3)
- 📖 Seeking Vengeance (Callaghan Brothers #4)
- 📖 Guardian Angel (Callaghan Brothers #5)
- 📖 Beyond Affection (Callaghan Brothers #6)
- 📖 Having Faith (Callaghan Brothers #7)
- 📖 Bottom Line (Callaghan Brothers #8)
- 📖 Forever Mine (Callaghan Brothers #9)

*

- 📖 Celina (Connelly Cousins #1)
- 📖 Johnny (Connelly Cousins #2)
- 📖 Michael (Connelly Cousins #3)

*

- 📖 Five Minute Man (Covendale Series #1)
- 📖 All Night Woman (Covendale Series #2)

*

- 📖 The Realist

*

- 📖 Celestial Desire

*

- 📖 Letting Go (02/15/17)

Time Travel Romance

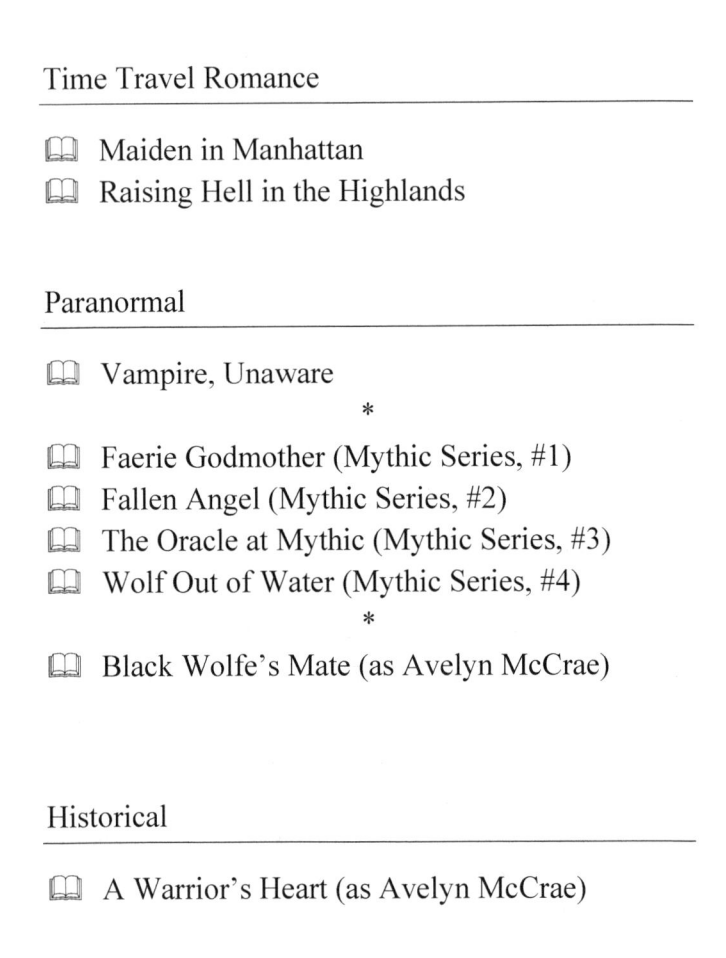

- 📖 Maiden in Manhattan
- 📖 Raising Hell in the Highlands

Paranormal

- 📖 Vampire, Unaware

*

- 📖 Faerie Godmother (Mythic Series, #1)
- 📖 Fallen Angel (Mythic Series, #2)
- 📖 The Oracle at Mythic (Mythic Series, #3)
- 📖 Wolf Out of Water (Mythic Series, #4)

*

- 📖 Black Wolfe's Mate (as Avelyn McCrae)

Historical

- 📖 A Warrior's Heart (as Avelyn McCrae)

About the Author

Abbie Zanders loves to read and write romance in all forms; she is quite obsessive, really. Her ultimate fantasy is to spend all of her free time doing both, preferably in a secluded mountain cabin overlooking a pristine lake, though a private beach on a lush tropical island works, too. Sharing her work with others of similar mind is a dream come true. She promises her readers two things: no cliffhangers, and there will always be a happy ending. Beyond that, you never know…

Made in the USA
Middletown, DE
30 December 2016